Moms Who Lie

"Moms Who Lie" Psychological Thriller Series - Book 1

Brett Monk, McKenna Langford

Contents

Welcome to the world of ***"Moms Who Lie"***.

I hope you're ready for an enjoyable and gripping ride, full of twists and turns and lots of suspense and excitement. McKenna and I have been having SO MUCH FUN creating this story for you!

So first, I want to say, get comfortable and pace yourself.

This is a five-book series and there are MAJOR CLIFFHANGERS at the end of each book.

But I promise it will be worth the ride and that we'll tie up all the loose ends by the time we're done. ;-)

AND in addition to the five full-length novels, there's also a special FREE bonus novella called ***"The Lying Begins"*** that's not available on Amazon or anywhere else other than the link below. It tells the story of just what happened twenty years ago, the night of the prom when Maddy and Amelia were in high school together. Once you're thoroughly hooked on this story, you're definitely going to want to read it, too.

https://www.brettmonk.com

When you join my reader's community, you will not only get free books and other content by me and some of my friends, but you will get the inside scoop on discounted products and upcoming releases. Plus, I share some personal thoughts and "behind the scenes" photos and notes about my life, media adventures, and favorite grilling recipes. :-)

Community members also get to vote in polls and make suggestions for upcoming books and projects. You might even want to consider being a "beta reader" or an "advance review reader", both of whom get to read the books before they're available to the public. But for now, enjoy ***"Moms Who Lie".***

- Brett

Chapter 1

Warner

It's not every day that somebody goes missing here. Although to the outsiders, here seems like the perfect setting for a mystery as such. Toxey is one of those sleepy, small towns. It's a place where the sun hates to shine, front lawns refuse to stay trim, and there's a stark contrast between those who have money—and those who have less. Much less. There's only one public high school, a dreary, old two-story building where the paint is chipping and there's not a single desk without gum underneath it. Most of the people who live here have lived here their entire lives. The only time we ever get new neighbors is when someone accepts a job offer and uproots their old lives to start new ones here.

I have always figured living in a town this small means there isn't any room for people to keep their secrets. I think everyone I know is just as I see them on the surface—just as everyone else sees them. No one's lives are complex. No one has more to them than meets the eye. No one who is the "quiet type" claims to be "funny and annoying once you get to know them." I don't even really understand what it means to be shy, because I think to be shy, you have to be somewhere that feels foreign, new, or uncomfortable. Toxey isn't any of those things. Not to me. Not to us. We don't feel the need to hide things from each other. In fact, I'd be willing to bet that most of my neighbors would tell you too much about their stories if you were to simply just ask.

Maybe the problem is that we are so cozy and sheltered here in our minuscule corner of rainy America that when outsiders arrive, we are too quick to withhold our trust. We are too quick to place judgment. We are too scared of the unknown. We are too scared of what they're bringing with them. Life in Toxey can get boring, but it's safe. Any newbies showing up makes everyone else risk jeopardizing that safety.

So, when the girl went missing, it had to be an outsider who took her.

It had to be.

Right?

Chapter 2

Audrey

I'm stoked for my junior year. I'm stoked to be sixteen with a driver's license and a car that puts it to use. I'm stoked for cheer tryouts and to see my friends—even though I saw them plenty over summer—and I'm even stoked to see my other classmates and to get to know my new teachers.

One thing that doesn't have me super excited is... Lyla.

My twin is still being mopey and moody. I thought the summer had given her plenty of time to get over what happened to her, but apparently, I was wrong.

I pick up one of the four pillows on her queen-sized bed and throw it at her. Lyla dodges it without looking up from her iPhone—the thing she is *glued* to nearly twenty-four-seven.

"Ree, stop," she snaps at me. We're hanging in her bedroom, Netflix on the TV playing some teenage drama as she pouts on her bed and I dig through her closet to find her the perfect outfit for tomorrow—the first day of school.

"Well, you're not being any help," I complain. "I've shown you three suggestions and you've shrugged at all of them. Does that mean you *like* all of them? Does that mean they're all *just okay*, or does it mean you *hate* them all but you just don't want to hurt my feelings by telling me so?"

Her long, Ash blonde hair—identical to mine—is messed up and static-ey from her pillow hitting her, but she doesn't bother to fix it.

"I just don't see how it matters," Lyla says to me. It's annoying because last year it would have mattered. I just don't understand why everything had to change. She used to have the same exact personality as mine. Our identical humor and looks made us nearly impossible to be differentiated. The only way anyone ever knew for sure which one of us they were seeing or talking to, was by our scars and freckles. I have a small smattering of freckles across my nose and forehead, and Lyla's freckles are focused more under her eyes. I have a tiny, indented scar below my hairline on the left side of my head from when I cracked it open on the sharp edge of my grandma's coffee table as a toddler. Lyla has a scar in a jagged, thin line that starts from the top of her shoulder and goes down to the middle of her bicep from a scrap of metal getting lodged inside of her.

"What are you talking about?" I ask her, my voice full of 'tude. "It's the first day of school."

She shrugs again. I'm about ready to take her pile of new clothes and toss them out of her open window. Maybe *then* they'd matter.

A soft knock sounds on the doorframe, and I turn to see my mother, Amelia, leaning against it with her arms crossed. "Whatcha guys doing up here?" she asks, looking back and forth between her only daughters. I try to shoot her a look that says, *Help me.*

"Well I was just trying to help Ly pick out her outfit for tomorrow," I say with a resigned sigh. "But she doesn't care."

Lyla puts her phone down—finally—and gets a guilty look on her face. "That's not true," she tries. I don't know why she bothers lying to me. We have twin-telepathy, duh.

Mom tilts her head and gives my sister that look that she's been giving her a lot lately. It's like her way of silently nagging at her to move on and be happy. "No?" she asks Lyla. "Then what are you going to wear?"

Mom is part of the reason we like fashion so much. She's always had an amazing sense of style. She knows how to look sophisticated, yet casual. Glamorous, yet natural. Sporty, yet chic. Her creative mind is what also allowed her to become the owner of her own boutique interior design firm downtown. It's literally called *Amelia Bailey Designs*, and it makes her a *lot* of money. Pretty much every person in Toxey is waiting for her to help remodel their fifty-something-year-old home.

Lyla crawls to the edge of her bed and scans over her previous options of outfits I had selected. "Um, I like the jeans one," she decides.

I smile brightly. "Yay! That one is my favorite, too!"

"Amelia, I can't find my new socks," Joey calls from somewhere in the hallway. Joey is our eleven-year-old foster brother. Fostering is something our dad, Gentry, has always wanted to do, so he and Mom got put in the system, and Joey's been with us for three years now. Mom and Dad won't tell me much about Joey's birth parents, but I guess Joey used to be in a pretty bad living situation a few cities over.

Joey appears in the doorway, anxiety plain on his deeply tanned face. He's starting the sixth grade tomorrow, and he's super nervous because it's at a middle school.

"It's in a bag on the shelf in your closet, remember?" Mom reminds him. "Along with your new belt." She lightly ruffles the top of his dark brown, bowl-cut hair. He actually wanted his hair like that—apparently, his favorite YouTuber had recently gotten a bowl-cut, and Joey wants to be just like him.

"Oh," Joey replies, wandering into Lyla's room. He walks up to me and flicks me on the elbow, then he goes over to Lyla to try and do the same, but she snatches his hand in hers and twists him so his hand is behind his back. He lets out a disappointed whine.

"Nice try, buddy," Lyla teases, giving him a little push. "Get out of my room."

We're pretty sure Joey doesn't know any other way to show us he likes us other than doing the opposite of what we tell him. He constantly walks into our rooms, uninvited, and finds a way to hit us, pinch us, or kick us. He never does it hard, but he does it hard enough to where it has definitely gotten annoying. Lyla is better at putting up with it than I am.

"Why are you such a twerp?" I ask him with my face twisted in a scowl.

Joey sticks his tongue out at me. "*Why are you such a twerp*?" he mimics in a high-pitched, whiny teen voice.

I look at Mom with an exasperated stare.

She sighs and steps away from the door frame. "Joey, come on, leave your sisters to get ready for their first day. I can't believe I have *two juniors* and a *middle schooler*!" she groans. "I *must* be getting old."

But compared to the other moms of the kids my age, Amelia isn't old at all. She hasn't even turned forty yet. She had me and Lyla when she was only twenty-one.

I don't think I ever want kids.

Mom and Joey leave me alone with Lyla again and retreat down the hallway, Joey asking her what's for dinner.

I turn back to my sister as she tries to get back on her phone. I can have quick reflexes sometimes too, so I snatch it out of her hand when she's not expecting it and put it behind my back. "How about you stay off of this for three minutes and talk to me, okay?"

She looks like she would rather do *anything* else. I don't know why—it's not like I did anything to her. All I've done this entire summer is try to make her happier. For some reason, sometimes I feel like I'm doing the opposite.

When she glowers at me silently, I continue. "Are you even a little excited for tomorrow?" I'm a little nervous to ask her because I don't want her to snap at me like she has been doing a lot lately.

"Why would I be excited to sit in a classroom all day and learn stuff I'm never going to need to use later in life?" she asks. "High school is pointless."

I sigh heavily. "There are other good things about high school. Friends, boyfriends..."

Unlike me, Lyla has a boyfriend. His name is Jackson Mullens, and they've been together since the summer before our freshman year. Their relationship didn't really make sense to me at first, because growing up, Jackson was always really mean to her, and Lyla often came home from school crying some days because of it. Turns out he just had a really fat crush on her, I guess. He never gave *me* the time of day, which is kind of weird considering Lyla and I look exactly the same... But I suppose I didn't have nearly as many classes as she had with him.

Lyla doesn't even seem excited about seeing Jackson. Maybe that's just something that happens when you've been with someone for that long, but I wouldn't know.

I would die to have a boyfriend. I've never had one before. I've definitely come close, but I have pretty high standards. No one has impressed me enough, especially since I've known all the boys in Toxey since I was a toddler. Kind of makes them less interesting when you already know everything about everyone. That's why I'm excited to graduate high school and go to college somewhere outside of town—so I can meet new people. I think I want to go to California. There are so many pretty people in California.

"It's just not going to be the same." Lyla says to me.

"What do you mean?"

She gives me that knowing look, like I shouldn't even have to ask this question. Which makes me remember exactly what she's referring to, so I cringe visibly and turn away from her. "Well, I'm going to go put on my outfit that I'm wearing tomorrow and you tell me what you think, okay? And you have to tell me how I should do my hair, too."

I saunter out of her room before she can even protest. That's how it is between us. I tell her to do stuff and she has no choice but to listen. She isn't big on arguing; she's always preferred to go with the flow. I think she would rather do things she hates than risk getting in an argument with people she cares about—that's another one of the differences between us.

"I don't care how you do your hair, Audrey," Lyla calls to me. "And I don't care what you wear tomorrow, either."

I freeze in my step just outside her bedroom door.

Huh. That's new.

Chapter 3

Maddy

A knock sounds loudly on my bedroom door. "Ma, are you up? Come on!" It's my son, Warner. He's starting his senior year of high school today.

Senior. Year. Of high school. *Where has the time gone?*

"I'm awake!" I grumble. I'm still in bed, but I'm awake.

I hear Warner sigh and mumble something under his breath as he walks away. I don't know what it's like to have a teenage daughter, but I honestly feel like teenage boys might be more dramatic than them.

I roll out of bed and hop in the shower, using my fancy new sample of shampoo and conditioner that is supposed to make brunette hair look extra shiny and vibrant, then I get changed in my black, short sleeve V-neck, black tight skinny jeans, and my comfy-yet-stylish chunky heeled boots. There isn't really a strict dress code at the hair salon I work at, but they do require you to wear all-black every day.

I am at my bathroom vanity blow-drying my long, dark chocolate hair, and I must have not heard Warner knocking again, because he does that sneaky thing with his thumb on the lock and unlocks my door from the outside, and barges his way in.

I jump, startled, seeing him through the reflection of my vanity mirror. I turn off my blow dryer and turn around to him.

"Warner! You scared the crap out of me."

"Have you seen my helmet?" he asks me, looking all first-day-of-school ready with his brown, shaggy hairstyle and simple T-shirt and jeans.

He is trying out for the varsity football team this week. He's obviously going to make it because he did last year, and even the year before, when he was only a sophomore. But Blackfell High tries to be fair and makes everyone try out every year.

Warner's voice is full of attitude, like he thinks it's *my* fault that he can't find his football helmet.

"I don't know," I say defensively, narrowing my eyebrows at him. I try to get back to the mirror and continue getting ready, but then I see him through the reflection again.

He's rolling his bright blue eyes—the same color as mine—and hanging from the door frame, pulling himself up a little bit. "I'm gonna be late for school if I can't find it," he complains. "I can't show up without it."

"Don't do that. You're gonna break the door," I tell him. This house is super old and shabby. Only Warner and I live here, but there's barely even room for that..

"No I'm not. You're so dramatic."

He turns to leave.

"Warner, wait!"

He turns back around, but acts like it's the most inconvenient thing in the world for him to do so. He flings his hands in the air and waits for what I have to say.

"I'll probably be home late tonight. I'm going out when I get off."

"Okay?"

"*Okay*... so will you be okay for dinner? I think there are some freezer meals in the fridge and maybe some leftover Thai food."

"Yeah, Ma, whatever." He sounds exasperated.

I squint at him, and he stares at me expectantly.

"What?" he asks.

I think about starting an argument with him. Telling him I don't like it when he talks to me this way. But it's his first day of school, and I know he's stressed out about it. Teens get so worked up over that kind of thing. "Nothing," I cave. "You can go."

He looks like he's just been let out of detention as he turns and dashes back into the small hallway leading to the living area.

I don't know if his attitude today *does* have everything to do with the first day of school, though; he acted like this with me the entire summer. We used to be pretty close, but it seems that throughout his high school years, he has only grown to resent me more and more. I don't quite know why, because I give him everything—or at least I *try* to. I know we don't have a lot of money, but I do all I can. It's not like he has a dad providing for him.

But maybe that's why he resents me so much. I told him I don't know who his father is. He doesn't need to know that. There's no point. His father isn't around to help. And I don't want him around, either. That's the way it has to be.

Chapter 4

Lyla

Most kids are thrilled to have their driver's license and a car to drive around in and show off to their friends.

Not me.

I'm never driving again.

It doesn't matter how many therapy appointments Mom and Dad try to put me in, it's not going to change my mind. It's already hard enough to get in a car at *all*, let alone be behind the wheel of one.

"Well, why are we even paying for a parking spot this year if you're not ever going to use it?" Mom asks me at the breakfast table before Audrey and I have to leave for school. It's the first day of my junior year. And I've been dreading it.

My dad, Gentry, puts his fork down, somewhat loudly, and it makes a clanging noise as he shoots my mother a glare. "Who cares that we're paying for a parking spot?" he asks. "It's only like fifty dollars. I'm pretty sure we can swing it." Dad's always been flexible about money and budgeting. Mom . . . not so much.

Dad is also more of the sensitive one between the two of them. He seems to understand me a little bit better than most, even though that's not really saying much—nobody understands me anymore. Including myself.

Audrey gets up from the white, modern farmhouse dining table we're all sitting at, her plate in hand. She's wearing flare cut jeans with a cute white top, and her blonde hair is in an extra high pony, almost as if she is trying to get in the mindset of a varsity cheerleader so that she can be better prepared for her tryouts today.

"Okay, that's our cue to leave before we have to sit around and listen to you guys start arguing again," she says as she heads into the kitchen.

Mom and Dad have been doing a lot of arguing lately. I'm not sure why, because they never really have before. At least not in the sixteen-and-a-half years I've been alive.

Dad sighs. "Okay, well, you kids have a good first day. I am headed out of town today, and I will be back in a few days."

I was in the middle of standing up, but I paused at his words, and now I'm standing in this weird half-squat position above the seat of my chair. "You're going out of town *again*?" I ask, my face falling.

When I look at Joey next to me, I see that his is, too.

Dad side-glances at Mom, then looks back at me. "I'm the only one that can do the job, bud," he says to me.

"But you leave all the time," Joey argues. He was enjoying some chocolate chip pancakes, but the news has upset him enough to put his fork down and stop chewing the current bite he still has in his mouth. Now, he kind of looks like he wants to spit it out onto the plate.

"It's just for right now," Mom answers for Dad. "It won't be like this forever."

"Ly, come on!" Audrey calls from the kitchen. She clearly doesn't care that Dad keeps going on business trips. She's too involved with school, cheer, and her social life.

I don't say another word to my parents before I carry my plate into the kitchen, drop it into the sink without rinsing it first, and then grab my brand new floral printed backpack and follow Audrey to her car. She got a baby blue Mini Cooper for our sixteenth birthday—with the white stripes—just like she wanted. I had gotten a cute white BMW just like I had wanted. Until the accident. After that, Mom and Dad bought me a white Toyota 4Runner. I told them they should sell it, but they won't listen.

When I get in my sister's car, that uneasy, stony feeling is inside my gut, as usual. I don't think that it'll ever go away, but thankfully it's gotten a little bit easier to manage over time. It sucks that Audrey has to be my ride to school every day, because she is the person that I trust to drive the *least*.

"Are you sure you don't want to try out for cheer?" she asks me as she backs out of the four-car garage and turns onto the street. I am in the passenger seat, my seatbelt fastened and my arms wrapped tightly around the backpack on my lap, as if for dear life.

"Uh, no thank you."

"It could be good for you," she tries.

A month ago, I couldn't even walk. I'm not about to try out for a jumpy, twisty, dancy sport. I don't think my body could handle it. "Yeah, no. I'm good."

I really don't feel like getting asked any other questions by her this morning, so I lean forward and plug my phone into her aux cord. Then I play some alternative music playlist on my Spotify. I like songs that have a rock sound and are sung by female artists. Audrey makes a face at my music choice, but I don't think it's because she hates it. I think it's more because it's not something she can sing along to. I don't need her to sing. I need her to focus on the road.

When we get to school, Jackson is waiting right out front on the steps, so there's no way I can possibly avoid him.

He hasn't done anything wrong. I'm just not in a good 'girlfriendly' mood.

I don't want to be here. I don't want to walk up those steps. I don't want to stroll down those halls. It's not fair.

Audrey parks her car in her spot, close to the front like mine is—was—and turns it off. I unbuckle and pull the handle to open the door, but I pause when I notice Audrey hesitating.

"Aren't you coming?" I ask her. "Aren't you like, dying of excitement?"

She nods, not looking at me right away. "Hey, you know it's going to be okay, right?"

I let go of the handle. I hadn't expected her to say anything like this. She tries to pretend like my accident never happened. As if it'll help me get over it quicker.

Now I feel a little awkward. Uncomfortable. "Oh... yeah, sure."

"Just try to have fun this year, okay? Forget about everything else. You deserve to have fun."

"You really are a natural-born cheerleader," I tease. "Mom and Dad should really be paying you to be my personal one."

She smiles in an accomplished way and makes a kissy face at me. Then she grabs her bag and we both get out.

We walk over to the steps together, but when I stop at Jackson, she carries on inside to go meet up with her friends. I guess they're my friends too, but I haven't really talked to them much since last year; Audrey was the only one who went and hung out with them.

Jackson finishes talking to a kid in our grade, Kyron Abbott. Then they fist bump each other and Kyron walks away as Jackson turns to me.

"You look cute," he greets, leaning in and kissing me right on the lips. I wrap my arms around him and kiss him back as a good girlfriend does. After we pull our heads apart, he doesn't let me go.

"You okay? Ready to do this?" he asks. His brown eyes are looking at me in concern—it doesn't matter how many times I have told him not to—and his jet-black hair is freshly trimmed. He's trying this new thing where he's not shaving, so he has grown in some slightly patchy stubble, but surprisingly, doesn't look bad. He's pretty proud of it because I guess not every teen boy is able to grow facial hair. It's a little scratchy on my face when we kiss, but I don't mind.

I groan at his question and try to get out of his grasp. "Yes, Jackson, I am good."

"Sorry," he says with a little bit of an attitude. "I just wanted to make sure, since it's the first day back and since—"

"I get it," I interrupt.

He lets go of me, holding his hands up in surrender. "Okay, okay. Conversation dropped."

"Thank you," I huff, but he's not listening to me anymore because another one of his friends has arrived and now they're fist-bumping and talking about tryouts today. Jackson is the star quarterback or something. He is also one of those guys who has a permanently angry look on his face, which you would think makes him look intimidating, but since we've all known him forever, nobody does. In fact, Jackson might be one of the most well-liked boys at Blackfell High—even his *teachers* love him. I can't count the number of times he's gotten away with not turning in his homework or a project on time because he schmoozes his way out of it.

His smooth-talking is what got me to like him so much my freshman year. We had science together, and even though I had pretty much hated him up to that point, he had been assigned the stool right next to mine at our lab table. Somehow, his boyish good looks, charm, and constant apologizing for the way he used to treat me had eventually been enough to win me over.

I fell for Jackson, and I fell for him hard. He completely changed from the mean, teasing boy I had always known as soon as we hung out for the first time. We had gone to Delilah's, like many people go on their first dates and anniversaries around here—there's not much else to do—and we had shared a banana split. I giggled when half-melted chocolate ice cream dribbled down his chin and he didn't notice it for four more bites. Then he laughed at the way I couldn't eat more than three bites at a time without getting brain-freeze. Then he told me he had always thought I was beautiful and that he had been dying for the chance to take me out. At the end of our first date, he also said he didn't want to do anything to ever mess this up. And since then, he hasn't.

Although I *do* sort of wish he would stop babying me as much as he has lately.

"What's up, Audrey?" Jackson's friend, Conner Schaefer, asks me. I raise my eyebrows at him. After a moment, he gets an embarrassed look on his face. "Oh shoot, my bad. I totally meant to say Lyla. Obviously."

"Yeah *obviously*," Jackson repeats. "I've only been dating Lyla forever. Why would I be hanging out front of school with Audrey?"

It's not like I'm not used to being mistaken for my twin, though. Audrey has always been a little bit more outgoing and liked than me. But if you were to ask her who she thought was more popular, she would say that it was completely equal. That we were basically the same person.

But Audrey and I have never been the same person. I've spent my entire life exhausting myself trying to keep up the act that I am like her. Because who wouldn't want to be like her? She's bubbly and funny and quick-witted, and everyone loves to be around her. I wanted people to see me the same way. But ever since the accident, I've realized that I couldn't care less anymore. I don't know if I ever will again.

Chapter 5

Amelia

After the kids leave and I have some breakfast in me, I go to the medicine cabinet in my bathroom and pull out my anxiety pill bottle. I pop the cap open and then pop one into my mouth, then I toss it back with the bottled water in my hand.

Gentry enters the bathroom a couple minutes later when I am touching up my makeup and hair before I head to my office.

"Joey got on the bus okay," he lets me know. "It's so weird to have him start school so late now."

"Hm," I reply. I don't really have much else to say about it. At least not with him. At least not right now.

Gentry sighs and starts gathering up his toiletries in his travel bag. "I feel bad doing this to him."

"Don't you mean them?" I say, in reference to our daughters.

"Well, them too, of course... But you know, they don't really care as much. They've got their own lives going on."

"Lyla seemed pretty affected by it this morning," I remind him. Sometimes I wonder if he completely forgets he has actual daughters at all. Ever since we started fostering Joey, Gentry has been mainly focused on him. I know it was my husband's life goal to be a foster parent and help kids in need, but I didn't know he was going to start lacking in fatherly care for his own children once he got one. I love Joey to death, I really do. But I still love my daughters as well.

"She'll be okay," Gentry says about Lyla. "She just looks for reasons to be mad at things."

He did have a point there. Ever since our daughter's car accident, Lyla hasn't been the same. I know she has PTSD, and I've sent her to therapy and even got her a prescription for it, but she doesn't like to take her meds and she claims that therapy doesn't help. I don't know what else to do other than wait and see if this is the new Lyla, or if the old one will come back. But this new Lyla? I'm not sure I like her attitude. She reminds me so much of my younger sister. Moody and defiant and with selective hearing.

Thinking about Lyla, my mind flashes back to the night of the wreck. I had driven right past it on my way home from work and nearly crashed my own car when I recognized her license plate. No one had called me yet. I had no idea what had happened to her. Her car was so . . . mangled. I thought she was dead.

"Mia, hey..." Gentry tries to snap me back to the present. I stare blankly at him. My eyes have filled with tears like they always do when I think about that night. I've been through some stuff, but I have never been as scared as I was when I found her car.

I turn away from Gentry, not wanting him to see me like this. "Sorry, sorry. What were you saying?"

He furrows his brows at me. "Nothing, it doesn't matter. Are you okay? I don't have to go. I can stay with you."

I wave him off. "Don't be ridiculous. Go to work. I'm fine. Promise."

As conflicting as things are with my husband right now, he will always and forever be my best friend. Nobody looks out for me the way he does. I don't think I could get through life without him.

"I like your hair like that," he says, changing the subject. I turn and look at myself in the mirror to try to see my snow blonde hair from his point of view. I always have it chopped to a long bob so that it's more manageable, and I like the way it frames my face this way. But today I have decided to put it halfway back in a little clip. I had seen a mom do it at the grocery store and I really liked the way it looked.

"Thank you." I point at him. "*Yours* is in need of a cut."

Gentry's hair is brown, but it's starting to get a little bit of gray in it even though he's only thirty-six years old. He always parts it down the middle, and he's always liked it to be a little longer than others, but right now he is starting to look a little bit like a nerdy hippie. A little bit like he looked in high school. I had known him all the way back then, but we hadn't spoken much. He had been my lab partner in chemistry my junior year, but we were in different friend groups, and even though I sort of had a crush on him, I didn't think my best friend back then would have approved of him, so I never went for it.

It wasn't until after graduation that I finally grew the courage to reach out to him. He told me he had never been expecting it. He said he thought pretty girls like me reaching out to nerdy guys like him only happened in dreams. But he is smart, charming and funny. He's not movie star cute, but he is still attractive to me. I like his slightly uneven face and the overly rounded tip of his nose. I've always admired his full head of hair, and at least I don't have to worry about having a cul-de-sac-headed husband when we get really old. I don't think.

When Gentry finishes packing, he approaches me in the kitchen and kisses me on the forehead. "You sure you're okay with me going?" he asks yet again.

"Gentry, go make your rocket ship software or whatever it is you have to do," I say with a little smile. I do not, at all, have any science-ey smarts in my brain, so whenever Gentry tries to tell me about his engineering job, I have no idea what he's talking about. Everything I learned in high school and college that was science or math related, I pretty much forgot as soon as I passed the test. I'm horrible at retaining information. I often feel like the only thing I'm good at is making things look pretty.

Gentry stares at me long and hard for a while before finally nodding his head and leaving me to get in his truck.

I sigh with relief the moment he is gone. With nobody else in the house, I finally have some time to actually be myself.

Then I have to leave for work and fake it all over again.

Chapter 6

Warner

Coach Reeves and I are tight, and I know I am going to get a spot on the team this year, so I don't know why I feel so anxious about today.

And go figure—I am the one that has to make sure my mother, Maddy, is up and getting ready for her job. Isn't that a little backward?

When I finish getting ready and finally find my helmet—it was in the storage closet on the back porch for some reason—I call 'bye' to Mom and walk out the screened-in front door.

Making perfect timing, I see Jackson walking across the yard next to mine over to me, so we ride to school together. He's been my best friend since we had the same PE class and played all the same sports in the seventh grade.

"Yo, Carpenter, you are looking insanely jacked, dude!" Jackson yells to me as he grows nearer, a huge, excited grin on his face.

We meet at my old red Jeep Wrangler—a hand-me-down from my mom—and I grin back at him. "Is there anything else to do in this town other than work out?" I ask. I'm not really good at accepting compliments. I don't know how to just say thank you.

We get inside my jeep and I start it up. As old as it is, it's in pretty good condition – I actually like taking care of it. It's a nice hobby, and it gets me out of my cramped house.

I was hoping to drive away before Mom came outside to get in her car, a black Hyundai Tucson that even though it's newer, is not in much better condition than mine.

I only notice she left the house because Jackson gets this glazed look in his eye as he stares over my shoulder. When I follow it, I see my mom putting something in her trunk.

"Jackson." I snap my fingers in front of his face.

"Good morning, Miss Carpenter!" Jackson calls to my mom, ignoring me. Mom turns and gives Jackson a large friendly wave and smile. It's embarrassing to me because it kind of looks flirty. My mom knows the effect she has on my guy friends, and I think she likes it.

When Mom starts looking like she's going to come over and try to start a conversation with Jackson, I peel out of there, kicking dust up behind me because the roads in our neighborhood aren't paved.

"Has your mom said she's going to marry me yet?" Jackson asks. I hit him straight in his pecs as I drive. He's not even worth me giving him crap for saying it. He does it too much.

"Ouch bro, I worked my chest yesterday." Jackson rubs where I hit him like I genuinely hurt him, and it makes me roll my eyes.

"So," he says, changing the subject. "This is your last year, dude. How does it feel?"

Jackson is only a junior. The only time we ever have class together is during electives. But we still have sports together—mainly football—and he lives only a street over from me. I give him rides to school every morning, because even though he has his license, his parent's haven't bought him a car yet.

"I don't know, kind of weird, I guess," I say.

"Have you applied to any colleges yet? Or are you even looking?"

My stomach sinks at the thought. "Yeah, I wanna go somewhere in Miami. I need sunshine in my life. I can't wait to get out of here."

"Florida? And your mom would really let you do that?"

Why does he know me and my mom so well? She's the reason why my stomach sinks when I think about it.

"I'm about to be eighteen. She can hate it all she wants, but legally, I can do whatever I want."

I really don't like the idea of her being alone here—she can't even remember to pay the bills on time—but I also can't stick around and take care of her forever. I am her kid. Not the other way around. Sometimes I wonder what it would be like for her to look out for me for a change. Apparently, she did that when I was younger, but I definitely don't remember it.

"Fair enough," Jackson says. "It'll be sick to come visit."

"What about you? Do you and your girl have plans to go to college together somewhere? Do you even plan to stay together after high school?"

Jackson gets a weird look on his face. "We haven't really talked about it. I don't think either of us has any idea what we're gonna do. Especially after everything that happened."

"Are you guys... good?" I ask. Usually, he seems a lot cheerier and eager to talk about the love of his life.

Jackson gets on his social media and starts making a video of our drive to school. I don't have any of my doors or roof on, so there's nothing but the cool summer morning breeze blowing in our faces.

He smiles at his camera. "Woo hoo! First day of junior year, let's get it!" He puts the camera on me so I stick my tongue out like I'm a member of Kiss. Then he ends the video, does some quick editing, and puts it on his story.

By the time he finishes with that, I am pulling into the student parking lot and parking in my assigned spot. Were a lot earlier than I expected because I hit all the green lights... and I definitely maybe was speeding a little, too.

"Hey so are we hanging out after tryouts today?" Jackson asks as I turn the car off and we both hop out all cool-guy style. Although Jackson is definitely cooler than I am. He's better at the whole social media thing and he's just way more outgoing too. It's weird because he's the junior, yet I feel like I'm younger than him.

Before I answer his question, I can't help but notice that he never answered mine about him and his girlfriend.

"I can't today," I tell him. "I have to get to the soccer fields at six." I am an assistant coach for a youth soccer team. It's my part-time job. The pay is pretty lame, but it's better than nothing. And at least I'm doing something I like. I think kids are super fun to be around. I always wished I had a younger brother or sister. I would have taken either.

Instead, it's just me.

Everyone turns their head to look at us as we head to the steps in front of the school entrance. It's something I'm used to when I am with Jackson. We smile and wave and say hello and hug our peers. Jessica Vaccari comes up and gives me a long hug, and when she walks away, Jackson flings his hand into my rib cage.

"She totally wants you," he says in a low voice. I shake my head and laugh. Any girl that gives me any time of day in front of Jackson, he tells me wants me. I think he just wants to see me off the market. But it's never happened in my entire life.

We stop walking at the steps, where we usually hang out in the mornings. But I can't today. "Hey man, I got to go talk to Coach Reeves and make sure tryouts will be done before I have to get to work today," I tell him. We fist bump and I head inside the school. While walking down the hall, my phone vibrates with a text in my pocket. I pull it out and roll my eyes when I see who it's from. Go figure, my mom would be the only one texting me right now. I bet Jackson has at least ten text messages, mostly from girls, even though he has a girlfriend. Everyone at Blackfell High loves Jackson.

Mom: *Good luck at tryouts today. I hope your first day of your last year of high school is perfect. Love you.*

Mom: *Oh, and also make good choices.*

Telling me to make good choices is my mom's favorite thing to say to me. It's funny. She says it so much, yet she can never seem to take her own advice.

I text her back just a thumbs-up emoji. Then I go to stick my phone back in my pocket, but I feel bad. Maybe she doesn't deserve me being that mean. So I pull my phone back out and send a smiley face emoji, too.

Chapter 7

Maddy

I go and meet Craig at our typical spot. It's a dive bar near my house, an old and dingy place called The Mix.

When I walk in, Craig is already seated at our usual high-top table next to the shuffleboard game. I smile at the sight of him, my heart skipping a beat.

"Hey you," I say when I reach the table and sit down.

He grins back at me and flashes me a wink. Then he slides an ice-cold beer my way.

"Hey Mads, looking gorgeous as ever."

I blush and pretend to be shy. But everyone in Toxey knows I'm not.

"Sorry I'm running late," I say after sipping the drink. "Work ran late, then I had to complain to Warner about how he didn't do all of his chores yesterday. You know, the usual."

He leans back in his stool, and I can't help but gaze at him longingly. I love his scruffiness and his ruggedness. I love how he makes it look so effortless to be so attractive. And I love how, for some reason, he wants to date me.

"How is he doing?" Craig asks about my son. "Is his senior year off to a good start?"

A good rock song plays on the radio overhead, and I slowly bob my head along to it. I can't help it when I hear good songs. The music nowadays isn't anything like it used to be.

"How should I know?" I reply to Craig bitterly. "For some reason, he doesn't seem to want to talk to me about anything anymore."

Craig nods his head at me like he understands, but I know he doesn't. He's never been married—not that I have either—and he doesn't have any kids of his own. It's honestly fine with me because if we do have a future together, I don't know if I would want to have a stepchild. Even thinking the word *stepchild* makes me feel old.

Craig raises his beer towards the ceiling to motion to the song playing. "Do you like this band?"

"Don't you?"

He smirks at me. "Duh! Nirvana is classic."

I lean closer to him across the table. "Ugh, I played one of their albums in my house the other day, and Warner legitimately made a face at it!"

"All anyone listens to is rap these days."

I shudder. I have never been a fan of it.

"Hey, Craig!" another one of The Mix's regulars says as he passes by our table. "Maddy."

I smile at Don. He's been coming here since the seventies.

Then I turn back to my date. "Are we going to play some pool?" I ask Craig.

"I'm sick of getting my butt beat by you," he complains.

I giggle and sip my drink some more.

Craig rests an elbow on the table. "So, what do you think about Warner going on that upperclassman trip?"

The upperclassmen camping trip is held at Blackfell high school every two years, and every junior and senior that signs up and pays for it gets to go. Warner used to talk nonstop about how excited he was for it, but so far this year, he's barely even mentioned it.

I shrug. The upperclassman camping trip wasn't around when I was in high school. "I'm excited for him, I guess. It's going to be weird to be away from him for so long."

The longest I've ever been away from Warner is about 48 hours, and this trip is two nights and three full days.

Hopefully, it goes by fast.

"You, uh, know who is going to be chaperoning this year?" Craig asks. Something about the twinkle in his eye lets me know he has juicy gossip.

"No, I don't. Do *you*?"

"Amelia Bailey and Dean Reeves."

Dread fills me. Out of all the people in this dump of a town, it has to be *those* two chaperoning?

"Huh," is all I can manage to say.

Craig raises an eyebrow. "Doesn't it strike you as kind of odd?"

I stand up, no longer wanting to be sitting still. "Whatever. I wanna play some pool."

Craig hesitates there in his barstool. I don't like the way he's looking at me. He has his half-grin on his face and one of his eyebrows remains sky-high. Even as he sips his beer, he doesn't look away from me.

"What?"

Craig shakes his head and slowly gets to his feet, too. "Are you alright?"

I put my arms around his neck and give him a quick, affectionate peck on the lips.

"Why wouldn't I be?" I ask. I'm lying, of course. I don't want Amelia Bailey and Dean Reeves to go on this trip.

Craig looks pleased that I have kissed him, even though I never know if that's really the case. We haven't exactly defined our relationship, but we've been seeing each other for three months now. I don't want to come on too strong by asking him what we are, so I'm just trying to go with the flow.

I feel happy when he takes my hand and leads me over to the pool table. As we play the game and it's his turn, I quickly whip out my phone and go to the school's website. I need to know how I can make myself a chaperone on this upperclassman trip, too.

Chapter 8

Audrey

I love first days of school. I love the excitement and promise that hangs in the air. How everyone wonders what is in store for them at this stage in their lives.

"Audrey, hi!" my friend, Sophia Key, cries to me when I enter the school. She's by her locker with a couple other friends of mine, Danielle Garner and Olive Gaines. When they turn and see me, they wave and smile. I rush over to them and hug them all, the four of us in a group hug.

"Sophia, your hair!" I say. She's gone from completely blonde to completely brunette. "You seriously rock it!"

She flips it behind her shoulder. "Thanks. Love your outfit."

I'm wearing cute flare jeans and an off-shoulder white top. Technically, the dress code says we aren't allowed to show our shoulders, so I'll just wear my cardigan inside the classrooms.

"I missed you guys!" Danielle says. She had been gone the last three weeks of summer, on a trip to Hawaii with her family.

"Where's Lyla?" Olive asks. An awkward silence settles over all of us at her question. It's not the Lyla part that brings it on, it's the words left unsaid.

I adjust my backpack on my shoulders. "She's outside with Jackson."

"How—how is she?" Danielle asks with wide concerned hazel eyes. Danielle is really big on being overly emotional and empathetic with people. I know it comes from a good place, but a lot of people think she's fake.

"The same," I tell them, wanting to change the subject. Everyone wants to talk about Lyla, all the time. And ... well, the accident.

"Guys, let's not turn into a bunch of sad downers," Sophia urges. She's the tall, skinny model of the group who can appear really heartless at times. She doesn't like to let anyone in and always puts on a facade. People think Danielle is fake—but I know that it's Sophia.

"Kay, so let's talk tryouts," Olive offers, loudly chewing bubblegum and looking up at us all since she's so short.

I clap my hands together. "Yes, I can't wait!"

Sophia grabs mine and Olive's arms since we're who she's standing in the middle of. "We're all going to make varsity, got it? No exceptions."

I know she doesn't mean it, but her words make me nervous, anyway.

"Oh my God!" Olive gasps, looking at someone, then leaning her head into our little group. "Have you seen what Bryson Anthony did to his hair?"

I sneak a peek; Bryson, known for his insanely cool dreadlocks, has chopped them off and is completely buzz-cut.

"Whoa," Danielle comments. "I-I think I like it?"

"He looks hot," Sophia says.

I giggle. I don't know if Bryson is my type. I don't know if any of the guys at this school are.

"Are there any new kids this year? Does anyone know?" I ask,

"Oh yeah there is," Sophia replies with a slightly constipated facial expression. "I saw her the second I got here. Some chick who looks like she's a hundred years old and totally cracked out."

"Oh, great," Olive and I say at the same time. Then we look at each other and giggle.

At tryouts after school, I meet up with the same three girls—I'm pretty much always seen with them. And Lyla, too, when she can stand it. If her accident had never happened, she would be in these tryouts, too.

We're sitting in the gym, all the girls trying out sitting on the hardwood floors and stretching ourselves out.

Sophia kicks me with her foot in my thigh. "There she is," she says to us. "Don't look now, but it's the new girl. I can't believe she's trying out."

I'm the only one with my back to the rest of the girls, so I hate that I can't see what the new girl looks like. I've heard multiple people talking about her, though. Granted, anyone who is new at Blackfell High gets talked about. It's a very rare occurrence.

Eventually, the cheer coach, Mrs. Greene—a young, sassy, black-haired vixen who all the boys drool over—walks into the gym and tells us to get on our feet, and the cheer tryouts begin.

We jump. We flip. We dance. We learn routines. We toss each other in the air. I even get tossed in the air—I'm not super short but I am pretty lightweight. I sweat my butt off, and meanwhile, Sophia makes it look effortless, and she keeps giggling and nudging either me or one of our other friends with her shoulder to make fun of the new girl behind her back.

I feel bad for her. Apparently, her name is Sydney Hutton. She's a junior, like me, and no one can really figure out where she came from, what neighborhood she moved to, and why she showed up here in Toxey in the first place. She's a completely tortured-looking mystery of a girl.

One, I can't help but notice, who won't stop staring at me. Maybe I'm going crazy, but every few seconds she is glancing over at me and trying to give me a friendly smile. The only thing I can think of is maybe she met Lyla earlier, and she is mistaking me for her. I have no idea.

It goes on like this all week during the tryouts, too. Every day we show up, try our hardest—Sydney is terrible, and I'm not even saying that to be mean—and there she is, just peeking over at me every so often. And every time I get home from school later, I forget to ask Lyla about it. Maybe they have a class together or something.

When Friday rolls around, I am a nervous wreck. I think I did really well in the tryouts, but I know there were girls who did better than me.

"This is the moment we've been waiting for!" Sophia says to us in the locker room as we dry our sweat, chug gallons of water, and wait for the list to be posted on the bulletin board outside.

"No matter what happens, we all killed it," Danielle says, smiling around at everyone.

"Well, most of us did," Sophia jokes. I lean over and swat her knee, but I can't help the small smirk on my lips. It was just odd that the new Sydney chick even bothered trying out—it had been clear from day one that she wasn't going to make even the JV squad.

I look over at Sydney to see that she's in her own little world, though, drinking water like she's never going to get enough out of the gross fountain everyone refuses to use.

Well, mostly everyone.

Sydney is actually incredibly beautiful. She has an exceedingly sharp jaw structure, naturally thick, arched eyebrows, and full, pink lips. She does look a little old to be in high school, but it might just be because of how harrowed she looks. Her cheeks are sunken in. Her sandy-colored hair is always greasy and stringy and looks like a brush has never been run through it, and when she's not trying to shoot me a smile, her facial expression is hardened. She always looks to be deeply in thought.

Mrs. Greene finally enters the locker room, beaming at all of us and looking thrilled to show off the results.

"I am so proud of each and every one of you!" she calls. "It was a really tough call on who to give the spots to this year, but in the end, I feel like I made the right decisions. Those who didn't make the team—there's always next year"—

"Unless you're a senior," Olive mutters under her breath.

- "and those who made JV but not varsity, you should still feel just as proud of yourself, okay? I saw some real talent out there!"

I reach over and grab Danielle's hand and squeeze it tightly, not even caring that my palms are sweating when hers aren't. She squeezes mine back.

Mrs. Greene steps aside and points to the locker room door. "Alright, go on and see now."

We all get up, squealing and racing to the door to try and get to the list first. Bodies slam into each other. Sweat gets swapped. None of us care. The list is most important.

I'm a very dedicated girl, so I push and shove my way through and even beat out Sophia to seeing the list first.

My name is the first one under varsity.

Chapter 9

Amelia

I know it's ridiculous to be nervous going to a chaperone meeting for the girls' upperclassman trip coming up. But I am. I'm going to try my best not to let anyone see it—but I am.

I park my black Range Rover in the school's parking lot, check out my reflection in the rearview mirror—my hair is in a classy, tight bun and my makeup is light and natural—then I force myself to get out and smooth my skirt.

"Okay," I breathe to myself, heading across the street and up the school's front steps. I do my best to have to come into this high school as little as possible, but having two teenage daughters can make that hard at times. And who knows if I will still have Joey when he starts high school, too?

One can hope.

I go through the unlocked doors, even though it's after hours and the sun is nearly setting. It's weird to be in here like this. I hate the ominous feeling I instantly get as I look around at the lockers. How so much has changed since I went to high school here, yet so much of it is exactly the same. The lockers have been painted. The tile has been torn out and redone. The walls are no longer a sickly yellow color. But it still smells the same—old and musty. The wooden trim along the ceilings and doorways hasn't been redone, either. And all the places they kept bulletin boards and display cases are still in the same spots.

I head into the gymnasium, remembering that the last time I was here as a kid was for my junior prom. I didn't go to my senior one.

I shudder as after I walk in, the big metal doors swing closed behind me. I am not fond of the memories made in this gym.

What I am even more not fond of, is the woman sticking a *Hello My Name Is...* sticker on her black V-neck shirt. Madeline Carpenter.

I keep my head held high, as I always do, even though anger is stewing up inside of me.

I can do this, I tell myself. *I can do this.*

I go get my nametag, fill it out, and stick it on my blouse, then when I turn to go take a seat in one of the folding chairs, I accidentally bump into someone.

Someone I know, but never talk to anymore.

"Oh, Dean, I'm sorry!" I say to the tall, familiar man in front of me.

Dean grins at me like he's seeing an old friend.

I wouldn't call myself that.

"Mia, how have you been?" he asks.

My stomach dips. Only the people from my childhood call me *Mia*. "I-I've been good, thanks."

He nods slowly.

I clear my throat. "So, you have my daughters this year," I comment.

"Yeah, I do," he replies. "In my first and fourth hour, I believe."

"Mm."

Dean continues nodding his head, his eyes darting around like he's looking for more words to say. "So ... are you excited for the trip?"

I side-glance at Maddy. He does, too.

Before I can make my reply, the principal begins introducing herself, and I go and take my seat, three rows and as far away from Madeline Carpenter as I can get.

When Dean gets his nametag and goes to find a chair, our eyes meet. But then he takes the seat closest to him, next to where Principle Mathers is talking.

I promise I do my best to listen to the debriefing we are all receiving about the trip. The principal is going over all of the rules and regulations, as well as what lessons are going to be taught to the kids and how the groups are going to be broken up. It's just difficult to fully concentrate when I have so many thoughts running through my head. Like of Dean, and how surprised I remember being when Dean moved back to town only a few years back and took up the teaching job. Or how his hair still has the same amount of fullness it did when we were kids. Or how the only signs of aging he has are some small lines on his face that didn't use to be there. If anything, it's only made him more attractive.

I also can't stop thinking about my high school experience, seeing as I am sitting in Blackfell High right now. All these memories keep flooding back no matter how much I want to suppress them.

And I'm also thinking about how the last time I checked, Maddy definitely wasn't on the parent chaperone list. If I had known, I'm not so sure I would have signed up. I'm not the most outdoorsy type, anyway, but I try my best to be active in Lyla and Audrey's school community. And since I didn't have a trip like this when I was young, maybe this was sort of my opportunity to go.

Even if I hate the woods.

When I get home later, Lyla and Audrey are still out—Lyla with Jackson and Audrey with her cheer friends—and Joey is in the kitchen working on his math homework.

I plop myself down on the couch in our gorgeous front room, a space redesigned by myself. The walls are a perfectly warm off-white, which matches the modern, plastered, floor-to-ceiling fireplace in the middle of the east wall, a simple natural wood mantle adding the perfect touch of contrast. There are simple adjustable black wall lights on either side of the fireplace, which create the perfect ambiance for a quiet, relaxing evening, and a taupe sofa sits across from two comfortable leather armchairs, and an organic, live-edge coffee table is in the center of the room on a light, soft, textured rug. The front room is off-limits to my children. They'd dirty it up in a heartbeat.

I go to Gentry's name in my phone and give him a call. He answers on the second ring.

"How did it go?" he asks me, sounding genuinely interested in hearing about the boring chaperone meeting. That is another wonderful thing about my husband—he is always willing to listen to me.

I sigh heavily and rest my chin in my palm. "Oh, it was ... something."

"Uh oh, what's that mean?"

Where do I even want to start? "I don't know. I guess I didn't realize how much time was actually going to be spent

... outdoors." He laughs deeply, and I smile. "I know, I'm ridiculous aren't I?"

His response is sarcastic. "Not at all! I'm sure most of the moms thought a three-day camping trip would be mostly inside."

I want to laugh with him, but the knot in my stomach won't let me. "Speaking of moms."

"I thought you liked all the ones that signed up."

He knows me too well. "I guess they had room to add one more."

"Who?"

I don't even like saying her name. "Maddy."

"Oof, that sounds like a grand ol' time."

"Gentry," I whine, slumping into the couch and looking up at the ceiling. "What do I do? How do I get her to change her mind, or get kicked off the list?"

"Mia, I'm sure it won't be as bad as you think."

"Maddy is an awful woman," I argue. "What if we have to ... I don't know, share a *bunk* or something?"

"Who's Maddy?" a voice asks behind me. I whip my head around and see Lyla and Audrey hovering in the archway by the front door. I hadn't even heard them come in.

It had been Lyla who spoke—I think.

"And why is she awful?" Audrey chimes in.

"Girls, hi," I say to them, sitting up and clearing my throat. "Gentry, your daughters are home. I'll call you later, okay?"

"Okay, tell them I love em. Joey, too."

We hang up.

"Your father says he loves you."

"So who is she?" Lyla asks again, ignoring me.

"Is she coming on the camping trip?" Audrey joins.

"She's nothing," I say. "No one."

Lyla dangles a sneaker-covered foot through the archway over my precious, clean rug. “Don’t make me come in there,” she threatens with a smirk.

“Lyla Rose,” I scold. But then I cave. “She’s just this woman I don’t get along with. Not to mention she’s completely irresponsible and will probably do a horrible job looking after a bunch of teenagers in the woods.”

“Oh, so you mean she’s a *cool* mom?” Lyla asks. “How do I make sure to be on *her* team?”

I stand. “You’re going to get it, young lady.”

Audrey shoves her sister playfully. “Don’t worry, Mom,” she tells me. "I want to be on your team.”

As I walk by them, I give Audrey a kiss on the top of her head. “And that’s why you’re my favorite.”

Lyla gasps, so I stop walking and turn back around to her.

“When you tell me you want to be on my team, you’ll be my favorite, too.”

She sticks her tongue out at me, then turns and heads up the stairs.

Audrey holds out her hand. “Your favorite daughter would like twenty dollars, please. It’s a lot of work to be in this position.”

I roll my eyes at her and go get dinner started.

Chapter 10

Lyla

The new girl, Sydney, is in my history class. For the first couple days of school, she sat in the last row over in the corner. But today, she decides to take her seat right next to me.

It's a little bit before the bell rings for class to start, so everybody is talking with their friends and watching video reels on their phones.

Sydney smiles at me. "Hi," she starts.

I look at her uncomfortably. She is the only new girl we have this year—so far at least, and everyone has been talking badly about her. I don't even know how she is able to smile right now. High schoolers can be so cruel.

"Um, hello," I reply.

"I'm Sydney."

I nod my head at her. "Yeah, everyone knows that. It's hard to not talk about the new girl," I explain. "The kids here obsess about new students. It's annoying, really."

She shrugs. I want to tell her that some friendly advice would be to maybe wash her hair once in a while and at least put some effort into her outfit choice—she seems to always wear old and baggy clothes—but that's if she wants people to stop being mean to her.

"I don't mind being talked about," she says.

"Oh. Well, then, you came to the right place."

Around me, I can tell that people are eyeing us curiously. Before today, Sydney sat at her desk and didn't say a word to anyone. It seems to me like I'm the first person she's wanted to make conversation with. I have no idea why. Maybe it's because she saw me sitting here not talking to anyone?

"Do you have a twin?" Sydney asks.

I smile at her. "Yes, that's Audrey."

She tilts her head in thought. "Huh. You're nothing like her."

I raise an eyebrow. This is probably the first time I have ever been told that. "Really?"

Then again, Sydney doesn't know who I was last year. All she knows is the person she's meeting now.

Suddenly, I think about how it's kind of nice. I can be whoever I want to this girl. I can be exactly how I feel like being and not have to worry about her saying something annoying like, "This isn't you!"

"Seriously," Sydney says. "I don't have any classes with the other one, but she's always walking through the halls, part of that Sophia girl's posse. She constantly looks like she's trying too hard to impress people."

I chew on my bottom lip. Last year I walked with that posse. "They've all been friends since they were kids," I explain. No point in mentioning that they were my friends too. It just doesn't feel like it anymore. It feels more like it's a good idea for me not to have any friends at all.

"Isn't it funny how the pretty girls are just somehow drawn to each other?" Sydney asks as a bell rings.

Our teacher, Mr. Wyatt, stands up from his desk and walks to the front of the class as the mumbling dies down. I shoot Sydney a shrug and go to face forward and pay attention—not that I have any desire to actually do any work.

"It came to my attention recently in a podcast that I was listening to, that many people have no idea where the states are on a US map," Mr. Wyatt starts off. He is a tall, basketball-star-sized man, with broad shoulders and possibly the largest feet I have ever seen. His dress shoes look like they could be used as snowshoes. So far from what I've gathered by being in Mr. Wyatt's class, he has a way of making everyone listen to him. Maybe it's because his height gives him a threatening vibe.

Mr. Wyatt walks up to the table in front of the whiteboard and grabs a stack of papers. Some kids groan, including myself. I already know what to expect.

Mr. Wyatt smiles at us. He knows we are all going to fail. "So. I just want to see how much you all know. I'm going to pass out these blank US maps to you, and I want you to not only label every state, but also any capital you know, write that too. Each extra capital you know will earn you some extra credit points."

The class erupts into conversation with each other. "I'm gonna fail!" one of them cries.

"I don't think I can even name all fifty states," someone else says.

Mr. Wyatt chuckles, loving the desperation in the air. "Here. I'll make it even easier for you. You can work in a pair. Two heads are always better than one." He hands a stack of papers to each row so they can take one and pass it back. "Just go ahead and work with a person next to you. You can put your desks together."

Sydney is sitting in the last row against the wall, so I have no choice but to have her as my partner since there is no one on the other side of her. Besides, the person on the other side of me is some Dungeons and Dragons guy who has his Dungeons and Dragons best friend to pair up with.

I move my desk toward Sydney as she looks over the map.

"Every single person has to have their own map!" Mr. Wyatt calls to us. "You can't just share one and put both of your names on it. Writing things on your own will help you retain the information better."

Then he walks over to his stereo and plays a CD that covers popular pop songs, but the singer transforms them into rock songs. Oops, I Did It Again is the first song that comes on.

"So ... how much do you know?" I ask Sydney. "I know where our state is, and California, Florida, and Texas, but I'm pretty sure that's it."

"I actually learned a song in elementary school about the fifty states, and it stuck with me. So I can at least name them all."

"That should help!"

Thank goodness, I think. Because I am pretty positive I wouldn't be able to remember all fifty states. How sad is that?

Sydney seems eager to keep the conversation with me going. "Hey, you were in that accident last year, weren't you?" she asks.

My stomach dips. How had she found out about that so quickly? I thought she didn't talk to anybody.

"I overheard people talking about it in the library the other day," she adds.

Huh, it's like she can read my mind.

I tuck some hair behind my ear and focus my eyes on the map only. "Yeah," I tell her, not really wanting to. "That was me."

"Did you really almost die?"

I'm surprised that she wants to talk about me. There are way worse things that that incident caused.

"I guess so," I huff. "I was in a coma for two weeks. I broke my leg, crushed some of my ribs, had internal bleeding, and this." I show her the long scar on my arm. "A piece of debris from the accident lodged itself in my arm. Thank God I was unconscious because if I had seen myself bleeding, I would've thrown up everywhere."

It feels weird talking about the incident like it's not a big deal. Like it was from long ago. I think it's also kind of weird that Sydney has no problems asking me about it. Most people get sort of weird and vague around me, and they try to find ways to bring it up indiscreetly. Sydney is more upfront about it.

"That's horrible," she says to me, leaning in to get a closer look at my arm. "But the scar is cool."

I offer a small smile. Nobody has called it cool yet. "It's the best way to tell me and my sister apart now," I say.

"Good to know."

I figure since nobody else seems to know anything about the new girl, maybe I can ask Sydney some questions about herself.

"So where did you move from?" I start.

"I've sort of been all over," she replies. "Hey, do you know anything about state capitals? Because if you don't, I doubt we're going to be getting any extra credit points."

I smirk at her and shake my head. She cringes at my answer and gets back to working on the map. I just lean over her desk and copy what she's putting down.

"Do you have a boyfriend?" she goes on to ask.

Back to talking about me, again, I guess. "Oh. Yeah ... His name is Jackson."

"Whoa," she says when she looks at me.

"What?"

"You told me that with not even a glimmer of a smile. Most girls blush and burst into a giggling fit when they talk about their boyfriends."

This girl is good at reading people. "We've just been together for a while now," I explain. But I know that's not the truth. Things have felt differently with Jackson lately. Just like they feel with everybody else.

I can tell by the look Sydney is giving me that she doesn't buy it. "Do you love him?"

I scoff. "Yes?"

"Why are you saying it like a question?"

A new song comes on the stereo, a cover of a Backstreet Boys song. Or maybe it's *NSYNC. I don't really know the difference between the two.

It feels like the room is getting hotter and like Sydney is giving me the third- degree.

"I don't know. That was just a random question," I say. "What about you? Do you have a boyfriend?"

"Nope. Does Audrey?"

"No. Have you ever had a boyfriend?"

She blows some air out of her nose and a half-hearted laugh. "It's complicated."

The entire rest of the class goes on this way. Sydney constantly asks me questions about my life, trying to get to know me, and every time I try to do it in return, she doesn't give me a straightforward answer. I don't know why she is so secretive, or if she has something to hide, but it's slightly infuriating, and when the bell rings and I pack up, I can't help but feel like there's a reason all of my classmates think there's something weird about her.

Still, it had been nice to talk to somebody new. It has been nice to not have to act like my old self.

Not to mention we got one of the highest scores in the class. Turns out pretty much nobody knew any state capitals, but Sydney knew a majority of where each state went. One group even got our own state placement wrong. The entire class was cracking up at that.

Audrey has her last tryout today for varsity cheerleading, so I don't have a ride home. I could take the bus, or I could ask one of my old friends for a ride, or Jackson, even, but he is at tryouts for football. Instead, I walk. It may be three miles away, but the exercise is probably good for my leg. And at least I won't have to be in a vehicle.

As people pass me on the street in their cars and in the school buses, some of them roll down the windows to yell things out at me. Mostly, "Hi, Lyla!" But then there are the bullies who say mean things like, "Where is your car?" or, "Too scared to drive?" or, "Where is Trinity?!"

With shaking hands, I dig through my backpack to try to find some headphones, but I'm pretty sure I left them back in my locker.

"I will just take the long way home," I mutter to myself. Then I cut between two houses to get off of the road, that way nobody else can see me.

Ten minutes later, when I am finally feeling a little bit better, still walking, I get a text message from Jackson.

Jackson: *Are you really walking home again?*

I don't reply to him. He shouldn't be texting me while he's at tryouts anyway. My guess is somebody took a photo of me and sent it to him. I would have thought having the weird new girl at Blackfell High would have been enough for everybody to stop talking about me and focus on her.

I guess not.

Audrey doesn't get home until after Mom does, right before dinner. She strolls in through the garage, a triumphant expression on her face.

Mom is in the kitchen chopping some onion and trying not to cry, and I am sitting at the dinner table, pretending like I'm working on my English homework when really I am doing absolutely nothing.

Joey is at the table with me, diligently working on his reading assignment. The Diary of Anne Frank is sitting open next to him.

Mom squeezes her eyes shut, but tries to look at Audrey at the same time. "So?" she asks her daughter.

"Did you get the results today?" I ask, too.

Audrey takes her backpack off and hangs it on a hook in the mudroom, then she steps into the kitchen with her lips pursed, trying to hide her smile.

"Oh my God, you totally made it, didn't you?" Mom asks her.

"U-G-L-Y, you ain't got no alibi!" Joey starts singing.

"Shut up," Audrey snaps at him. Then she looks back at Mom. "I made it!"

Mom and her squeal excitedly as Mom gives her a hug. I'm happy for her too, but I don't feel the need to freak out with them.

When Audrey looks over at me to see my reaction, I give her a simple smile. "I knew you would," I say.

"It was really hard, though," she said. I thought for sure I wouldn't a couple of times."

I roll my eyes.

Mom goes back to preparing dinner. "I am so proud of you. Are you going to tell your father, or should I?"

"I already texted him!" Audrey says. Then she walks over to the counter and sits on the barstool. "There was this girl that tried out, Mom. You should have seen it. She went every single day, even though it was clear from the beginning that she wasn't going to get a spot." Audrey starts giggling at the memory of it.

"That bad, huh?" Mom asks.

"Oh yeah. It was actually comical. I swear, if somebody got a video of it, it would have gone viral."

"Who was it?" I ask.

"That new chick. Sydney, I think?"

I know that Audrey is one hundred percent certain of what the new girl's name is, but she is just trying to pretend like she is too cool to care. It's something she does that annoys the crap out of me.

Also, I feel bad for Sydney. I wonder how quickly the rumors are going to be spread about her. How quickly she's going to start being made fun of for her bad cheerleading skills.

I try to pretend like I am working on homework again, but Audrey doesn't want to stop talking about it. "Have you met her?" she asks me.

"She's in my history class."

She acts relieved. "Okay, good. Because she kept staring and smiling at me like we were friends or something. I was totally confused. You're not friends with her, are you?" I can hear the disapproval clearly and her tone.

"I don't even know her. It's only been, like, three days since school started."

"She's weird," Audrey informs me. "Like, really weird. I'm telling you, Mom, something is off about her."

I open my mouth to jump to her defense, but I already know what will happen. Audrey will say some remarks about how I must like her, and how I was probably lying when I said I don't really know her. Then she will make fun of me. She will call me a loser and tell me that I am really letting my life go downhill this year.

So instead, I say nothing.

Chapter 11

Warner

I almost don't recognize Lyla when I go up to hang out with her and Jackson.

"Lyla, wow," I say as I bump fists with Jackson. Audrey is here, too, the four of us sitting on the steps in the front of the school during our lunch.

Lyla tenses beside her boyfriend, like she's expecting me to say something mean about it.

I don't. "I dig it."

Lyla has chopped her hair off. It went from hanging down at her waist, like Audrey's, to now being just above her shoulders. Something about it makes her look older. Different.

"You do?" Audrey and Jackson say at the same time.

Oh, now I get why Lyla had gotten defensive.

I raise an eyebrow. "Yeah. Why wouldn't I? It looks good."

"At least someone thinks so," Lyla says to me.

"Do you not like it?" I ask her. "Did you have to cut it? Get gum stuck in your hair?"

"No, I love it. It's everybody else that is against me," she says, looking between Jackson and Audrey.

"I'm not against you, Ly," Jackson says. "It's just … going to take some time to get used to."

"Yeah, and you don't look like me anymore! Everyone is going to be able to tell us apart. So how are we supposed to play tricks on people?" her sister complains.

"Then you should cut your hair, too, if it means that much to you," Lyla snaps at her.

Audrey looks offended and strokes her long mane. "We have such pretty hair, Ly. I would never do that to myself."

I get the feeling that if Audrey could, she would be some sort of shampoo and conditioner hair influencer on Instagram.

Lyla gets a slightly constipated look on her face, then she turns to me and lets out a long breath. "I heard you made football captain. Congrats!"

Audrey's eyes widen. "Oh, yeah! That's amazing news! I can't wait to cheer for you!"

I can't help but smile, even though I'm never good at taking compliments. I can't believe Coach Reeves thinks I have what it takes. It's a huge honor. "Thanks. I'm pretty excited about it," I tell them.

Jackson punches my arm. "We are going to dominate this year."

"Oh!" Audrey suddenly gasps at me, making us all turn to look at her. "Also! How do you feel about your mom being a chaperone on the upperclassman trip?"

Lyla smiles. "Oh yeah, welcome to the club."

Stones drop in my stomach as I look around at all three of them. It's only Jackson who seems just as clueless as I am. "What are you guys talking about?" I ask.

Lyla and Audrey exchange looks. "Has she not told you, or something?" Audrey asks. "Our mom is chaperoning, too. And she told us that she saw your mom at one of the meetings the other day."

I itch the top of my head as I try to process this new information. "Uh… I guess I—I haven't seen her in a couple days," I admit. Then I feel bad for saying it, because I don't want them to be worried that I am some sort of homeless, parentless kid or something. Mom is just always working or always out. I don't think she can stand being alone for one second. So I try to save it. "I mean, she's just really busy."

"Busy trying to find herself a worthy boyfriend?" Jackson asks, shooting me a wink.

A side-eye his girlfriend. "Dude. Lyla is sitting right next to you."

Jackson playfully nudges her. "She knows I'm only messing around. Besides, everyone can agree that your mom is hot."

Lyla looks up at the sky and Audrey nods her head enthusiastically. I internally groan. I still can't believe that my mom is going to be going on the trip, and I am angry that she never bothered to mention it to me.

I can already picture it now. All of my friends are going to give me crap and talk about how they have a crush on her, and then Mom is going to try way too hard to be cool, and she's probably going to get me and herself in trouble. Not to mention, she probably won't let me out of her sight.

"You okay?" Lyla asks me.

I roll my shoulders back and try to look happier. "Oh, yeah, totally."

She squints at me. "Does your mom like camping?"

"I have no idea. I don't think I've ever seen her go on a camping trip before," I say.

"We have no idea why our mom is going, either. She hates the outdoors," Lyla says.

"She does?" I ask.

Lyla nods. "Oh, yeah." Then she chuckles a little bit, too, something I haven't seen her do much of lately. "One mosquito bite, and she's going to be hiding inside one of the cabins the entire rest of the trip, I guarantee it."

Audrey gets defensive. "That's not true," she snaps at her sister. "You are being dramatic. She just wants to spend some quality time with us. And you know, Mom, she's always willing to try anything at least once."

Listening to them talk, it's easy to tell which one of them gets along better with their mother. I am more with Lyla on the parent-child relationship scale.

I check the time on my phone and see that the lunch bell is going to ring in a couple of minutes, and I still want to get to my locker before my next class. So I adjust the straps on my backpack and step away from everyone. "I gotta go, but I guess I will see you out on the field, ladies."

"Lyla isn't on the cheer team this year," Jackson corrects me. I look at Lyla, surprised, and see that she is scrolling through her phone.

"Oh. Then I will see you on the field, Audrey."

Audrey waves at me, and I head up the steps and go inside the school. As soon as I am on my own, I take my phone out and compose a text to my mother.

Me: *We need to talk.*

I don't want her coming on this trip. I can't have her ruining it for me. I've been desperate for months now to have some time away from her, and this was supposed to be my chance to do that.

When I get to my locker, I see that new girl, Sydney, lingering nearby it.

Dread fills me.

I try to pretend like I don't notice her as I put my combo in my lock and pop it open. Then I pretend to be really invested in the books I need to grab for my free period.

Still, she comes up to talk to me, anyway. "Hi, Warner!"

I peek at her around my locker door. Sydney is tall, and kind of pretty, I guess. But she always looks like a complete mess, and everyone thinks she's really weird. Me included.

Since our lockers are near each other, she struck up a conversation with me on her first day here, and she's been trying to talk to me ever since.

"What's up, Sydney?" I ask. I am not a bully. In fact, I am usually the type of guy that will stick up for someone whenever I see them getting bullied. So I play nice with the new girl. I'm sure it can't be easy being her.

"I was wondering when I would bump into you again," she says to me. "How was your weekend?"

"My weekend?" I pile some stuff in my backpack and close the locker. "It was good, yeah."

"Mine was, too," she says, even though I didn't ask her.

I slowly start walking to see if maybe she will get the hint that I need to leave, but she starts walking beside me. So I guess now we're going to walk to my free period classroom ... together.

"Cool," I say to her. The bell rings, and of course, the entire lunchroom has to empty out into the hallway just as Sydney and I are standing before it. I wave at some friends as they pass by, a lot of them side-eyeing Sydney and giving me a look like, "why are you talking to her?"

Then Sydney and I turn a corner and start heading up the stairs. "So you're football captain?" Sydney continues.

"I guess so."

"That's great! I didn't make the cheer squad this year."

I give her an apologetic glance. "Oh, that sucks, dude. I'm sorry." When we get to the second floor, I stop walking, hoping she gets the signal that this is where we should part ways.

She shrugs and looks to the ground for a moment. "It's no big deal, really. I just wanted something to keep me away from home longer. I guess I will have to find something else to do instead."

I nod at her. I don't know anything about what her home life is like, but I don't want to dig into the conversation about it right this second. "There are tons of other things you could do. Lots of clubs you could join. And you don't have to try out to be on the track team, if that is something you like."

She makes a disgusted face. "Cheerleading is about as physical as I would ever want to be."

I raise an eyebrow at her. "You know that in cheer, they have to run around the track pretty much every practice, right?"

She puts a hand to her heart. "Oh! Well, thank goodness I didn't make the team then!" She starts giggling.

I give her a pity laugh.

Then she pulls out her cell phone. "Well, give me your number. I'll text you later about some of the clubs I'm interested in and you can tell me if they are cool or not."

I scratch the back of my head, looking around to see how many people could be witnessing the fact that the weird new girl is asking for my phone number. "Oh, um ... okay."

Sometimes I hate that I'm so nice to people. I don't have any idea how to tell her to get lost because I don't want to hurt her feelings. So I rattle off my phone number to her, and she punches it in, then she gives me a flirty smile.

"Great! I'll text you."

Then she turns and saunters off into the throng of students.

As I walk the other way to head to my free period, I want to punch myself. I should've just accidentally given her the wrong number.

Chapter 12

Maddy

Ever since Warner found out that I'm going to be chaperoning on his upperclassman trip, he's been talking to me even less. He stays late at school for football practice, then he heads to Delilah's or to his friend's house, or he works at his part-time job being an assistant soccer coach. Then when he gets home, he hops right in the shower and locks himself in his room.

I'm not much of a cook, so I rarely have dinner for him—I tend to just give him some cash to pick up food from wherever—but I'm wondering if maybe I should start cooking, if that's what it's going to take to get him to talk to me.

So when I get off work, I head to the grocery store. I pick an easy recipe—some frozen pasta dish for two that all I have to do is heat up in a skillet. Then I grab his favorite soda, Mountain Dew, and I get myself a bottle of wine, and I go home and start cooking.

When Warner walks through the front door, I watch as he tries to pretend like he doesn't even see me as he heads toward his bedroom.

"Hold it right there!" I say.

He stops moving and hesitates for a moment before turning around to look at me.

"Aren't you going to ask me what I'm doing?" I ask, trying to keep my voice pleasant.

He cocks his head at me, asking the question only to appease me. "What are you doing?"

I'll take what I can get from him.

"Believe it or not, I am cooking us dinner."

"I already ate."

Shoot, I hadn't thought to check that first.

"Okay..." I try anyway. "But you're a growing boy. I'm sure you work up quite an appetite from all that football playing. Just have some with me."

"I have a lot of homework."

"Already? It hasn't even been a full two weeks since school started."

He shrugs. "Yeah, but it's my senior year. There's a lot more I have to do besides just homework."

"Like what?" I put my hands on my hips.

"Like my SATs and ACTs, and preparing for college, and making money so that I can go to college."

That horrible, sinking, guilty feeling in my stomach makes itself present again. I hate that I didn't save up any money for Warner's college education. I just thought, when I was younger, that I wouldn't ever have kids. I didn't want any because I didn't want to take a risk that I would turn out anything like my parents. Luckily for me, at least, I am definitely different from my parents. But now poor Warner hast to pay his way through some small community college.

"It'll take, like, ten minutes for you to shovel a few bites into your mouth," I complain.

He rolls his eyes and drops his backpack to the floor. I am starting to think that I'm never going to see my teenage son without an attitude ever again.

Warner walks over to our two-person dining table and flips on the switch for the ceiling light above it. Nothing happens.

Over in the kitchen, I remove the heated up pasta from the stove and wince. "Oh, dangit. That lightbulb is out, Warner. I keep forgetting to buy a replacement."

"We don't have extra lightbulbs lying around anywhere?"

I pause. "I don't know."

Warner walks out the back door and goes to the storage closet out there. I hear him rummaging around as I get plates out of the cabinet and dish us up our servings. Then I grab his Mountain Dew and crack it open, and I uncork my wine and pour myself a glass. Warner comes back in with a new bulb. "You should really check to make sure we don't have things before you go and buy more," he says to me.

"You know what, good point." Normally I would've argued with him and told him not to tell me how to budget., but I'm trying to get him on my good side again. I want my sweet Warner back.

He climbs up on a chair, unscrews the light cover, then replaces the bulb for me. Then he turns the light back on and sits down. But when he notices that dust has fallen all over the top of the table from changing it, he sighs, gets up, wets a paper towel, and wipes the table down.

"Thank you," I tell him encouragingly.

"No one else will do it if I don't."

Ouch.

So, I'm not a big fan of cleaning. Who cares? It's not like anyone ever comes over, anyway.

I ignore his comment and bring the food over to the table. Then I go back and get our drinks and bring those over, too.

"Mountain Dew?" he asks.

I smile at him. "Your favorite, right?"

"Mom, I cut out soda. At least while in football. I need to drink a gallon of water a day, at least."

I don't know why a simple sentence like this is what makes a lump form in my throat. I swirl my pasta around with my fork and nod my head, staying silent. Dinner is not going at all how I wanted it to.

Warner digs into his food, not even bothering to thank me for cooking. We sit there in silence until his whole plate is gone.

He stands up. "Well, this was fun."

He goes to walk away, but I grab his wrist and turn him back to me. "Warner, wait."

"Mom," he says in an exasperated tone.

"Are you seriously still mad about me going on your class trip?" I ask, feeling hurt.

"Are you kidding me?"

"What?" I hiss.

"Yes, I'm still mad! I don't want you to go!"

I'd take a slow, deep breath in, willing myself not to let him see me cry. "Why not?"

"Do you seriously think you would actually be any help? You don't know anything about camping, and you don't know anything about looking after a bunch of kids! You can't even look after *me*!"

I can tell that my son has been building this up inside of him for a while now. He is a good kid, and I know he hasn't said anything until now because he was trying to hold it in. But for some reason, I've made him so angry that he can't do that anymore.

"That is not true!" I let go of his wrist and stand up. "All I do is look after you! All I do is work all day so that I can give you money to buy yourself food and stuff for football, and so you can go on this trip in the first place!"

"Yeah, and then you are never home in the evenings. I literally never see you! How is it even possible to look after me if you're not even here?"

"I'm trying to give you your freedom, so you can hang with your friends and be independent."

"Yeah right."

"Warner!" I am getting fed up.

Someone knocks on the front door and the both of us jump.

"Looks like one of your boyfriends is here," Warner mutters under his breath. Then he picks up the backpack he had dropped carelessly on the floor and starts heading down the hallway to his room. I sigh and walk over to the door to answer it.

A girl is standing on my porch.

"Oh," I say. I'm not sure who I was expecting, but definitely not a stranger. "Hello."

She smiles at me brightly. "Is Warner here?"

Oh my goodness. A girl has come to my house asking for Warner. This is a new one for me.

I smile back at her. "Yes, actually, he is." I step away from the door and only leave it open a crack, so the girl doesn't think she's invited inside. Then I call out to Warner.

When he comes out of the hallway, he has a confused expression on his face.

I point to the door. "There's a girl out there to see you," I say quietly, so whoever she is doesn't hear me.

Warner peeks his head out the window to see who it is, and I can't read the expression on his face when he heads over to the door. Before he answers it, he turns back to me. "Um, I'm going to go. I'll see you later."

He steps outside and closes the door, and I rush over to the window to watch as he and the mystery girl step down off the porch and head towards the street.

As much as I feel like breaking down and crying over my pathetic attempt to get closer to my son, I decide that I will just do something to distract me, instead. I grab my keys, hop in my car, and go hang out with everyone at the bar.

Chapter 13

Audrey

My sister can pretend that she doesn't like attention all she wants, but I know that's not true. She wouldn't have cut all of her hair off if she didn't. I have the feeling she was worried that people were going to stop talking about her accident and move on from it, so she had to do something drastic again to bring the focus back to her.

I have to admit, I'm getting really sick of hearing about her. Part of me wonders if she was jealous that I made the varsity team, so she wanted to do something that would take away some of the excitement over me.

When I talk to my friends about it, most of them agree with me. It's only Danielle who tries to convince me that Lyla is just going through a rough time right now and is figuring out how to feel okay again.

So now, not only am I mad at my sister, I am also mad at Danielle for being on her side.

"So, do you not care at all that she totally dropped you?" I ask Danielle as the four of us sit at our lunch table. Normally, Lyla would be with us, and so would Jackson and his friends. But Lyla isn't even sitting with Jackson's table, either. She hardly ever shows up in the cafeteria during lunch anymore.

Danielle shrugs at me. "It's sort of sad," she admits, "but I can't pretend to know what Lyla is going through, and neither can you guys. Just give her space and let her do her thing."

Sophia glares at her. "Oh, come on, Danielle," she argues. "We all know she only cut her hair because she was jealous of all the attention I was getting from turning brunette."

Danielle frowns. "I really don't think that's the case."

Sophia rolls her eyes. "Whatever."

When the lunch bell rings, I have to head my separate way from them. They all have next period together, and I am alone in my English class.

I stop at my locker, which is next to my sister's, but Lyla is nowhere to be found. I get out my English book and shove it in my backpack, still feeling heated over my discussion with my friends.

When I close my locker door, I scream and jump back.

Sydney is just standing there, waiting for me.

"You scared the crap out of me," I tell her.

She gives me an apologetic smile. "Sorry! I thought you saw me."

"How would I have seen you? You were behind my locker door."

She shrugs. "Anyway. Congrats on making the team."

I have no idea why this random chick is talking to me.

"Um ... thank you?" I don't hide my distaste for her.

But somehow, she's clueless about it. "You're welcome! It's such a bummer that we don't have any classes together. I have history with your sister, though."

I fight the urge to roll my eyes. "That's cool, but just because you know her doesn't mean you automatically know me, too. We're not the same person, you know that, right?"

For some reason, she has the audacity to look at me like I'm the dumb one. "Duh."

I narrow my eyes at her for a moment, then I shake my head and turn around to walk away.

"Wait!" she calls. I keep walking, so she hurries to walk beside me. "I just came over here to tell you that I'm gonna be throwing a huge party when my parents go out of town."

This gets me interested. Everyone at Blackfell High is always looking for a party to go to since there is little else to do in this town. And getting to know where the weird new girl lives seems intriguing as well. I don't doubt that it would give my friends and me lots of stuff to make fun of her about.

"Party?" I ask as we walk.

"Yeah. And I know you and your friends are the girls to talk to in this school, so I figured I would tell you about it myself. Invite whoever you want. It can be huge."

"When is it?"

"I don't know yet. I have to wait until my parents buy their plane tickets. But as soon as they do, I'll let you know." Then she pulls her phone out of her back pocket. "Give me your number and I can text you the details."

I say it to her.

"Perfect!" She smiles at me and flips her greasy hair. "I'll text you." Then she finally leaves me alone.

"Wait, so you were actually talking to the new girl?" Sophia asks me after school. We don't have cheer practice today, so we're standing outside my car while I wait for Lyla to get here so we can drive home together. I just finished telling my friends about how Sydney had randomly come up and started talking to me, and then I told them about the party she plans on throwing.

I shrug at Sophia's response. "There wasn't really any way to avoid it. She was literally standing right outside my locker. Scared me to death, actually. She's so strange."

They laugh. "Yeah, she is!" Olive says.

"Anyway," I continue, "I figured it could be funny. We should definitely tell people about the party. Don't you guys want to know what the inside of her house looks like?"

"Based on the way she takes care of herself, I don't expect her house to be much cleaner," Sophia jokes.

"You guys, that's so mean," Danielle says, but there is a smile on her face, anyway. As nice as she is, she agrees with us about how weird the new girl is.

"Why don't you go be her friend then," Sophia says to her. Danielle begins stuttering, then Sophia laughs and gives her a little shove. "I'm just kidding. Besides, she's already found a friend." She looks over at me and winks.

As annoyed as I am, and as worried as I am that I'm going to be teased about this for a while, I keep my head high and brush it off like I don't care. "Shut up," I say to them. "We all know I would never actually be friends with somebody like her. I'm just trying to find somewhere for us all to party."

Then Lyla finally arrives at my car, and all of us turn to her.

"Hi, Lyla!" Danielle says with a sweet smile. The rest of us just stare at her.

She adjusts the straps on her backpack uncomfortably. "Hey guys," she says.

"Long time, no talk," Sophia comments. My sister avoids her hateful stare.

"Yeah, sorry. It's kind of been a crazy start to the year for me," she lies.

"Okay ... well, I'm gonna go," Sophia says to us. "I gotta do ... something that isn't this." Then she walks away, and Danielle and Olive wave to us and go follow her.

"What's their problem?" Lyla asks me as we climb into my car. Then she buckles her seatbelt and holds her backpack tightly to her chest like usual.

"What did you expect?" I ask. "You have barely said a word to them since school started. They're mad at you."

She looks up at the roof of my car and leans her head against the headrest. "They're mad at me?"

I reverse the car and start driving. "Um ... yes."

"I'm sorry, but where were they when I was in the accident? They came to see me in the hospital all of what, once?"

"Sophia doesn't like hospitals, you know that."

"What about the other ones?"

"They were too sad. Everyone was really sad, Lyla. You know that."

"How about you stop defending them and maybe be on my side?"

I grip the steering wheel tighter. "How do you expect me to do that?" I ask. "You aren't exactly being my best friend lately, either."

She gives me her puppy dog eyes. "Wait, you're mad at me too?"

Did she really not know?

I drive in silence, not really knowing how to reply to that.

She puts a hand gently on my shoulder. "Is it because I didn't try out for cheer? Or because I cut my hair?"

"I don't know. This year just.... It isn't going how I thought it would. I guess it just sucks when I had this perfect image in my head, and it ends up turning out nothing like it."

"I don't think any of us could have expected everything to turn out the way that it did."

I nod. "Still. Things are just... different now."

"I know I've been distant. I am working on it, I promise you. As for things being different ... I don't know. Maybe different is a good thing."

I don't see how, but I don't want to keep arguing with her, so I say nothing instead.

Chapter 14

Amelia

Joey is in one of his moods today. It's a Saturday, and Gentry isn't home, per usual, and the girls are off with their friends doing their own thing.

My foster son gets like this sometimes. He comes from an incredibly abusive family, and he had to deal with a lot of trauma before being placed in our household.

Right now, Joey is sitting on the couch with his arms crossed. His favorite show is on the TV, something about superheroes—I can't keep up—but he's not watching it.

"Isn't there anything you feel like doing today?" I try to ask him, sitting on the coffee table in front of him.

He shrugs, still not looking at anything.

"Is school going okay?"

He's been in the sixth grade for two weeks now, and he hasn't had much to say about it. He just comes home, has his two snacks, then gets started on his homework. When I ask him how his day was, he gives me one word. "Fine."

Joey shrugs again, which leads me to believe that maybe it's not going as well as I thought.

"Do you like all your new teachers?"

"I don't know."

It's not a good answer, but at least he's speaking to me now.

"Have you made any new friends?"

Radio silence again.

I huff. “Joey, talk to me.” I grab his knees and wiggle them a little. He slowly brings his eyes to meet mine, and only for a second.

“I don’t have any friends.”

One simple, small sentence, and it has a massive effect on me. My stomach sinks and my heart falls. Joey has always felt like an outcast since coming to stay with us. I know it’s because of my neighbors, and because of his other classmates. You can’t exactly be the new kid in Toxey without everyone judging you for it.

“None at all?” I try. “What about Kayden Farley? You guys used to hang out all the time last year.”

“We don’t have any classes together and we don’t even have the same lunch.”

I pout. “Well, that’s lame, but you guys can still hang out after school.”

He shrugs again.

“Is that why you are in a bad mood?”

“I don’t know.”

The guessing game. Lovely. “Is it because you miss Gentry?”

He nods his head slowly. “Yeah, but that’s not all of it.”

“I’m sorry he’s been gone so much. I’ll have a talk with him and see if there’s anything he can do to stop having to go out of town so much, does that sound good?”

He shrugs again.

My heart aches for him. I wish he was enjoying school, and I wish he was able to hang out with his foster father more. He could use some one-on-one man-time around here. It can’t be much fun having to always be surrounded by three girly-girls.

An idea pops in my head, making my eyes brighten. "I know!"

The excitement in my voice makes Joey's head turn to me. "We should go to the swimming hole today! You've been wanting to check it out, right?"

I can tell he still wants to be in a bad mood, but that he also loves the idea of going. "Is that the place you used to go when you were little?"

I smile and nod my head at him. "My little sister and I used to go all the time. You'll love it."

"You have a sister?"

"Yes, I do. Her name is Nora. We don't see each other very much because she lives really far away."

"Can she come visit?"

I bite my bottom lip. "I'm not so sure about that." Then I get to my feet. "Go on. Go get your suit on and put on some sunscreen too, will you?"

Joey hesitates, but then a smile slowly spreads across his face as he stands up.

"Maybe we can even grab some ice cream after. Sound good?" I throw in.

"Yeah." He tries to hide his grin, then he turns around and dashes up the stairs to get changed.

I haven't been to the swimming hole in years. Not since I was in high school. I don't know what I expected, but I certainly wasn't anticipating there being a parking lot in front of it, and a marked trail showing us the way. When I was young, the swimming hole was out of the beaten path. You had to know somebody who knew how to get there in order to see it. It was a secret hang out spot for all of us teenagers.

I park the car, and Joey and I get out and follow the path, his mood still quiet, but no longer sad-like.

"It's not too far of a walk," I tell him, giving his shoulder a squeeze.

He nods and looks up all around himself, admiring the greenery.

After a short while, we come across a curve in the path, then we approach the clearing.

"Oh my goodness," I breathe. It's much more packed than I thought it would be. Families, children, and teens of all ages are gathered around, either lounging on the rocks or swimming around in the water. Across the bridge, up where the cliffs get really high, I see that it is fenced off.

I point to the cliff. "See that, Joey?" I ask. He looks at it. "My sister fell off of that when we were young. I don't think I had ever been so scared. She was a terrible swimmer."

"Is that why they closed it off?"

I hum, uncertain. "Maybe. I'm sure she wasn't the only one to have a fall." I continue looking around at everything and notice that there is one cliff that sits slightly lower, where people are still allowed to jump from. Along with that, there is now a snack bar and a lifeguard on duty. I can't help but shake my head in disbelief. The swimming hole has become a tourist trap.

"Can I go in?" Joey asks.

I smile at him. "Go for it. I will find a spot to set up our stuff."

He smiles and wanders off. I walk amongst everybody's blankets, chairs, and coolers, hoping to find a shady spot, but I am unsuccessful. So I lay my beach blanket down in the sun, far off away from the edge of the water, and plop myself down.

I look up to check on Joey every so often while reading a romance novel. The cheesier the romance novel, the better. I like how obviously fake and how predictable they are. I like when I read books where I can easily tell what the outcome is going to be. I hate the unknown.

For a while, I was worried that Joey was going to have to swim either with me or by himself the entire time, and that he would get bored or feel lonely again, or that other kids were going to walk up to him and start teasing him, but to my delight, a young boy approaches Joey in the water and the two of them begin looking at something on a boulder and poking it with sticks together.

My heart soars as I fold the book in my lap and watch them. All I want is for Joey to be happy. I want him to be so over loved and overcrowded with people who make him smile so that he doesn't ever have to think about how bad he used to have it. I want to be able to give him the perfect life, and I try hard to do it. Part of me wishes I could march right into his school and start paying kids to be nice to him, but I know that's not the way the world works.

It's a little uncomfortable being here at the swimming hole because yet again, I can't stop thinking back to my childhood. And about Nora. We used to be so close. I honestly don't know how I would've gotten through my childhood without her. It's too bad that Lyla and Audrey are so much older than Joey, so he can't have a close connection with his sisters like I did with mine.

There is something I just don't like about this place, too. Being back here brings me darkness. It makes my head go back to a terrible time in my life. I work hard to keep my past in the past, and reliving my childhood doesn't exactly make it any easier.

CHAPTER 15

LYLA

I told my mom I am going to go hang out with Jackson today and that he is picking me up. But it's a lie. Instead, I wander over to a park in the next neighborhood over. It has a cute pond, and I want to go feed the ducks.

I don't mind spending time with myself, but if Mom knew I was, she would get all protective and worried about me. And if Audrey knew I was hanging out alone, she would complain that it's not good for me and then she would try to drag me to whatever it is she and her other friends are doing.

It's not that I don't like Danielle, Sophia, and Olive anymore. I just feel like I no longer have anything in common with them. I don't care about the same things as them. It's completely ridiculous that one single moment had such a large effect on my entire life, but I can't help it.

"Here ducky ducky ducky's," I say when I plop myself down in the green summer grass on the pond's edge. Other families are here too, their kids playing on the playground nearby while parents sit on benches and chat with each other. Over in the grass, a couple people are letting their dogs run around together. Over on the other side of the pond, under the gazebo, it looks like a thirteen-year-old girl is having a birthday party. Popular TikTok songs keep playing on their Bluetooth speaker.

I toss some bread into the water even though there is a sign that says not to feed the ducks. But why wouldn't I? They need to eat, too. What's so wrong with helping those who need it?

The ducks start quacking excitedly and swim in my direction, making me feel warm inside. I love watching them gather together and fight each other over the bread. And I love when I toss more in, and they realize that they have another chance to get their own piece.

My phone vibrates in the back pocket of my shorts—ones I made by cutting up a pair of old skinny jeans. Apparently skinny jeans aren't really in style anymore and I had been dying for new shorts. I did a lousy job, but if I roll up the hems, I can hardly see the uneven cuts.

I pull my phone out and see that it's the person I'm actually supposed to be with right now who is calling me. My boyfriend. "Hey," I answer.

"Are we hanging out today?" Jackson asks.

"Uh..."

"We made plans on it, remember?"

"Yeah, I know." I pull on some grass and pluck it out of the ground. Then I grab more bread and toss it in the water. I chuck it with a little more power this time, feeling frustrated. I'm not really in the mood to talk. Nor am I in the mood to hang out with Jackson.

"Okay then. What's the problem?" Jackson asks.

"Why are you assuming there's a problem?"

"Because you don't sound too excited about seeing me."

"I just... I don't know. I sort of want to be alone today." If he cares about me like a good boyfriend is supposed to, he will understand.

"What do you mean you want to be *alone*?"

So much for that.

"I just don't feel super social."

"Yeah, that seems to be happening a lot lately."

"Look, if you are going to make comments like that and act all annoyed at me, then I'm going to get off the phone." I don't want to put up with him right now.

It takes him a second to talk again. "Can't you just come over? I miss you. I want to see you. I'm sorry for being mean, or insensitive, or whatever. It just kind of sucks to hear you say that you would rather be alone than hanging out with me. I am supposed to be your boyfriend."

"You are my boyfriend."

"Well, do you want me to be?"

His question makes my palms sweat and my appetite disappear. Even looking at the bread is grossing me out now.

He speaks again. "No answer. Cool."

"Jackson, stop," I sigh. "Of course, I want you to be my boyfriend."

"Are you sure? Because ever since the accident, you haven't been yourself."

"You have no idea what it's like."

"Then come over here and tell me about it. Seriously. You never even talk about what happened that night. I'm here for you, you know that."

I do appreciate his attempt to consult me. But at the same time, it's not exactly easy to get over to his house. He lives all the way on the other side of town. "Audrey isn't home to give me a ride, so I have to ask my mom."

"Come on, babe," he grumbles. "You have a car. You have hands and legs. You have your license. Just get in your car and come see me."

My chest tightens at the thought of it. He knows how I feel about driving. He's just upset that he doesn't have a car of his own yet.

"I'm not doing that," I snap at him.

"*Seriously*?"

"How can you even ask me to? Are you for real?"

"Ly. All I'm asking is for you to *drive* over to my house. It's not that hard. How else are we going to make this relationship work if you can't drive to see me?"

"We see each other at school and stuff. You have friends that can give you rides places. Usually I have Audrey that can take me places, too. It's not the end of the world if I don't feel like driving. So stop asking me to."

"Not driving your car isn't going to bring Trinity back."

My mouth drops open and I say nothing. I can't even comprehend what would bring Jackson to be so cruel to me right now. I have no idea why he would say something like that to me. He's never been the type of boyfriend who wanted to intentionally cause me pain. At least not before.

Jackson sighs. "I didn't mean it like that."

"I gotta go." I hang up the phone on him.

Tears silently stream down my face as I continue feeding the ducks. I hate hearing Trinity's name being mentioned. Every time I do, it kills another little part inside of me.

She's dead.

Trinity Cruz was another one of the girls in our friend group. It was always me, Audrey, Sophia, Danielle, Olive, and Trinity. We were on cheer together, we had a bunch of classes together, we sat together in the cafeteria, and we did everything outside of school together.

The night of the accident, Trinity and I, who were always closer than the rest of the group, were driving back to her place after seeing a movie. Then the drunk driver hit me, I got knocked into a coma, and apparently, Trinity died on impact.

Me being behind the wheel had caused somebody else to die. I don't care that it was a drunk driver who hit us. If I hadn't been driving, it would have never happened.

Someone sits down next to me, making me jump.

"Hey, are you okay?"

I turn my head to see Sydney. She's wearing a giant pink T-shirt, faded white socks up to the middle of her shins, and ratty sneakers. Her hair is up in a tangled ponytail and her face is bare of any makeup.

"What are you doing here?" I ask her as I wipe my tears.

"I live around here. I saw you sitting here at the pond feeding the ducks—which is super adorable, by the way. I figured I would come say hi. I just now realized that you're crying, though. I'm sorry to interrupt you, if you're trying to be alone or something."

"Oh, I'm fine."

"Do you feel like talking about it?"

I shrug.

"You should. I am a completely unbiased party. I know nothing about anyone in your life or at our high school. So, feel free to vent away."

I think back to the map project we did in history class together. I remember the feeling I had when answering questions about myself. I like how I could be real with her then. So, I figure, why not be real with her now?

I dive into detailed conversation about why Jackson and I had gotten into a fight. Then she talks about how boys are stupid and gives me some stories of relationship drama she had at her other schools. The more we talk and laugh and get to know each other, the more I realize I like having Sydney around. She's super laid-back and funny, and I can tell she genuinely cares about the things I'm saying. She's not one of those people who is just waiting for her turn to talk.

"Jackson is friends with Warner Carpenter, right?" she asks me after a while. When I look at the time on my phone, I realize I've been talking to her for almost three hours.

I raise an eyebrow. "Yeah, why?" I feel so much better than I did when I first got here. Lighter, somehow.

She gives me a devilish smirk. "Well I'm going to tell you a secret."

I grin back at her and lean in, eager to hear it. "What?"

"I think I have a crush on him. Is that weird? Is it stupid? I don't know. He's super cute, don't you think?"

I'm not surprised Sydney would have a crush on Warner. He is completely adorable. He's football captain and a senior—I don't think that there is a single girl at Blackfell that *doesn't* have a crush on him. Especially since he is so nice to everybody. Too nice, if you want my opinion.

"Wow, are you going to go for it?" I ask. I don't see Warner actually giving Sydney a chance, but I am curious how far Sydney is willing to go for what she wants. She already seems to know that everybody at our school thinks she's weird, but she's told me multiple times now that she doesn't care. That she is going to do what she wants whenever she wants and there's nothing anyone can do about it. I like that attitude about her.

"I don't know," she says, reaching over me to grab my loaf of bread. Then she pulls a piece out and starts tearing it up and tossing it into the water. "I guess I don't really know him that well. What do you know?"

"About Warner?" I ask. She nods. "Oh, well... I don't know."

"Come on. You must know *something* about him. Hasn't everyone around here known each other, like, their entire lives?"

"All I know about Warner is that my mom told me I should stay away from him."

This makes her eyes bulge out unattractively. “Really? Why?”

“I have no idea, honestly. Warner and Jackson are best friends, so I hang out with Warner all the time. I can’t find a single thing wrong with him.”

“Then why doesn’t your mom want you to go near him?”

“She probably thinks he’s a heartbreaker or something. I don’t know.”

“What, you didn’t ask her?” Her eyes are narrowed at me and her expression has changed. She’s using a condescending tone now like she doesn’t understand me, and I’m not sure why she is suddenly being so pushy.

“No… I didn’t. Who cares though? I wouldn’t trust my mom’s opinion. She’s not the one who goes to school with him. If you like him, go for it.”

My answer isn’t good enough.

“Well you should really talk to her,” Sydney says. “Because that’s weird. If there is something bad about Warner, I want to know about it. Right now, in my eyes, he’s too good to be true. And I’m terrified of people that are too good to be true. It’s like, what are they hiding, you know?”

I nod my head slowly, feeling a little bit uncomfortable now.

“What about you?” she asks me.

“What about me?” I have already given her lots of information about my life. More than she has about herself.

“What is so bad about you? What are your secrets? Because I also think *you* are super cool. Probably the nicest person at Blackfell. But you have to have *something* wrong with you. Especially since you’re sitting here on a Saturday afternoon all by yourself.”

I think she is being a little too intense for me right now. “No secrets here.” I grab the bag of bread and get to my feet. “I didn't realize how late it was already. My brother has a soccer game soon and I told him I would go see it."

She doesn't move to get up. "Okay. You're going on the upperclassmen trip, right?"

"Yeah, are you?"

"Yeah. We should try and ride the bus there together or something."

"Uh, yeah, maybe. I might have to sit with Audrey."

"Right, forgot about her," she says. "Well, want to text me later?"

She had found me on Instagram and messaged me the day after we worked together in history and it was annoying to keep checking my Instagram notifications, so I just gave her my phone number and told her to text me instead. Now she texts me all the time. "Yeah, sounds good," I tell her. "See you later."

She waves goodbye to me then turns around and stares out at the water.

As I walk home I can't help but think about how good she had been at keeping most conversation topics focused on me, making it so I could barely learn anything about her. I feel like the only things I know about Sydney Hutton right now are that she has had some crummy boyfriends in the past. That's it.

Next time I hang out with her, I'm going to have to dig deeper. If I'm really going to be friends with Sydney Hutton, I need to find out more about her.

CHAPTER 16

WARNER

Things are getting weird with the new girl.

And when I try to talk to Jackson about it, he laughs at me. He thinks it's the funniest thing in the entire world—the strange new girl has latched on to me. Jackson likes to joke and call her my stalker.

It's Saturday night, and he and I arc hanging out at a kickback at one of my friend's houses. Jackson and two others are the only juniors here.

"I'm serious," I say to my best friend. "Like, how did she even find out where I live?" We're sitting on the back porch and watching the others swim around in Zane's pool. Jackson laughs some more, so I punch him. "It's not funny, dude. I'm wondering if I'm gonna have to get a restraining order on her." I don't mean it, of course. Sydney is harmless, but I am having fun making Jackson laugh.

"Oh man, she has it *bad*," he says. I nod my head. "You know you don't have to be so nice to her. She probably thinks you're in love with her in return because you're such a softy."

I sip from my red solo cup. He sips from his. "I don't know," I say. "I guess I feel bad for her. Everyone else is so mean to her. I don't want her to be completely alone."

Another guy on the football team, Cody Lawson, does a cannonball into the pool and water splashes so far that it gets on me and Jackson.

"Bro, come on!" Jackson yells. Cody comes up out of the water and laughs at us. "You're lucky it's hot outside and I could really use the cool down! Just wait 'til I see you in those kayaks!" He's referring to the upperclassman trip we're going on next week. It's all anyone can seem to talk about. Before I found out my mom was going, I had been really excited about it, too.

"You're so lame," I say to him, shaking my head with a smile. But I think it's Jackson's lameness that makes him so well-liked by everyone.

"You're not the only one who thinks so," he replies.

"Are you referencing Lyla?"

He finishes the rest of his drink and sets the cup down. "Yeah, man. I don't know what's going on with her. She's been acting even weirder than that Sydney girl."

I chuckle. "I highly doubt that."

"I don't know, Warner, it's just not the same. She got mad at me today because I wanted to *hang out* with her. Isn't there something seriously messed up about that?"

I get a weird feeling in my stomach, but I ignore it. "Did you ask her how she feels about your relationship?"

Jackson gets on the defense. "What are you talking about?"

"I mean, does she still want to be with you? Is she being distant because she's not feeling it anymore, but she's just afraid to break it off?"

"Why wouldn't she want to be with me? I didn't do anything to her."

I'm not meaning to upset him. "That's not what I'm trying to say. I...I don't know."

Jackson gets to his feet and picks up his cup. "Do you want another?" he asks. I hand him my cup but stay seated on the porch. "After her accident," he continues. "I stayed the same. She's the one who's different. Yet she acts like it's the opposite. It sucks."

"Just give it time. You have to give her a little bit of a break, I mean...her friend *died*, you know? People tease her about it. She was in a horrible accident. She's probably just going through a lot of stuff right now."

He waves his hand at me and shakes his head, then he goes inside to refill our drinks.

When we go back to school on Monday, I am in the locker room with Jackson and the other players, getting changed for practice. Coach Reeves comes in and claps his hands loudly at us. "Time to get out there, boys!" he says in his booming voice. I stand up, feeling nervous and excited at the same time. The guys all shuffle out of the locker room to get onto the field, but Coach Reeves pulls me aside before I can go with.

"What's up, coach?" I ask.

Coach Reeves gives me a stern look. "How are you feeling?"

"About what?"

"About being captain."

"Oh! Great, really. Thank you so much. It's an honor."

Coach Reeves nods his head and puts his hands on his hips. I have a feeling that this isn't all he wanted to talk to me about.

I was right.

"I heard there was a little party on Saturday night," he says.

How the heck did he find out about that? My stomach stinks. "A party?"

It was hardly a *party* anyway—there were only ten of us.

"You are supposed to set an example for all of your teammates. Don't forget that, Warner."

"I think I do a good job of that."

"Good. Because we're leaving for the upperclassman trip tomorrow..."

"Coach, I would never do anything to jeopardize my spot. I am excited to be captain."

"I know you won't let me down," he says. Then he slaps a hand on my shoulder.

I smile, wanting to joke with him a little bit. "Besides, you know my mom is going to be there, right?"

"Maddy Carpenter?" he asks. "So?"

"So it's going to be impossible for me to get in trouble anyway with her around. She's not going to let me out of her sight for a single second." I laugh, hoping he doesn't take me seriously. After a second, he chuckles too, then he pushes me towards the door.

Outside on the field, a couple of people are sitting on the bleachers to support us during practice. Among them is Lyla, Jackson's girlfriend. Jackson is gripping the railing of the bleachers down on the ground looking up at her, the two of them talking. I wonder if they were able to work out the fight they had over the weekend. Based on the way Lyla sits down and sulks when Jackson walks away from her, I'm guessing no.

"You guys good?" I ask Jackson as he jogs over to join us all before we start our drills.

"It's whatever," he mumbles.

I have absolutely no idea what that means, but I nod my head at him, anyway. Then I go stand up next to Coach and we start our practice.

Later when I catch a break to go gulp some of my water down, Lyla is still sitting there on the bleachers looking miserable.

"You okay up there?" I call to her. When she snaps her head to me, she still looks upset, but I think it's only because she thought I was Jackson. When she realizes it's me, her expression softens.

"You're doing great."

I step towards her. "That's not what I asked."

She frowns.

"I asked if you're doing okay."

"Oh. Sorry," she says. "Uh, I guess?"

"Oh yeah?" I smile. "Because you don't really look like it."

"Football isn't really my thing. No offense," she answers. "It was much easier when I was on the cheer team so that I had something to do while Jackson was practicing. Now if I want to hang out with him after school, I have to sit here and endure this."

I laugh a little. "You guys have plans to hang out after this?"

It looks like Lyla goes to fiddle with her hair down by her collarbone, but then she realizes she doesn't have long hair anymore, so she looks at her hand briefly then sets it down by her side again. "Yes. He has some groveling to do, so we're going to get milkshakes at Delilah's."

"He told me you two got into it over the weekend."

She looks confused. "He did? What did he say?"

"Carpenter! Get over here!" Coach calls to me.

I point at Lyla and shoot her a smile. "Hey, good talking to you, Lyla. I feel like I haven't really gotten to in a while." Then I go join everybody on the field.

Chapter 17

Audrey

"You can't be serious!"

But I am oh so serious. "What do you mean?" I ask my twin. "What's wrong with *these*?" We are in my bedroom trying to pack for our trip tomorrow. She had stopped in to see if I had stolen her flannel—the one with the missing button—but then she saw me throwing a pair of heels into my suitcase.

Lyla bursts out into laughter. I hadn't been meaning to, but at least I'm making her happy.

"You can't bring heels to a camping trip!" she cries. "Where do you expect to wear them to? You're going to break your freaking ankle."

I pout and pull them out of my luggage. I guess she has a point. "I don't know... I thought maybe there would be a party somewhere one night."

"I highly doubt that will be happening," she says. "From what I've heard, the parents and teachers watch us like hawks."

I groan. "What is the point of going on the stupid trip anyway, then?"

Lyla laughs some more. "Anyway. Do you have it?" she asks again, referring to the flannel.

I stand in front of my suitcase. "I don't even know which one you're talking about."

She raises an eyebrow. "Oh really? Then why are you suddenly standing in front of your suitcase so that I can't look inside of it?"

"I'm not standing here on purpose."

She stares me down, then in a split second, she dashes over to my luggage.

"No!" I squeal. So what if I am borrowing her stupid flannel? She has plenty of others!

We wrestle with each other, but eventually I give up and my sister lunges into my suitcase and pulls it out.

"A-ha!"

"But that one looks *way* better on me!" I complain.

"We look the same!" she argues.

"Not anymore," I point out.

"Dad!" Joey's voice yells excitedly from downstairs.

My eyes get big as I look at Lyla. "I think Dad's home!" Then I run past her and race down the stairs, thinking she would be right on my tail. Dad has been gone even longer than normal on this last trip. I feel like I haven't seen him since the middle of summer.

When I turn around, Lyla isn't coming with me.

I walk into the kitchen and see Dad hugging Joey and Mom at the same time. I go over and join in on it.

"There's my girl," he says. "Or one of them, anyway. Where is your sister?"

"She's packing for the trip!" I tell him. "We leave tomorrow!" I'm glad I'm getting to see him, at least for a little bit, before we go. But I don't feel like admitting to him that Lyla knows he's here and still hasn't come to say hi.

"I know, I have such a little time to spend with you guys!" Dad says. We all break apart from our hug and Dad picks up his duffel bag and grabs his suitcase handle. "Tell you what. I'm going to go drop my stuff off in our room, get out of these clothes, then I will grill us up some burgers and dogs in the backyard. You two come swim outside when you finish packing."

Feeling excited to hang out with my family—which isn't something I usually feel—I go upstairs and inform Lyla of the plan. She doesn't look even remotely excited to go swimming, but I am too happy to let her bring me down, so I don't ask her why.

We finish packing, then I change into my yellow bikini and Lyla puts on a leopard print one piece. When we head outside, Mom and Joey are already in the pool while Dad is grilling, an ice-cold beer bottle in his hand.

I put my toes on the first step of the pool, wanting to feel the temperature before getting in further. Lyla walks over the edge, looks down at the water for a second, then jumps in without even testing it first.

Joey cheers her on then turns to me. "Come on, Audrey! You should jump in too!"

"I'm not getting my hair wet," I inform them.

"You're such a girl!" Joey barks.

"Is that supposed to be an insult or something?" I chuckle as I slowly move to the next step. The water isn't exactly warm, but I guess it's not freezing cold either.

Lyla comes up out of the water and flips her hair back. Then she swims over to Joey and dunks his head under, and the two of them instantly begin wrestling with each other and splashing around.

Mom holds her hands out in front of her face and squints, not wanting to get water in her hair either. "Wait, wait, wait!" she shouts at my siblings. "At least wait until I get away from you!" She tries to wade quickly across the pool and away from their splash zone.

"You want cheese on your burger, Mia?" Dad asks her.

"Doesn't matter," she replies.

"What do you mean? You either want cheese or you don't."

Mom looks annoyed. "Just... whatever, Gentry. It doesn't matter. I am fine with cheese, and I'm fine without. Just make some of each."

Dad turns away from the barbecue for a moment to stare at her. My mom avoids his gaze and pretends to be really interested in flicking some water with her middle finger as she leans against the edge of the pool.

"You got it, babe," Dad says. But he doesn't sound super enthusiastic.

When he finishes up the food, he sets up a topping station on the outdoor counter, and we all get out of the pool and dry off so that we can go load up our plates. Usually, we're not the type of family to always sit at the same table for dinner, but tonight we do. We opt for the one outside, so we can enjoy the cool evening air.

"I really do love your hair like that, Ly," Dad says to my sister. Then he looks at me. "You should do that."

"I like mine the way it is, thank you," I say through my teeth.

"Fair enough, fair enough. It's just weird to see you guys looking different, for once."

"Thanks, Dad," Lyla replies.

"Joey, school going good?" he asks.

Joey has a face full of hot dog. He was taught manners, so he points out his mouth to show that he can't answer.

Dad laughs. "You know what? We will circle back to you." Then he looks to Lyla again. "How is Jackson? I haven't seen him in a while."

She shrugs and looks down at her plate. "I don't know. I'm thinking about breaking up with him, actually."

"What?!" I ask. Mom and Joey look up at Lyla in surprise with me.

Lyla shrugs like it's no big deal and like the conversation we're having with her is totally casual. But it is so far from it. My sister and Jackson have been together for, like, *ever*. She used to be crazy in love with him.

"Really?" Mom asks when Lyla doesn't reply to me.

"Yeah. I don't know," she says. "Maybe. It wouldn't be until after the trip because I don't want things to be awkward."

"Ly, I think that's a bad idea," I have to say. "You don't *actually* want to break up with him."

She turns her head to me. "I don't?"

"You're just... sad right now. You're not thinking clearly. Once you get back to your normal self and you get past everything that happened last year, you will realize that you still want to be with him. You'll see." I'm trying to be encouraging and thoughtful. I want to be able to give her good advice and help her not do something she will regret.

"My normal self?" Lyla asks.

"Yeah," I reply.

"That's the thing, Ree—I don't think I will ever go back to normal."

Chapter 18

Lyla

The day we take off on our upperclassman trip has finally arrived. There are four buses everyone is going to be split up onto, and everyone on those buses will be grouped together for the remainder of the trip. Each group is assigned a color: purple, orange, yellow, or blue.

The groups are randomly selected—aside from the fact that the chaperones who were parents were somehow able to work out a deal to get their kids on the same team as them.

"Shouldn't there be rules against our parents getting to be in our group?" Warner asks Audrey and me as we prepare to board our bus, which has a massive yellow banner on it indicating what color team we're on.

"Right?" I ask him back. "They could, like, play favorites. That's hardly fair."

Audrey disagrees. "You don't want your mom on your team? I hope Mom plays favorites with us. I'm here to win!" Then she gets on her iPhone and takes a picture of the bus to put it on her social media story.

"If you don't post it on Instagram, it didn't happen, right?" Warner jokes.

Audrey shoots him a dirty look. "I want to be able to look back at this when I'm older. What if our kids go to the same school growing up and get to experience it, too?"

"I'm not having any kids," Warner and I say together. Then we look at each other and laugh, but I quickly stop when I see Jackson heading my way.

I turn back to the bus. "I'm going to go get myself a good seat. Are you sitting with me, Audrey?"

She raises an eyebrow. "Duh."

I give her a thumbs up and get on. Mom is already sitting in the first seat behind the driver, a grin on her face at the sight of me.

"Are you excited?" she asks.

"Just totally *thrilled*," I say with sarcasm. Then I go to nearly the very back so that I am as far away from her as possible and sit down.

Thankfully, not only is Jackson not the same color as me, Sydney isn't, either. Both of them are on the purple team, like Warner, so they're on a different bus.

It's not that I don't like Sydney, but I can't spend the entire trip hanging out with her. It might sound shallow, but I don't want everyone thinking that I'm super close with her. Especially Audrey—I will never hear the end of it if she finds out.

And when it comes to Jackson... I don't know. I'm still going back-and-forth on if I should break up with him or not. There is a chance that my sister is right and that I will return back to my old self someday soon, but as much as I try to, I never see that actually happening. And Jackson doesn't seem like he likes the new me all that much. So I'm just going to try to spend the entire upperclassman trip avoiding him as much as possible.

I sit in my seat and fiddle with the yellow rubber bracelet around my wrist, my name written on it in black sharpie. I wonder vaguely if it's to help identify our bodies if one of us ends up lost in the wilderness, unable to find a way back from camp.

When all the kids are on the bus and Audrey is sitting next to me, Mr. Reeves climbs up the steps to join our group. "Alright!" he cries. "I'm excited to hang out with you all, Team Yellow!"

I look at his wrist and see that he also has a yellow band on.

"Everyone have their bracelets? Their belongings? Is everyone on the right bus?" He walks down the aisle and checks every seat, making us all hold up our wrists to show that we are indeed on the yellow team. "Great! Let's have a good trip!"

The class cheers and claps their hands and Audrey joins in excitedly. I get on my phone and scroll through social media. The upperclassman trip is all anyone is posting about. It appears that even the juniors and seniors who couldn't come on the trip have just decided to stay off of social media altogether, probably too upset that they are missing out. I can't find a single post that doesn't have anything to do with it.

"What do you think it will be like?" Audrey asks as the bus starts driving and Mr. Reeves takes a seat next to our mom.

"What will what be like?" I ask, only half listening.

"The trip!" She excitedly gives me a little shake. "I can barely remember what everyone said two years ago about the last one! I just hope it's fun."

Well, it's not going to be *all* fun. We're still getting graded." Apparently, every single school subject is still going to be covered so that we don't miss out on any *learning* these next three days.

She shrugs. "I know that, but still. I'm excited to hang out with the seniors."

"Are you going to try hard to find yourself a boyfriend?" I ask. I know my sister prefers to date older guys.

She gives me a sly smile and shrugs, saying nothing.

During the drive deep into the mountains and into the woods, to the middle of nowhere, I can't help but notice my mom and Mr. Reeves together. They keep talking to each other and laughing. It sort of seems to me like they're flirting, but that would be crazy, right? My mom would never flirt with a man who wasn't her husband. She is a classy woman. She loves Dad.

About an hour into the drive, Mom and Mr. Reeves start getting *really* giddy and hyper, and they turn around and try to get the bus to sing campfire and road trip songs with them. Most of the bus surprisingly joins in, but Audrey and I stare at each other in disgust. "This is so embarrassing," Audrey says. I nod in agreement.

"What is *with* them?"

"No idea." Audrey looks at Mom and Mr. Reeves again. "Do they even know each other? I've never heard Mom even talk about Mr. Reeves before."

I haven't either. Even when I mentioned that he was going to be my English teacher this year, Mom hadn't acted the slightest bit like she even knew who he was. In fact, I think she even said, "Oh, I hope he's nice."

When Mom and Mr. Reeves finally stop trying to make a scene is when the rest of the bus decides we're going to sing our *own* song. We choose one that's super annoying, guaranteed to irritate them. It's a song that I'm not even sure has a name. It has one verse that repeats itself in a loop, over and over. It's the song that never ends. We all sing it as loud as possible, growing in volume each time we repeat the same verse.

Eventually, it's the bus driver who gets annoyed. He gets on his speaker and tells us all to settle down, then he turns on some country music louder than he's probably supposed to.

Audrey and I sit back in our seats, cracking up with everyone.

When we calm down, my sister sighs. "I wish—"

She stops abruptly. Then she looks worried.

"Wish what?" I ask. She hesitates. So I ask again. "Wish *what*?"

She bites her bottom lip. "I wish Trinity had been able to experience this," she finally admits. Then she shakes her head. "I'm sorry, I'm sorry! I didn't want to say it. I just... forgot for a second."

The smile is quickly wiped off of my face. Out of all of us, Trinity had probably been the most excited about going on the upperclassman trip. She actually loved camping and went with her dad all the time growing up.

"It's fine," I say. But my happy mood is gone. I turn towards the window and stare outside of it the rest of the way to camp. At one point, I feel around the front pouch of my backpack, making sure the item I brought is still safely secured where it's supposed to be. I will be needing it very shortly.

Chapter 19

Maddy

Of course, stupid Amelia Bailey, who always gets whatever she wants, ends up getting to be on the yellow team and sit with Dean. I know it shouldn't annoy me. I know I shouldn't care. But I do. Why does everything always have to turn out her way?

Every time the yellow team's bus passes ours or vice versa, I peek in and see Dean and Amelia talking, both of them smiling big at each other.

Aren't you married, Amelia? Shouldn't you be giggling and smiling at your husband instead?

Meanwhile, here I am with *my* chaperone partner, Mr. Sawyer, a man who is an outdoor enthusiast and is taking this whole trip way too seriously. I had to sit next to him because of how full the bus was, and the entire ride so far, he's talked to me nonstop about our upcoming plans.

"You know," I feel the need to point out to him. "I read about all of this several times over in the packet the principal handed out during the meeting."

Mr. Sawyer, a senior grade teacher in the subject of economics, nods his head like he understands what I'm saying, but clearly he doesn't because he keeps talking. "Good! Glad you read it! I swear, some teachers and parents have *no idea* what we're going to be doing. Like with the kayaks..." He keeps going, but I tune him out. I don't know how I'm going to be able to go for *three* days like this. Already, I'm wondering why I even bothered to come at all.

I turn around in my seat to check on Warner. Thankfully, he's on the purple bus with me at least. He's sitting towards the back on the same side as me, next to Jackson. He hasn't said one word to me since we got here this morning, but I get it; he wants to seem cool in front of everyone. Talking to his mother would be the opposite of that—even though I consider myself to be cool, too. Plus, I think his guy friends all think that I'm cute. I could see them all whispering excitedly to each other when they figured out I was going to be on the purple team with them.

While my head is turned back looking at my son, the bus goes over a bump, and I fly towards Mr. Sawyer, straining a muscle in my neck. I cry out in pain and start massaging it. The bus doesn't stop rocking. We have officially gone off the paved road and are driving over loose gravel. Every few yards we get, I bump into Mr. Sawyer again and his sweaty forearms keep rubbing off on me.

"Oh no, the ride's getting rough. Thank God I brought my nausea medication," Mr. Sawyer says, trying to sound like he's joking as he opens his fanny pack and pulls out a bottle of drugstore medication.

Good, hopefully it knocks him out.

The yellow team's bus passes us again, and when I look through the window, Amelia and Dean are *still* conversing. What could they possibly have to talk about? And why is Amelia even on this trip, anyway? She's not outdoorsy. Never has been. In fact, when I saw her earlier, I'm pretty sure she was wearing a *skirt*. Who wears a skirt in the wilderness? I can't help but get the feeling that she's up to something. That could be the only explanation for it.

Why couldn't she have moved away from Toxey instead of her sister, Nora? I had always liked her better. I would've much preferred hanging out with Nora on this trip instead.

Something that annoys me about Amelia the most is that she reminds me of my mother. And my mother is a horrible human being.

"Now, those boys are being *much* too rowdy," Mr. Sawyer says. "Be a doll and go tell them to settle down, will you? You can get up and walk back there. It's completely allowed. If I do it, I will throw up on someone."

Heat creeps into my face immediately. I don't want to do that. I'm not here to be some bossy little teacher wannabe. I'm just here to spend time with my son. And...

No. That's it. Just spend time with my son.

"Go on," Mr. Sawyer encourages. "It's good to establish that you're in charge, anyway. Show them that they need to listen to you."

Sorry Warner, you're probably going to hate me even more after this, I think to myself as I stand up and make my way back. I have a feeling that, with Mr. Sawyer, this is going to be one long trip.

Chapter 20

Warner

I get on the purple bus with my lame purple wristband in front of Jackson. As we go down the aisle between green seats, I see Sydney sitting alone in the middle. She waves at me immediately and gets a giant smile on her face. I offer her a small smile back, feeling like it would be too rude of me to just ignore her completely, even though that's what I desperately want to do. Then I keep walking. Thankfully, I find a seat closer towards the back and Jackson sits next to me.

Unfortunately for the purple team, not only is my *mom* on my bus, but so is Mr. Sawyer—my Econ teacher. I remember being warned sophomore year to not get on his group if I could help it. Apparently, he acts like this is one big Boy Scout trip. I heard he even tries to get his students to learn bird calls and knot names.

The only thing that brings me a small ounce of joy is the fact that my mom has to endure an entire trip hanging out with Mr. Sawyer. Hopefully, she was already regretting her decision.

For the first twenty minutes of the ride, I sleep with my head against the window. Then when we hit a couple of bumps, I wake up and join in on hanging with Jackson and some of our other friends. We talk and laugh and crack a bunch of jokes until, out of nowhere, I watch my mom walking down the aisle towards us.

She gives me a bright smile and for one horrible second, I think she's back here just to chitchat with me. But instead, she turns to Austin Booth and Chance Hobbs, who are being rowdy as they try to play fight each other over their seats.

"Hey, boys," Mom says with a flirty smile. "As much fun as you all look like you're having, your teacher sent me back here to settle you down." She grimaces like this is the *last* thing she wants to say to us. "I, personally, don't care what you all do back here, but I'm just passing along the message."

I groan out loud.

"Thank you, Mrs. Carpenter!" Jackson is quick to say, perking his head up and smiling brightly at my mother. "So sorry we bothered you!"

I hit him, but he ignores it. Then a bunch of other guys start to apologize to her, too. Austin even smirks at her and says, "You should probably stay back here with us and make sure we behave ourselves."

If he was within reach, I would hit him, too.

Mom giggles in an unnatural way, clearly flattered by all the attention she gets from my teenage friends. Then she heads back up to the front. When I stare at her as she goes, I notice Sydney turned around in her seat, trying to get my attention.

"Is that your mom?" she asks loudly.

"Unfortunately," I call over to her.

I meant it as a joke, and I almost forgot my mom was even in earshot. Thankfully, I don't think she heard me because she doesn't turn around.

Four rows away, Sydney giggles. When Jackson notices the two of us talking, his eyes widen.

"Oh, Sydney! Do you want to talk to Warner?" he asks with a smile.

I hit him again. "Dude, *no*," I warn quietly.

But he continues speaking to her anyway. "Hey, come switch me seats then!"

Everyone turns to listen to Jackson. Because everyone *always* listens to Jackson when he speaks.

Then they all get to watch as Sydney smiles and stands up in her seat. "Okay, thank you!"

Jackson gets up too, and the two of them start moving to make the exchange.

"Jackson!" I hiss at him, grabbing onto his backpack as he starts walking away from me. He thinks he's so funny. I'm going to make him pay for this.

Sydney takes his spot and plops down on the rubbery green seat next to me. She's all dressed and ready for the upperclassman trip— she has on hiking boots, denim shorts, and a windbreaker. Her hair is in an off-centered high pony, bits of it sticking out all over the place. She looks so happy to see me that I can't find it in me to be rude to her.

"Hi," she says in a squeak.

"Um, hi." Maybe I will just fall back asleep, and when I wake up again, we will be at camp.

"I *thought* your mom looked familiar. She's super pretty."

I nod my head uncomfortably. "Yeah, people tell me that all the time."

"She looks so young! How old is she, like twenty-something?"

"Seeing as I am almost eighteen, that's not really possible."

She squeezes her eyes shut for a moment. "Right. That was stupid of me." Then she giggles obnoxiously. I might be imagining it, but I think she even scoots a little bit closer to me.

I go to my Spotify app and reach in my backpack to pull out my wireless headphones. Maybe if I slowly put them in my ears, she will realize that I don't feel like talking.

"So does she like camping?" Sydney continues, asking about my mom. "Is that why she came on the trip?"

"No, she hates it. I have no idea why she's here."

"Oh, really?" She raises her eyebrows. "That's weird."

I shrug. I don't really know what I'm supposed to say to that.

But it doesn't stop her from continuing more. "Does she have a boyfriend?"

This question throws me off guard because I feel like most people who don't know me would have asked if my mom was still with my dad. It's as if she already knows that I don't know who my father is. I wonder who she talked to about me. And *why* has she been talking to people about me? Why does she seem to like me so much? How the heck am I supposed to get rid of her?

"Oh, I don't think so," I answer. "But if she does, I wouldn't know about it. I don't like her telling me about her love life."

"Why not?"

"Because it's weird."

"Why is it weird? She's your mom. Don't you wanna know who she's dating?"

"Do *you* know who she's dating?" I ask as a joke.

"Why would I know that?" she asks, giving me a funny look.

"Never mind," I say. Around me, I can still feel everyone's eyes on us. They all know I'm not interested in Sydney and that she has a crush on me. They think it's amusing that they're getting to witness this right now. Some of them are even sneaking photos of us.

It makes me feel bad for Sydney. I want to tell them all to stop, but I don't want her to realize that they're doing it in the first place. I don't like bullies.

Sydney stays in my seat for the remainder of the ride to our camp. At one point, she even falls asleep and puts her head on my shoulder. This would have been cute if she was a girl that I was interested in. Instead, it just feels uncomfortable and awkward as I sit there frozen, afraid to move too much in case I wake her and she starts talking to me again.

My classmates and some juniors keep taking pictures of us while she sleeps on my shoulder. Someone even throws a small crinkled-up piece of paper at her. Luckily it misses.

"Knock it off!" I hiss at them as quietly as possible. Just because Sydney is weird and different doesn't mean that everyone has to be mean to her. It's messed up.

"Oh, that is too cute," Jackson says when he turns around and sees us. He even stands up in his seat to get a better look. I shoot him the dirtiest glare I can muster, then I pick up my cell phone and go to Lyla's contact.

Me: *You better come get your man before I kill him.*

Lyla: *Oh great. What is he doing now?*

Me: *He's making me endure something I really would rather not be enduring.*

Lyla: *I might've seen it on Snapchat. Sydney?*

Me: *Help!*

Lyla: *LOL! I'm cracking up. Part of me wondered if you guys were like a thing.*

Lyla: *I have to admit. I'm jealous.*

Lyla: *I thought I was the only one she was obsessed with becoming friends with.*

I send her the crying-laughing emoji, then we continue talking back-and-forth. I don't normally text Lyla for casual chitchat, but for some reason, I find myself enjoying it. A lot.

Chapter 21

Amelia

"And then the pizza guy was even getting in on it!" Dean jokes. The two of us burst out into a fit of laughter over the memory we're discussing. It seems that for the majority of the bus ride, we've been reminiscing about how we grew up next door to each other. He had always been my little sister's best friend, so he was at our house almost as much as he was at his own.

"Oh my God, I completely forgot about the pizza guy!" I cry. We keep laughing to the point where my stomach aches and my cheeks hurt.

I hadn't expected to get placed on the same bus as Dean, and I wasn't sure how it was going to go when he first sat down next to me. But so far, it's been incredibly fun and easy. Nothing like what I had been imagining.

"So tell me, Dean," I decide to ask. We've talked plenty about our past. I want to know about his present. "Are you married at all? Do you have a family of your own?"

His smile falters slightly at my question. Maybe he wanted to keep talking about our past for the entire bus ride. Regardless, he answers me. "Not married. No kids. I haven't been able to settle down like you."

I smile and roll my eyes. "*Settle down.* Such a strange expression."

"Why? Are you not?"

"I mean, I'm married and I have three children, but I don't know why that means I've settled down, you know? Why is it that when someone gets married and decides to have kids, it's like their lives are destined to become boring? Like everything important has been done and all that's left to do is just... I don't know, get fat and die."

Dean laughs some more. I like that I can make him smile; I didn't know I could be so funny.

"Well, you're far from either of those things," he tells me. "So I guess you're right. You're not settled."

I give him an appreciative smile. "Thank you," I say before changing the subject again. "Speaking of not settled..."

He seems to know what I'm thinking. "Maddy Carpenter?" he asks.

I nod. "How do you feel about her being on the trip?"

He shrugs. "It's weird. Definitely weird."

"I agree. And it was so out of nowhere, too, don't you think?"

"It's like..." Dean scratches his head. "I don't know. Never mind."

I grab his forearm. "No. What? Tell me," I insist. Then I realize I am holding onto him and quickly let go and smooth out my skirt. I know it wasn't practical to wear a skirt on a camping trip, but it's the kind that has shorts underneath it—I can look cute and athletic at the same time.

He looks down at his forearm for a second before looking back up at me. "It's just been a long time since the three of us have been in the same place at the same time, is all."

But I know that's not what he had wanted to say. Part of me thinks that he is curious as to whether or not Maddy decided to join the class camping trip *because* she found out Dean and I were going to be a part of it. Like she couldn't stand the thought of us going somewhere without her.

But not one out of me, Maddy, Nora, or Dean, has stayed in touch over the years. None of us talk or do anything together. I didn't join the trip as a chaperone just because I found out Dean was going to be on it. It was purely a coincidence. So why would Maddy even care?

Still, I can't help but think about it.

As we exit the freeway and turn into the woods, my heart skips a beat and my stomach drops. I turn completely away from Dean and stare out the window.

"You okay?" Dean asks, sensing something.

My mouth feels dry. "I just didn't realize we would be going out this direction," I tell him, seeing a sign for the Boldosa Redwoods. Then I swallow audibly. "I... I don't really do that well with... the woods."

Even though I can't see him, I can picture him narrowing his eyebrows. "You don't do well in the woods, and yet you came on a camping trip? Makes complete sense."

I chuckle and turn to face him again. "I know I seem crazy."

He doesn't disagree with me. "You know, it wasn't mandatory."

Now I'm finding myself wondering if *he* thinks I only joined the trip because of him. But he has to know that that is the *last* thing I would want.

"I did it for my girls. And because I didn't get to go on the trip when I was in high school. I wanted to know what it was like. And it will be good for Gentry and Joey to have some alone time together back at the house. I'll be with my girls and the boys will be with each other."

He nods slowly.

I get a little defensive. "Besides, I shouldn't have to justify myself to you, anyway. It's none of your business why I don't do well with the woods and came on the trip, regardless."

He holds his hands up in the air in surrender. “Fair enough. I won’t ask again. But just so you know, I am pretty good with nature. You’re in good hands by being on the yellow team with me.”

It shouldn’t make me feel better, but it does. I have no idea why.

Chapter 22

Audrey

The first thing I do when I step off the bus is take in a giant breath of fresh air. Sure, I don't get outside a lot, but I'm super happy to be here regardless.

"Oh my God, this is so exciting!" I say to Lyla. But when I turn to look at her, I find that she isn't next to me.

Pouting, I look around to see if I can spot her, but she's nowhere to be found. What I see instead, is my other friends running towards me. We all join together in a circle and hold hands as we giggle and jump up and down.

"You guys are here!" I cry excitedly. Danielle and Sophia are in the orange group and Olive is in the purple group. None of them got to be on my team.

"My bus ride was so lame!" Olive says. "I literally didn't have anyone to hang out with! I'm mostly with the seniors!"

"Jealous," I say, nudging her playfully.

"We have to set our tents up next to each other!" Sophia says. Then we do some more excited giggling and jumping together.

"Hate to break it to you, but you will be making your tents near your own groups," Mrs. Winston, our science teacher, says. "This is a chance to break out of your comfort zone and experience hanging out with new people,"

"But Mrs. Winston, we have to make sure the cheerleaders get to practice their routine at some point!" I protest.

She shoots me down fast. "It's three days, Audrey—Lyla—whichever one you are. You will be fine until we get back. Now go find your tent mates and get to your camping spot. They've already all been assigned."

My friends and I groan and look at each other as Mrs. Winston walks away.

"She is such a stick in the mud," Olive says, then we all crack up at her camp pun.

"You guys, come on," Sophia says, opening up her phone and getting it ready for a video. "Come, be in my TikTok. We have to show off our cute camping outfits."

I spent a pretty penny on my new hiking boots; Mom and I went shopping together. Lyla opted out—she said she would be fine wearing her Converse. I don't know why she wouldn't want an excuse to buy new clothes, but I guess I'm not her. And she's not me.

"Wait, there's Wi-Fi, here, right?" Danielle double checks, pulling out her own phone.

"There has to be," I say. I had already talked this over with Mom. "That way we can submit our stupid assignments and contact one another in case anything happens to us."

"Thank God," Sophia says, fixing her hair in her reflection on the camera. Then she starts the video, going around and saying who we all are and showing our outfits. "Can't believe we are finally here!" she says to the camera. Then we all squeal and the video ends.

"Girls! Get to your tents!" another chaperone snaps at us. We roll our eyes and start saying our goodbyes to each other.

"I like your boots."

I turn to see who's talking to me and find a handsome blonde senior boy smiling at me—his name is Ryan Copeland.

And he is insanely gorgeous. As in, he is one of the few seniors I could actually see myself dating. I've always wanted him to notice me. But naturally, he has always acted as if he's too cool to do so.

I look at him through my lashes and put on my flirty smile. "Thanks," I say.

"Audrey! Come on!"

I turn again to see who's talking to me this time and find that Lyla is over at our assigned camping spot, close to where the main gathering center of the camp is, between two large redwoods.

I roll my eyes at her, not sure why she's so eager to get the tent set up—It's not like either of us are going to have any idea what we're doing.

When I turn back around to Ryan, he is no longer there. With my heart falling, I slouch and slowly make my way to my sister.

Chapter 23

Maddy

It's going to be impossible for me to keep my eyes on Warner if Mr. Sawyer doesn't leave me alone. Every corner I turn, everywhere I look, there he is again, barking at me some instructions on whatever it is we're supposed to be preparing for the trip.

And Warner isn't the only person I am trying to look at; I also want to see what it is Amelia and Dean are up to. Their groups' tents are on the other side of the main gathering spot of the camp. The two of them are very hands-on with their students, helping them one by one get their tents set up. It annoys me that neither of them looks over in my direction to see how *I'm* doing with *my* group. It's like they're in their own little world. Something about it makes me want to scream.

It's eleven AM when our group finishes getting their tents set up. I'm already sweaty and dirty, and I'm fairly certain I already have fifteen mosquito bites. I try not to act too bothered though because I want everyone to think that I'm laid-back and outdoorsy. I'm nothing like Amelia Bailey. The wilderness doesn't get to me.

"Nice work on the tent, buddy," I say to Warner, who is with Jackson.

"Thanks, I did all the work," Warner says, glaring at his friend.

I put my hands on my hips and tap my foot at Jackson. "Weren't you in Boy Scouts when you were little?"

"He was probably hoping you would come over and help us," Warner says. Jackson shoves him a little, so I jokingly grab the whistle hanging from the lanyard around my neck and blow it. "Hey! No shoving!" I say with a smile.

"Maddy—Mrs. Carpenter, can you *please* not blow your whistle unless there is actually trouble?" Mr. Sawyer asks in the distance.

I turn to him. "It's *Miss* Carpenter, actually," I correct. Then I give him an exaggerated eye roll. He might be in charge of these teenagers, but I will not let him be in charge of me.

Why am I not even getting paid for this? I wonder.

"You tell him, Mrs. Carpenter," Jackson says to me. I turn and beam at him.

"Alright!" Dean suddenly yells from the center of the camp. He has a megaphone with him, but his voice is loud enough that he is still able to grab everyone's attention without it. "Team leaders, does everybody have their tents set up?" He looks around at us, finally making eye contact with me. I nod my head and try to give him a piercing expression, but all he does is nod back at me and move on to check the orange team.

"Great!" he says when he's gotten everyone's answers. "It's time for our upperclassman trip to finally begin!"

Everyone claps and cheers. I can tell the students are excited to get on with the activities and start having some fun.

Dean looks at his clipboard and assigns everyone their first activities. When it's called out that our team, team purple, is going to get to use the kayaks first, I hear everybody on the other teams groan in disappointment. Apparently kayaking is the activity everyone is most excited for.

Jackson curses in his excitement, and I whirl my head around to give him a look. He turns red and clears his throat. "I mean, *heck* yeah!" he corrects.

Warner puts his head in his hand. "Mom, don't you have other kids to go check on?"

I roll my eyes at him—there's no need for him to be embarrassed. I'm not even being that bad. At least I'm not being Amelia, who's pretending like she's an outdoor enthusiast when we all can tell she isn't. Every time a mosquito flies in her direction, she squeals and sprays it with her bug spray.

And no, I'm not just bitter that I forgot to bring bug spray.

Mr. Sawyer and I lead the purple team to the trail, heading into the woods and over to the lake, where all the boats are tied at the docks, set up by the volunteers and teachers who got here ahead of us.

"You do know how to kayak, correct?" Mr. Sawyer asks me as we approach them. "We have to teach them all how to do it."

I sigh in irritation. "It can't be that hard to figure out." Then I march onto the dock with confidence and grab one of the lifejackets out of the pile. "Alright, purple team!" I begin. Then I pause. "Shouldn't we call ourselves something other than *the purple team*? That's so generic."

"The Eggplant Emojis!" someone yells among the group of students.

"Love that!" Mr. Sawyer says at the same time that I point at everyone and go, "Don't think I don't know what that means!"

Then Mr. Sawyer and I look at each other.

"What does it mean?" he asks me.

I shake my head. "What are some other options?!" I call out to the crowd, ignoring him.

"The Purple Posse!" someone calls.

"The Purple People Eaters!" somebody else says.

"The Grapes of Wrath!"

I laugh, amused. "These are excellent!" I say. "Let's take a vote!"

I have everyone applaud at how much they like each name, and it ends up being The Purple People Eaters that win.

Mr. Sawyer looks something over on his clipboard. I think I'm supposed to have one too, but I prefer to be hands-free.

"I don't really know if we're actually allowed to be picking a name other than The Purple Team," he says to me.

"Don't be such a downer," I tell him. "Unless you want our team names to be The Purple Party Poopers."

The kids closest to us who can hear me look at each other and crack up. Even though Mr. Sawyer looks offended, he doesn't push back anymore.

"Okay, the kayaks seat two each, so pair up!" he says. Immediately, the kids look around each other and start grouping together with their pair. I look at Warner, expecting to see him with Jackson, but instead, I see him with a blonde-haired girl. Jackson is with one of Warner's other friends, Ryan. He and Jackson are laughing over in Warner's direction.

I steadily get in a kayak thinking that Mr. Sawyer will get in with me, but instead, he gets in his own one. "We need to be sure to cover all of them," he explains when he sees my uncomfortable expression. I pick up my paddle, feeling nervous, but I can't let them see it.

"What are you all waiting for?!" I call to the kids. "Grab a kayak and get in!"

They all start racing forward, and Mr. Sawyer grows panic-stricken. "In a structured and mannerly order, please!" he calls after me. "If any of you jump overboard or push one another into the water, there will be penalties!"

Boring, I think.

Once everyone is situated, Mr. Sawyer leads the way out into the lake. He turns his boat around so he's facing everyone and instructs them not to paddle until he says. I manage to somehow get to where he is at, already sweating profusely at the immense effort it takes to paddle. I'm probably doing something wrong. Especially when it comes to trying to turn the thing around. I run into Mr. Sawyer's boat several times as I do it, and the entire purple team laughs at me.

I laugh, too, because I figure if I can't beat them, I should join them. And they're liking me so far already.

Mr. Sawyer tries to give the kids detailed instructions on how to paddle in their kayaks and where they are allowed to row. We have the Lake Oshwana completely to ourselves, which makes me wonder if the entire campsite has been mapped out and reserved just for us. I haven't seen any other cars or people around since we first pulled into the parking lot on our busses.

I don't really care how the kids kayak as long as nobody drowns because I'm not sure I know how to do CPR. We were given lessons at one of the trip's trainings, but it was hard for me to pay attention because Dean was the one teaching the lesson. I don't understand how that man is good at everything he does and why he has to be so good-looking when he does it.

The kids all start kayaking, getting their practice in so we can have a race with another team later on in the trip. I have to admit; it is entertaining watching them all giggle and talk with each other and have a good time. Even Warner is smiling, which I rarely get to see anymore.

The only person who isn't enjoying themselves is Mr. Sawyer. Nobody had listened to his instructions on how to do the activity in a structured format, so he is pouting off to the side, continuously blowing his whistle at people who look like they're having too much fun.

"Maybe Purple Party Poopers *would* have been a better name," one of the students says as they row by me with their friend. I shoot them a wink. Knowing my rebellious, anti-rule following ways, I'm probably going to get out of this get kicked out of this trip before the sun even sets. But would that really be the worst thing in the world? At least I could stop torturing myself over the fact that Warner wants nothing to do with me and that Amelia and Dean get to spend the entire trip together.

Mr. Sawyer blows his whistle again. "Hey!" he shouts. I follow his gaze and see that the girl Warner is with is playfully pushing him with her paddle. They both seem to be joking around and laughing, but then out of nowhere, the girl's push is a little too hard, and Warner goes overboard into the water.

"You heard what I said!" Mr. Sawyer barks. "I said no roughhousing! No one going overboard!" His face is bright red and angry.

Warner resurfaces, soaking wet.

The girl he's with slaps her hand over her mouth and reaches another hand out to help him. "Oh my God, Warner, I'm so sorry!" she cries.

"She pushed me!" Warner turns to tell everyone.

"I don't care!" Mr. Sawyer replies. He blows his whistle again, even though everybody is paying attention to him now. "You two, out of the water!"

Why did it have to be *my* son who gets in trouble the instant we get to the camp? I feel the need to defend him because technically, it wasn't his fault that he went in the water, but somehow I get the feeling he would just be mad at me for trying to help. So, I shrug instead. He's not going to like what his punishment is. Whoever gets in trouble, instead of detention, they have to help in the mess hall during meals. Hairnets, aprons, gloves, and all.

Instead of letting the girl help him back into his kayak, Warner takes off his life vest, tosses it into their boat, then swims athletically to the shore.

The girl he had been with is just as bad as I am at figuring out how to get the boat back to the dock without him. I watch as her schoolmates whisper and laugh at her. She seems strange to me—and everyone else, apparently—and not a girl Warner would normally associate himself with. I know my son is more a part of the popular crowd at Blackfell high, so what exactly is he doing with her?

Chapter 24

Lyla

The yellow team, or the *Precious Sunflowers*, as my mom keeps calling us, gets to play "Spotted Bingo" first. We have to follow my mom and Mr. Reeves through the wide Boldosa Redwoods with our bingo cards in hand and cross out whenever we see an item listed on our nature walk. Some of the items on my bingo card are mushrooms, animal tracks, a Banana Slug, and a spider web.

"What is scat?" a kid from the back of the group calls to the teachers.

My mom and Mr. Reeves smile at each other. "Animal poop!" Mr. Reeves says brightly.

"You want us to look for poop?" another kid complains.

Next to me, Audrey giggles. "That's disgusting," she says. My card doesn't have *scat* on it. It would probably be an easy one to mark off, but I don't even care. I'm not playing, anyway. I have something much more important I need to get done. I just need Audrey to leave me alone for two seconds so I can do it.

I don't want to be caught, because this could be my only chance to get this task done out of the entire trip. And I don't really care for anyone to find out what it is I'm doing either. So I'm careful as we go about our hike through the woods.

Whatever Mr. Reeves and Mom points to has to be incredibly exciting in order for me to break away.

Thankfully, my chance seems to come when my mom is convinced she just saw a deer off in the distance. When everyone's heads are turned to see where she's pointing, I give her a silent thank you in my head and turn the opposite direction and dive into the trees. Audrey has found somebody to occupy her for the time being, so she shouldn't notice I'm gone for a while—girl on the cheer squad had walked up to her and started asking her advice about a couple of their moves on their current routine they were working on.

The redwood trees are very pretty, and it *is* nice to admire them without being told I have to. And not walking with a group of over thirty kids is a lot more peaceful, too. Like the way nature was meant to be enjoyed.

I walk deeper into the woods, off the beaten path, looking all around for a perfect spot. I can still hear my groups' voice in the distance, so I'm not worried about losing them. Somewhere behind me, a tree branch cracks and I whip my head around to see who followed me. I figure it will be Audrey or a classmate who wanted to also go rogue, but instead, I see no one. I turn around and keep walking, but I feel strange. I can't shake the feeling of a presence behind me, but every time I look over my shoulder, I can't see anyone.

Maybe it's just a bird, or a rabbit, I think to myself. Or maybe I'm just so worried about getting caught sneaking off that I am almost willing it to happen. Or maybe even... it could be crazy, but maybe Trinity *has* come on this trip with me after all.

I freeze in my step when I find the perfect tree. It's has a trunk wider than the span of my arms, and there's a perfect break in the canopy of trees up above me where a ray of sunshine is beaming down on it, illuminating the ground in front of the tree as if something was calling it to me. It's as if this tree knew I was coming and was showcasing itself to me that it was the perfect place. I drop my backpack down and get on my knees before it. The earth is cold and damp, and twigs and small rocks are digging into my legs, but I don't care. Small insignificant pains don't bother me anymore.

"What do you think, Trinity?" I say out loud. A breeze ruffles some tree leaves up overhead, signaling her answer. I smile, feeling the lump form in my throat. I don't want to cry, because when I rejoin all my classmates, I don't want them to be able to tell. But it's difficult to try and remain strong. No, not difficult.

It's impossible to remain strong when it comes to my dead friend.

I begin digging up the ground with my bare hands. I thought it would be easy to do, but I quickly learn that if it's going to be deep enough of a hole, this is going to take me a while. Fine by me though, as long as I can still hear my groups' voices and don't have to play the ridiculous game of Bingo.

I stop digging when I'm certain the hole is deep enough. Mud is going to be caked under my fingernails until I get my next manicure. I'm pretty sure I even have it on my face from wiping away sweat with my dirty hands, but I don't care. The sun is still illuminating the spot for my burial.

I unzip the front pocket of my backpack and pull out the small photo album. "I know how much you wanted to be here with us," I say to Trinity, looking at the pictures on the inside as I continue to try not to cry. Even looking at her hurts. "Now, in a way, it's like you *are* here."

I slowly lower the album into the ground. As I look down at it, a tear trails from the inner corner of my eye down to the tip of my nose. Then I watch as it drips right on to the cover.

"It sucks without you. You were my only real friend." More tears come. I slowly scoop up some dirt and begin filling the hole. They continue to fall down my face no matter how badly I don't want them to. "You were the only one that knew me. The real me. You were the only one I didn't have to pretend with. Remember when we made fun of my sister and Sophia for getting so worked up about nationals last year?

We couldn't believe how seriously they took a stupid sport that they will never play outside of high school again. Or remember how we would go to the park, just us, and climb on the playground and scream out our frustrations about everyone? About how sick we were of living in a small town. About how annoying it was that our friends cared so much about being popular."

Then I chuckle a little. "Or about how they never ever put anything new on Delilah's menu? You wanted to try lavender ice cream so bad, but the nearest place to get it was like, a three-hour drive."

I stop reminiscing when the hole is filled. Then I pluck the nearest flower and place it on top of the dirt pile. I stay there, my knees on my hands as I look down at it. I thought doing this would make me feel better.

It doesn't.

"Why isn't this helping?"

I burst into body racking sobs, falling back on my butt, the pain of Trinity's death nearly consuming me. "It's all my fault," I say through my gasps for breath. "It's all my fault."

When I finally manage to get my stuff together and stand up from the ground, I wipe my eyes and listen for the group. Then my stomach drops. I no longer hear them.

Trying not to instantly start worrying, I walk in the direction I had come. If anything, I can just get to the trail and follow it back to camp. But as I keep walking, I'm not so certain I'm going the right direction. Which way is north again? Does the sun set on the east or the west?

I stop walking. "Okay…" I slowly say, trying to think of the most practical thing to do in this situation. I pull out my phone and note the time—2:14 p.m. How long have I been missing from the group? How long had I've been crying? I can't remember what time it was when we left the campsite.

I go to the compass app on my phone, but quickly realize it's useless to me if I don't know which direction camp even is. Aren't you just supposed to go north when you get lost? Didn't I read that that was the rule?

"Don't freak out," I tell myself. "Everything is fine. Everything is fine." I keep walking, trying to trust my gut. Another twig snaps behind me and I whip around, my heart feeling like it's about to fly out of my mouth. *Are there bears in the redwoods? Oh who am I kidding, there's bears in* every *woods. What other animals are out here though that can eat me?*

If I call out for help, is that only going to attract myself a predator?

I try calling Audrey again, just in case my phone somehow works. Instantly, the call fails. Every crack, creak, and rustle of branches begins to make me more and more terrified.

I keep walking through the woods, thinking the worst possible scenarios in my head and doing the exact opposite of not panicking. It's only after I finish thinking, *Thank God I'm wearing the stupid rubber bracelet with my name on it so they can identify my decomposing body months from now*, that I hear someone calling my name.

I race towards the sound of it. "Over here!" I yell. Then I trip over a tree root and fall face-first into the ground.

I try to untangle my foot from the branch and stand myself back up. I can still hear them calling out to me.

"Lyla?"

I jump and turn in the opposite direction. That had been a different voice, and it had been much, much nearer.

"Hello?" I call.

"Lyla, where are you?!" the far away voice says again. I turn around myself wildly. Whoever else had just spoke to me sounded so close. I hadn't imagined it, had I?

I go back to following the other voice instead.

"Over here! Hello?!" I yell back.

Eventually, after more walking, I finally find myself reunited with a park ranger and a chaperone from the camp.

"Do you know you have about four different groups of adults looking for you right now?" the park ranger says with a hand on her hips. Then she radios someone on a walkie-talkie, letting him know that I have been found.

The volunteer from camp seems apathetic about the whole thing. "Looks like you're going to have fun tonight!" she says, even though I have no idea what she's talking about.

When we arrive back at the campsite, my mother marches right up to me and throws her arms around me. "My goodness, Lyla, what on earth are you thinking?" she asks. "You know better than to leave the group behind! You don't know anything about the outdoors!"

Mr. Reeves stands behind her with his hands on his hips. "What exactly were you doing?" he asks.

I look behind them and see several kids staring at me and talking to each other. I notice the phones, too, a lot of them aimed at me, some of them not even trying to be discreet about it. *There crazy Lyla goes again, doing something else to draw attention to herself.*

It's not like I meant for this to happen. I don't want the attention. I just want to be left alone.

"I'm sorry. I... just stopped to tie my shoe!" It's the lamest lie in the entire world and I know they're not going to buy it. But I refuse to tell them the actual reason I had separated from the Precious Sunflowers.

"And you had to wander into the middle of the woods before tying it?" Mr. Reeves asks as mom let's go of me and stands beside him.

"Um... I'm a really slow shoe tier?"

"Lyla!" Mom snaps. That's her *don't mess with me* voice.

"Sorry." It's all I'm going to offer.

"Yeah, well you're going to be," Mom says. "Looks like you've just signed up to serve dinner in the mess hall tonight."

The punishment isn't nearly as bad as I thought it would be. I'm guessing that I can't get sent home because Mom already paid for the trip upfront, and there would be a lot of angry parents if their kids were sent home. I know I look ridiculous in my apron in hairnet, and I know everyone is going to make fun of me and take pictures, but as long as they aren't trying to figure out why I really went in the woods, I will put up with it.

"Don't *we* look cute," Warner says, standing in between Sydney and me as we prepare to serve whatever slop is in the big metal trays at the counter in the mess hall. The students, teachers, and chaperones are all seated in random spots since this is one of the few places we're not required to sit with our teams. As they talk amongst each other, the hall echoes with their voices. The tables are made of plastic and aluminum with the benches already attached, pushed together to create four long rows like we are in a knock off version of a Harry Potter novel.

"I think this hairnet looks really good on me," Sydney jokes, shooting me a wink. I bet she's thrilled to be hanging out with Warner. I don't have any idea what got them in trouble. Part of me wonders if she planned for this to happen to the two of them.

"Oh, it's definitely an improvement." Warner says. This gets a chuckle out of me. Then one of the kitchen ladies barks out instructions to us, and we lineup at our serving stations. I am serving the mysterious mushy brown stuff that is apparently franks and beans, then Warner is a little bit down the line where he has to hand out the pieces of corn on the cob with his metal tongs. Then on the other side of him, Sydney passes out little muffin rappers with corn bread on the inside. After we're situated, someone gives the signal that it's time to dish up, and the massive line begins.

"So, what are you in for?" I ask Warner as I slap spoonfuls of food onto my peers' trays.

"I went overboard in my kayak. Apparently, we can only swim at designated times or something."

I smile. "I got lost in the woods."

"Oh, I heard." Of course he did. That's all anybody wants to talk about.

"What's up, Ly?"

I look up and see my boyfriend glaring at me. I haven't spoken to him once the entire day. "Jackson, hi." I scoop him up his food. "Want me to sneak you extra?" I try to sound extra nice so that he's not as mad at me. It doesn't work.

"Not of whatever the heck this is," he snaps.

I cringe. "Good point."

He doesn't move. He just stands there staring at me, holding up the line. "What happened? Where were you today?"

My cheeks flush. "Can we talk about this later?"

He stares at me for a little bit longer, then he shakes his head and moves down the line to get his corn from Warner.

Now I'm *really* glad I am on dinner serving duty. Maybe I should request to do it tomorrow, too.

A few minutes later, Warner speaks to me again. "Hey, do you ever get the feeling that our parents hate each other?"

"Yeah, actually. What is that?" I ask him. Maybe his mom has told him something that our mom hasn't.

Warner shrugs. "I have absolutely no idea, but I feel like your mom can't say a single word without mine making some sort of disgusted face," he says. We laugh at how childish it is.

Then later, when my mom finishes getting her food after Warner's mom had already sat back down, Warner throws one of his corns at me to catch my attention. It hits me right on my bicep and thuds to the floor.

"Did you just throw *corn* at me?" I ask. Down the serving line, I can see Sydney staring over at us like she longs to be a part of the conversation.

"Look!" Warner commands, pointing down an aisle between two rows of tables. My mom is walking with her meal tray over to where all the teachers and chaperones are sitting. I watch as she grows closer and closer to where Maddy Carpenter is sitting, a visibly open seat right next to her. When my mom sees the open seat, she stops walking, and looks like she's considering. Then she resumes walking towards the very end of the table and takes a seat down there instead. Warner and I crack up as we watch.

"What's so funny?" Sydney calls to us. We ignore her and keep laughing.

Chapter 25

Amelia

Naturally, the yellow team is scheduled to go against the purple team after dinner for charades at the stage. There's two other campfire stations in the center of everybody's camping sites, and the orange team gets to go make S'mores and hang out with one another while the blue team has to sit around and talk about their goals for after high school. As much as I would have loved to prolong the charades competition with Madeline Carpenter's team, I also figure it's probably best to just get this over with.

Dean gets up on stage first to get the show started, since we teachers and chaperones can both hear the kids talking about how lame playing charades sounds. What other way would we be able to entertain a large group of teenagers in the middle of the woods at nighttime?

"Alright, my yellow team!" Dean calls, clapping his hands together and trying to get everyone riled up. Luckily, we have some football players in our group because they cheer on their coach. I hold out a basket for Dean, and he draws a folded piece of paper that tells him the thing he has to act out. "Now, if the rules of charades aren't clear to some of you, only the yellow team is allowed to guess! We have a timer of thirty seconds to get it right."

We collectively count him down and then set the timer, and he begins his silent acting. Instantly, someone is able to guess that he is a flying squirrel.

Then a couple of other members of the yellow team put on their performances in between the purples', but after that, no one else seems like they want to go up and act. I hadn't anticipated going up there on the stage, but I like to win, and I'm kind of excited to show off to Maddy that I'm not afraid to embarrass myself. I don't know why I care or why it matters, but for some reason, it just does.

The second I walk up on stage while some kids from the yellow team clap for me, Maddy lets out a loud, elongated "Boo!"

I glare at her, then look at my daughters, who are exchanging strange looks with each other. No other performers got booed until I came on stage. Feeling the need to stand up for myself, I walk over to the microphone. "Excuse me, Maddy, is it?" I start. She rolls her eyes. "It's important that we all be respectful to one another... and set a good example for the kids." I look over at Dean and see him nodding in agreement. At least I have him on my side.

"Oh, come on!" Maddy says, waving a dismissive hand at me. "I'm just having some good old-fashioned, Flynn, harmless, competitive fun!" Some of the kids on her team murmur their agreement. Then she stands up from the log she's sitting on and steps up on it. "Purple People Eaters!" She chants. "Purple People Eaters!" She keeps repeating it as she pumps a fist in the air, and quickly, the rest of the team is chanting it with her. I feel hot and sweaty and my throat has gone dry, and I stand there and wait for the chant to die down. How on earth am I supposed to put on an act after that?

Sighing, I turn and grab the piece of paper out of the basket Dean is holding.

"It's okay, you got this," Dean whispers to me. I give him an appreciative smile and open up the folded paper. A *blind painter.*

"Come on, Mom!" Lyla yells at me in the crowd, standing on two feet. Audrey quickly gets up and joins her.

"Yeah, Mom! Come on! Let's kick their butt!"

Feeling overwhelmed with my love and pride in my daughters, I began acting. With my daughters on my team, the two of them shouting out and getting incredibly into every action I do, the yellow team eventually gains more interest, too, and when the timer is up, we've gotten 10 guesses right from continuously picking papers from the basket.

"Looks like the yellow team wins!" the mediator on the stage calls out afterwards. The yellow team bursts into applause and cheers, and I run off the stage and go hug my daughters.

Chapter 26

Warner

When the campfire is finally coming to an end and everyone has a little bit of free time before they have to go to their tents for the evening, Coach Reeves finds me hanging out with some guys from the football team.

"Mind if I have a word?" he asks. His expression is hard. I can tell that Coach is in his teaching mode and not his coaching mode—those are his two versions of himself. They are very different. When Coach is coaching, he gets loud and either really angry or really excited. When he's in his teacher mode, he gets quieter and more serious. He's kind and sincere, and harsh only when he needs to be.

I am sitting around a nearly dead fire with Chance, Austin, and Ryan. Some senior girls are trying to get our attention on the other side on the log they're sitting on. They keep giggling and looking over at us. Chance and Austin love it, Ryan plays it to cool, and I, for some reason, don't find that I'm interested.

"Yeah Coach, sure." I stand up as everyone eyes us curiously. Coach Reeves walks away from the fire over into a small gathering of trees to the side, and I follow him dutifully.

"So you got in trouble today," he comments when we are alone.

Shoot. I should have known this was coming. He told me to make sure I don't get in trouble on this trip. I hadn't even made it more than three hours without getting busted.

"Coach, I can explain. It wasn't my fault—"

"What did we talk about yesterday?" Evidently, Coach doesn't want to hear any of my excuses.

"I know, I know, but—"

"You mentioned that you were grateful to be captain this year. But you know what, I don't think I believe you."

"Coach, that's not fair. It's super important to me." Is he going to take the position away from me? Because of Sydney?

"Then what is it? Are you acting out? Upset about your home life or something?"

I give up. "No, sir."

"You just like disobeying teachers' orders and doing whatever you want?"

"No sir."

"Warner."

I look him in the eyes, my blood boiling that this conversation is even happening.

Coach is mad. "One more chance. You got it?"

I nod my head repeatedly, feeling relieved.

"Are you dating that Sydney girl?" he asks, his expression softening a bit.

I make a face of repulsion. "Definitely not. She… she won't leave me alone."

"Well, I suggest you do something about that. You can't have her dragging you down."

"I completely agree. Don't worry, I will handle it."

He lets out a sigh. "All right, you can go."

"Thank you, Coach." I turn and try to head back to my friends. I'll think about what I want to do about Sydney later, but I could use some fun tonight.

I only make it about twenty steps when my mom's voice calls out to me. "Warner!"

Feeling exasperated, I turn to her begrudgingly.

"Can I talk to you? Inside my cabin?"

"I was just about to go hang out with my friends," I try. Immediately, I expect her to start a fight. Argue with me about how she just wants to spend time with me and how I'm not being a very good son.

I'm surprised when instead, she nods her head and crosses her arms. "Yeah, okay. Of course." Then she turns and starts walking away with her head down. I can sense that something is bothering her and that she's upset, and even though I *really* want to go hang with my friends and try to enjoy this upperclassman trip, I don't like the thought of her sitting in her cabin alone and sad.

There I go again, being way too nice.

I start racing after her. "Mom, wait up!"

When we reach Mom's cabin, I snicker.

"What?" Mom asks as we walk up the little steps to the little porch in front of the little door.

"This is basically a tent, just made out of wood," I say. "Does it even have AC?"

The cabins—if they can even be called that—look barely big enough to fit more than two people. They're run down an old-looking and some of them have the screen door hanging off of its hinges. As I think about the spiders and snakes that might have made their homes inside of them, I think I almost prefer my tent.

"It doesn't," Mom answers. She unlocks her door and inside we go. It's even more pitiful in here. There is a single bunk bed with twin-sized beds and a desk. Not even a dresser or anywhere to store her clothes. "How's the mattress?" I joke, walking over to it and laying down. It's rock hard.

"I know, I know, I don't know what I was thinking volunteering for this."

I put my hands under my head to prop it up a little so I can look at her. She's standing over by the desk, one hand on top of it.

"Well, at least the Purple People Eaters really like you," I tell her. "I think you make it seem like it's not that bad to have Mr. Sawyer as our other team leader."

I don't know why am even complementing her. It's just that my mom looks so strange out of her element. She looks vulnerable here. I don't like it.

I watch her corners of her lips curl up even though I can tell she's trying not to smile. "Well, are you having fun?"

I shrug. "I know that serving dinner in the mess hall was punishment, but it was actually pretty fun."

"Because you got to hang out with Sydney?"

"No, because I got to hang out with Lyla. I don't think I ever realized how much fun I have around her."

"That's Jackson's girlfriend, right?" she asks. Her voice is casual, but I secretly wonder if she's trying to remind me that Lyla is taken.

"Yeah. I don't normally hang out with her when Jackson's not around. She's different without him."

"Different how?"

I sit up and drape my feet over the side of the bed. "I don't know. And I also think she has sort of changed since she got in her accident last year."

"The one that killed Trinity Clearwater?"

"Yeah, but it was a drunk driver that killed her. Not Lyla."

"I see."

I don't normally come to my mom for advice, but since I'm here, I figure I might as well. "You know, Jackson doesn't even seem like he's interested in her anymore."

She sits in the tiny desk chair and crosses her arms. "How so?"

"They're always fighting, and Jackson is always complaining that she is different and he doesn't like it. Do you think they should break up?"

"Do I think they should? I'm not sure. Haven't they been together for a long time? Maybe they're just going through a phase."

What I'm about to say is going to make me sound like a terrible friend. "I sort of hope they do," I admit. "I like her, Mom. How messed up is that?"

I watch as her eyes widen while she processes what I just told her. Not only do I not ever tell her about the girls I crush on, but it's also my best friend's *girlfriend*. I know it's wrong.

"Wait a second," Mom starts. "You like Lyla Bailey?"

"Yeah."

"What about that girl in the kayak?"

I crinkle my nose. "Sydney? No."

"What about any other girl?"

"What *about* any other girl?" I deadpan. "There's nobody else I have feelings for. I don't want it to be Lyla, but it is."

She grips the back of the chair as she faces me. "Warner, sweetie. That's a horrible idea."

"I know she's my best friend's girl," I say. "But if Jackson doesn't like her anymore…" I'm hoping my mom will tell me that as long as Jackson doesn't have feelings for her, it's okay for me to go for her.

Mom shakes her head. “Absolutely not. Even if she wasn't Jackson's girl. Both of those girls, Lyla and Audrey. I wouldn't want you dating either of them.”

I feel defensive of them. “Why not?” I ask as I scowl at my mother. “You don't even know them.”

“I've heard things,” she argues.

“What kind of things?”

“Just *things*, Warner. Okay? They're not good girls and you'd be much better off with somebody else.” She stands up and starts rummaging through her suitcase that's sitting on top of the desk. “Regardless. You can't do that to your friend. Even if he breaks up with her. Isn't there, like, a bro code for that? And with both of you being on the football team… I would just hate for things to get complicated.”

I groan. “Speaking of the football team…”

She turns to give me a concerned look. “What's wrong?”

“Coach Reeves lectured me today about getting in trouble. He's been lecturing me a lot lately. And he was super rude about it today, too. It's not *my* fault that Sydney pushed me in the water. But he wouldn't even let me explain myself.”

Her face twists into an angry expression. “And why exactly was he lecturing you?”

“Because apparently, that's not how the captain of the football team is supposed to act.”

“But he didn't let you explain yourself. That's not fair.”

I fling my hands in the air. “That's what I said!”

But the more I look at my mom, the more I wish I hadn't said anything about him at all. She looks like she's about to march out of this cabin and go scream at him. That's the last thing I want.

“But it's fine,” I try to correct. “I get that I'm supposed to set a good example. He's just… Trying to do his job.” I get to my feet. “Anyway, I should go.”

She looks at her watch around her wrist. "Yeah, that's probably a good idea." Her voice is tight and her jaw is tense.

"Mom, it's fine, really," I tell her about Coach. "I was being dramatic." Then I wrap my arms around her, trapping her hands by her sides as I squeeze her, hoping that my sudden affection will distract her from how angry she is at Mr. Reeves right now. I notice her smiling right away.

Good. The happier Mom is, the less she meddles. And I really can't have her meddling in my life right now.

CHAPTER 27

Audrey

Inside of my tent with Lyla, while digging through my suitcase, I freeze.

Lyla, who is wiping off her makeup with a wipe, gives me a funny look. "What's wrong?" she asks.

"You know what?" I ask. She waits. "I'm going to go to Mom's cabin. I want to use her make-up wipes. Have you tried them?"

Lyla stops wiping her face with the ones she brought. "No? What's wrong with these? They work fine."

so freaking soft." I stand up as straight as a tent will allow and undo the zipper door.

"But Mom's cabin is all the way on the other side of camp," she tells me. "Curfew is soon."

"I'll be fine," I say. Then in my UGG boots, I crawl out of the tent and make my way to where my mom is staying. There are still a few kids and teachers lingering about out here—the curfew officially starts at ten p.m., and we're not allowed to leave our tents at that point. I say hi to a couple of people as I cross through the center.

The closer I get to the chaperone's cabins, the darker and quieter it gets around me. Their cabins are off a little way up a small hill, lined up in a row and looking like a set straight out of a horror movie. I have no idea which one my mom is staying in, so I head to the cabin on the very right and decide I will peek in through the windows and work my way down until I find her. It's super nosy of me, but I don't really care. It will be funny to see how teachers live outside of school. Maybe I'll catch them doing something embarrassing and I can tell my sister and friends about it. Maybe I can tell that cute Ryan Copeland guy, too.

I stand under the window of the first cabin. The windows are high up and small, so I have to get on my tippy toes to be able to peer into it. There's no one inside this cabin. But from the looks of the Nikes on the floor and a stack of reading books on the desk, I assume that it is Mr. Reeves's cabin. He definitely strikes me as the kind of guy that reads before bed.

I go around the backside and creep to the next cabin. That way I'm not spotted through any of their screen doors. It's so dark outside, however, that I don't even know if they would realize someone was standing outside if they *did* look out their windows. It probably looks like pitch black darkness to them.

As I stand under the second cabin's window, I can hear people talking inside. I assume Mr. Reeves is one of them because I recognize his voice and he's not outside and he's not in his own cabin, either.

Not liking the idea of him being in this tiny little cabin with my mother, whispering to each other late at night, I get on my tiptoes again and peek through the window. When I see Maddy facing the window talking to my English teacher, I duck quickly. Then I hold my breath and wait, hoping Maddy didn't see me. My sister said serving in the mess hall hadn't been that horrible, but I still don't want to do it. I cannot picture myself in a hairnet. And my friends will make fun of me for months.

Inside, Maddy is speaking to Dean in a hushed, irritated voice. I listen, but can no longer see them. "I don't care that you *were* his teacher. I don't care that you *are* his coach now. It does not give you the right."

Mr. Reeves, who had been sitting on her bed when I first looked in, his back turned to the window, speaks next. "I'm just doing my job," he tells her, sounding just as irritated. "Maddy, I respected everything that you've asked of me."

"No, you haven't!" Maddy hisses. "If you respected everything that I've wanted, then you wouldn't be here at all! Why are you doing this to me? Why did you come back?"

Forget about the make-up wipes, this gossip is so much more exciting than having a soft face.

"To take the teaching job," he tells her.

"I don't want to hear another one of your lies!" Maddy cries. I hear a creaking sound, and I can only assume that Mr. Reeves has gotten to his feet.

"Fine!" Mr. Reeves snaps. "To be closer to him! There, I said it. Is that so wrong?"

Maddy scoffs at him. "Are you kidding me?" she asks. "Of *course*, it's wrong!"

"*Why*?"

"Because I don't want you having a relationship with him, Dean!"

"He's my son, Maddy. If you're not going to let me be in his life as his father, then you have to let me have this."

I slap a hand over my mouth. From what I know about Warner and what everyone says about him, he's never known who his father is. His mother has always said she doesn't know, either. But she does know.

Warner's father is his football coach and my English teacher. Warner's father is Mr. Reeves.

Chapter 28

Maddy

I don't eat breakfast the next morning in the mess hall. Not only is it because I don't trust the food being prepared in these old and not well-kept kitchens, but because the knots in my stomach have taken away all of my appetite.

So instead of sitting with the teachers and other chaperones while they feast on their meals, I head outside and start preparing the activities for today in the center of camp. Then, when everybody comes outside after they finish eating and break into their groups, I decide that it's time for me to do this.

I walk over to the folding table where the teachers and chaperones are keeping all of their supplies and pick up the megaphone. Then I go and stand off to the side where no one else is standing nearby and figure out how to work it. It makes a loud squealing noise and several kids clamp their hands over their ears and duck. Cringing, I smile at them all and talk into it.

"Audrey Bailey, please come here." I scan the crowd for her and don't immediately see her. "Audrey Bailey!"

She emerges from a group of cheerleaders. Her big blue eyes look startled as she fiddles with her hair and makes her way slowly over to me.

I don't have the patience for this glacial pace of hers. "Chop chop!" I say into the megaphone.

She turns back to her friends and shrugs at them, then she moves to me with a little more efficiency. I turn the megaphone off and set it by my feet.

"Hi," she says quietly with a smile. I can see right through her fakeness.

I pull an item out of my pocket and dangle it in front of her face.

She gasps. "My bracelet!" She reaches out to lunge for it, but I pull it back before she can get her fingers around it.

"Yes, *your* bracelet," I say. "Do you want to know where I found it?"

"Um, not really," she squeaks.

I ball the rubber bracelet up in my hand and hold it close to my chest as I lean in closer to her. "I thought I heard someone outside my window last night," I say in a lowered voice. I look around us to make sure we're not being overheard, and when the coast is clear, I resume. "After I finished my chat with Mr. Reeves, the English teacher, I decided to go outside and do a little investigating. And lo and behold, there it was, just *waiting* to be found."

Audrey's face reddens. I love how I am making her sweat. I bet her heart is hammering in her chest like it is in mine.

"I—I must have dropped it while trying to find which cabin my mother was staying in," she claims. "Thank you so much for finding it for me. Miss Carpenter."

I step closer to her. I make myself as threatening and scary-looking as I possibly can. It's a look usually only reserved for when Warner is in big trouble. But I have a feeling it will work on her, too. "Whatever you think you heard last night, you're wrong. And whatever you're thinking inside that pretty little head of yours, you need to keep it to yourself. Am I understood? Because if you don't, bad, *bad* things will happen to you. I guarantee it."

She swallows and nods her head. "I won't say anything," she whispers. "I promise."

I toss her bracelet at her. She looks scared enough. I think I can trust her to keep her word.

Do I have a plan in case she *does* decide to blab to Warner or somebody else? No, I don't. I just have to hope and pray that it doesn't come to that. The last thing I ever want is for Warner to know who his father is.

Chapter 29

Lyla

I nearly collide with Sydney on my way out of one of the bathrooms this morning. I had just finished getting ready for the day and was going to join Jackson in the mess hall for breakfast. Things hadn't been great with him yesterday when I sat next to him during charades and when we went on a walk around the campsite together afterwards. It felt awkward and silent between us. But Jackson had told me it was only because I've been super distant, and if we just hang out more often, it wouldn't feel so strange. The only reason I agreed to give it a shot was because he didn't mention that he hoped things would go back to how they *used* to be. I think he's finally starting to understand that that's not going to happen. Especially after he got it out of me the real reason why I disappeared into the woods yesterday. I think it helped him realize that I'm not over Trinity's death yet.

"Lyla, hey!" Sydney says to me outside the bathroom. She looks like she's just heading in, her toiletries in hand. "Why didn't you tell me you were going to sneak away from the group yesterday? I would have totally joined you." She wiggles her eyebrows like she loves the idea of being rebellious.

"It was an accident," I lie. Then I look around us to see if anyone is watching us talk to each other.

"Yeah right," she replies, seeing right through me. Then she pouts. "You've hardly talked to me the entire trip."

I tuck some of my freshly blow-dried hair behind my ear. It had been nearly an impossible battle to fight for one of the power outlets inside the bathroom. "Oh, yeah." I say. "I think it's just kind of hard—you know, because we're different colored wristbands."

"Yeah, but we had free time last night," she argues.

"I was with Jackson. He needed to talk to me," I say. When I step around her away from the bathroom door and try to keep walking, she follows me.

"Okay, then maybe today? We can meet up and hang out?"

"I um... I don't know. Jackson has been extra needy lately." I'm starting to think I am going to need to brainstorm new excuse ideas to have handy for when she continuingly asks me to spend time with her.

Sydney stops walking. I turn around to look at her and notice that her face has clouded over. "We can do it in secret," she offers in a snobby voice. "It's okay, Lyla. I know you don't want your sister or your other friends finding out about our friendship."

Busted.

"Sydney..." I trail off, trying to think of what I can say to make myself not sound so awful. She's right. I *don't* want anyone knowing I'm friends with her.

"It's fine." She adjusts how she's holding all of her belongings in her arms. "I get that you don't want them to know. I don't get why you care so much, but regardless, I can keep your secret."

I feel bad. I step towards her. "I just—my sister, she's so—"

Sydney waves her hand at me, so I stop talking. "Just text me later and we can figure out where to meet up. You can tell me all about your mean and manipulative sister and friends."

She goes back to smiling happily, turns around, and heads to the bathrooms.

I'm actually excited when it's announced that the yellow team gets to use the kayaks today. Audrey and I have been looking forward to learning how to use them. When we reach the dock, a bunch of girls and guys are taking pictures and videos of the lake to post on their social media. Beside me, Audrey doesn't join in. She's just standing there with her arms crossed, staring out into the water, looking in deep thought.

I nudge her. "You okay?"

She snaps out of it and smiles at me. "Yeah. Totally. I call the front seat!"

We get in the kayaks, and after our short lesson on how to use them, we're given free range of the lake. We just have to keep an eye on the time and come back in when we're scheduled.

I have to struggle to keep up with how quickly Audrey is paddling. She seems determined to get as far away from the teachers as possible.

"Do you think the water is cold?" I ask, trying to make casual conversation with her.

"Ew, *why*? Do you want to go swimming in it?" Some of the other kids had used their free time to swim in the lake, but a lot of the girls thought it looked disgusting and refused to join in, Audrey included.

"No. I was thinking about how Sydney had pushed Warner in. I just wondered if it felt cold."

"Warner?"

"Yes?"

Audrey keeps paddling.

"Can we, like, slow down?" I ask her, my arms burning. "Or take a break? I don't get regular exercise like you do anymore."

"Oh, yeah. Fine." She takes her paddle out of the water and sets it down. I do the same, expecting her to turn around in her seat and keep talking to me. I'm confused when she sits there and stares out into the nothingness.

I can't help but wonder if she saw me talking to Sydney this morning and now she's mad at me.

"Are you okay?" I ask her again.

It takes her a while to answer me. "Yeah."

"It doesn't really seem like it. You're being weirdly quiet."

She turns her body around to give me a fierce gaze. "You have your quiet mood sometimes," she points out. "Why can't I?"

I raise my hands in surrender. "Fine. I was just checking, geez."

Something is definitely wrong with her. Quiet isn't exactly in my sister's vocabulary. She is always hyper and chatty, borderline ADHD, if you ask me. It takes something pretty big to make her act like this. But I won't try and push her. I am her twin and her best friend—she will spill it to me, eventually.

I hope.

Chapter 30

Amelia

After lunch, the kids have some free time while the chaperones prepare the next set of activities. Dean and I walk back down to the docks together to straighten up the kayaks and tie them properly so they don't float away and we don't get fined.

"Does your family go kayaking a lot?" Dean asks me. "Lyla and Audrey were really good out there."

I smile. "We haven't actually ever gone," I tell him. "They've always wanted to try it, though. And they get their athletic skills from my husband, not me."

Dean laughs. He got to see this firsthand when I was trying to get around with my own kayak earlier. Eventually, I gave up and asked if I could just join in with his. It was so much easier after that. And Dean and I especially had fun sitting together and secretly making fun of everybody who had been just as bad at kayaking as me.

We climb on the dock together, noticing how some kids are using their free time to go swimming. Dean and I start at the furthest kayak and move it into the dock properly, then the both of us tie up one end. It's a workout, and it's humid today, so already I can feel myself starting to sweat.

"Gentry doesn't really strike me as an outdoorsy kind of guy," Dean comments. When I look up at him, he's smiling at me.

"What is that supposed to mean?" I ask as we move to the next kayak.

Dean shrugs. "I don't know, it's just what I said. He just doesn't seem super outdoorsy, that's all."

For a fleeting moment, I wonder if Dean is taking a dig at my husband out of jealousy.

"He is really big on camping," I inform him. We tie up the second kayak, then move to the third. The dock is slightly wobbling, and I have to struggle to keep my balance. It's going to be super embarrassing if I fall into the water in front of him.

"Ha," Dean comments. "*He* should've volunteered to chaperone then."

I roll my eyes as we tug the next kayak closer. "Oh, stop. I already told you that he is hanging out with Joey this weekend."

Dean straightens up the paddles and wipes some beaded sweat off of his forehead with the back of his hand. "Right, right."

"You know, you're *weirdly* good at this." I say the words before I even think about them. I hadn't meant for that to slip out.

"Good at what?" he asks. "Putting kayaks back?"

I bite my bottom lip to hold back my nervous smile. "Yeah. That."

He lets go of the kayak we are currently working on and stands up straight. "I don't believe you," he tells me. "What were you going to say?"

I cave. "You're weirdly good at acting like nothing ever happened between us," I finally admit. Dean has been nothing but a friendly gentleman so far this entire trip. Every time we talk about the past, he never tries to bring up ours.

Dean tilts his head at me, looking surprised. “Oh. Well... that was a long time ago, Mia.”

I nod my head profusely. “No, you’re right. It was,” I agree. “I just... I don’t know. I thought being here with you would feel weirder.”

Before he can say anything back, there’s a rustling in the trees nearby, and we both turn and see Sydney Hutton stepping out of the woods, apparently all by herself. She heads over to the trail leading back to the camp, her phone in her hand as she types up a message to somebody.

“I’m not trying to be mean,” I can’t help but say as I stare after her. “But that girl is quite odd, isn’t she?”

Dean nods his head. “Oh, I thought that, too. I’m sure it’s hard being the new girl, but I don’t know. There’s something else about her.”

“She seems to be... alone a lot. Do you think she has any friends?”

I know she’s on the purple team, but every time I’ve seen her, she’s been hanging out on her own.

“You know, I’m not certain. But I’m going to definitely pay more attention to that when we get back to school.”

“Mom!”

I turn around and see my daughters heading towards me.

“There you are!” Audrey cries. Lyla approaches me first, Audrey in tow. I watch as Audrey’s eyes flicker to Dean a few times.

“Hey girls, how are you?” Mr. Reeves asks.

My kids ignore him and stare only at me. Lyla crosses her arms. “We want to know why you and Maddy Carpenter are being so mean to each other.”

Heat creeps into my face and I avoid turning around to look at Dean's reaction. Even this morning, when I had spoken through the megaphone to let all the students know it was time to wash up for lunch, Maddy had made a scene. She ripped the megaphone from my hands and spoke into it herself. All she did was repeat my instructions, only twice as loud and with more authority. I took the megaphone back from her when she finished and added a, "Please and thank you," since Maddy hadn't said it.

I also suppose it's quite obvious we don't like each other from the way we mean-mug each other every time we cross paths.

"Uh, I don't know what you're talking about," I try.

"Don't play dumb," Lyla snaps. My mouth drops open.

Mr. Reeves clears his throat. "You know what, I have to go prepare our team for the scavenger hunt," he explains. Then he waves to us and heads back down the trail leading to the camp.

I turn to my daughters and narrow my eyes. "In front of your teacher?"

"We just want to know why you to hate each other," Audrey repeats with innocent eyes.

"Yeah, *something* must've happened between you two," Lyla adds.

I blow out some air from my mouth to get the hair out of the front of my eyes. Then I cross my arms. I should have known that they would continue to pry. Everybody in this town loves to gossip, regardless of their age.

"She's just an awful woman," I say. Already, I know it's not going to be enough. I just wish it was.

"But how?" Audrey asks. "What made her that way?"

My stomach dips violently at the way Audrey worded her question. "I—how should I know how she turned out that way?"

"Well, why do you *think* so?" Lyla asks.

I always knew deep down that I wouldn't be able to keep this quiet and to myself forever. Not if I was going to continue to live in Toxey.

"Fine. If you *must* know, we used to be friends. It was years and years ago. And we had a falling out."

They look at each other before looking back to me. "You guys were friends?" Lyla asks.

"What kind of falling out?" Audrey chimes in.

"That's all you need to know," I tell them. What's my business is my business. They don't have to know everything.

Everybody has their secrets.

Chapter 31

Warner

I'm in the mess hall sitting with the seniors when I hear a familiar voice. "Hey, Warner," Audrey says, taking a seat beside me with her food tray. Tonight's meal consists of grilled cheese sandwiches and tomato soup.

"Oh, hi, Audrey," I say, surprised to see her. Audrey and I aren't exactly close. I talk to her sometimes because she's the sister of my best friend's girlfriend, but other than that, I don't really know her.

"I can't believe we go home tomorrow already," she says.

"For sure," I tell her. "I wish the trip was longer."

"I didn't know you two hung out," my buddy Ryan says to us. He's sitting across the way, stuffing his face full of grilled cheese.

Audrey and I look at each other and smile. "Uh, sometimes," Audrey answers.

Yeah, sometimes, I think to myself. *So why are you here now*?

Audrey spends the entire meal sitting next to me, tearing her grilled cheese into little pieces and nibbling on them as we chat. We talk about football and cheerleading and how our parents seem to not like each other, and even a little bit about her sister and how she's been doing with Trinity's death. Audrey is a nice girl and easy to talk to. I can't understand why Mom thinks that she and Lyla are both rotten. I just don't see it. Maybe my mom is just worried that if I did date one of them, I'd maybe get married to them and make *my* mom have to be related to *their* mom.

At the end of the meal, Audrey's cheerleading friends—I think their names are Danielle, Sophia, and Olive—come grab her and tell her that they need to go practice.

"Okay, well, I guess I will see you on the field," Audrey tells me as she gets to her feet.

"See you on the field," I say. She smiles and waves at me and my friends and then turns and walks off with the girls, her long blonde ponytail swinging behind her.

"That was weird," I say to the guys.

"Does she have a crush on you or something?" Ryan asks.

I raise an eyebrow. "I don't think so," I say. But his question does stir up an idea inside of me: could it be possible that maybe Lyla mentioned something to Audrey about how she has a crush on me? And maybe Audrey only came to talk to me because she was trying to figure out if I liked her back? What if Audrey was simply talking to me because she was trying to play matchmaker?

"You guys should definitely date," Austin says. "It would be so fitting. You and Jackson would be best friends, dating a pair of twins. It's cliché and perfect."

"I don't know about that," I say. Unfortunately, Audrey isn't the twin that I want.

"Why not?" Ryan asks. "She's cute."

"You date her then," I suggest.

"Maybe I will," he deadpans. Chance and Austin crack up and give him a high five. I shake my head and chuckle, part of my brain still thinking about the possibility of Lyla liking me back. I scan the mess hall to see where Lyla and Jackson are sitting. When I find them on the other side at the first table, neither of them are talking and they look completely miserable.

We head to the campfires after dinner like we did last night. Thankfully, instead of charades this evening, the purple team gets to go to the S'more's station. Jackson and I joke around and stuff our faces the entire time. I laugh as he lights marshmallows on fire and chases girls around with them. Something about the way Jackson behaves seems to me like he's *meant* to be single. He likes to talk and flirt with girls, and while Lyla isn't really the jealous type, I can't help but wonder why Jackson even wants to be with her if he still craves attention from other females.

Sydney comes and stands next to me the moment Jackson gets far enough away so that it looks like I'm alone. She doesn't say anything at first. Instead, she just stands there roasting her marshmallow, pretending like she doesn't even see me. I'm still mad at the stunt she pulled with the kayaks and don't really want to talk to her. But at the same time, I'm not very good at telling people off.

If she tries to talk to you, just man up and confront her, I think to myself. I've been trying to work up the courage to do it this entire trip. I can't keep leading Sydney on and making her think I want to be around her, because I don't.

"Hi, Warner," she says in a quiet voice after a while. When she pulls her marshmallow out of the flame, it's completely black. She turns and wipes it on a boulder.

I nod my head but don't say hi back. That's progress, right?

I pull my marshmallow out of the flame and inspect it, then when I decide it's the perfect browned color, I pull it off and put it on my graham cracker and chocolate sandwich.

"Um, listen. Do you think I could talk to you for a moment?" she asks me.

Now I don't even want the S'mores anymore.

I sigh heavily and turn to her. "No, Sydney," I start, "I don't think you can."

"Are you still mad at me about the kayak thing?" she asks. "I'm sorry. I didn't mean to do it." Her face is creased with worry as she waits for me to say something.

"It's not just that," I begin.

"Well, well, well. Look who it is," Jackson's voice says behind me. I turn around and see him approaching the two of us, a smug smile on his face. He's probably going to start cracking more jokes about how she two of us should date. It's his favorite running joke.

Sydney glares at him. "I'm trying to talk to Warner," she snaps at him.

Jackson puts his arm around my shoulder and laughs. "Of course you are," he says. "You're *always* trying to talk to him. You're obsessed with him. It was funny at first, but now it's just getting plain weird. Why did you push him into the lake? Did you think if you drowned him, then nobody else would get to have him?"

"Jackson," I warn. He finally has my back, but now I don't want him to speak at all.

Sydney grips her marshmallow spear tighter as she glowers at him.

Jackson continues. "Everywhere my friend here turns, there you are again. How do you do it, Sydney? They make TV shows and movies about girls like you, you know. About stalkers.

"I'm not stalking him," she argues.

"I think you are," Jackson argues. "You need to leave Warner alone."

Sydney's eyes move from Jackson to me. I can tell by the way she's staring at me that she's hoping I will come to her rescue. That she's expecting that I will. Part of me wants to be nice and tell her I don't think she's a stalker and that Jackson is being too harsh, but I know if I want her to leave me alone, I have to say nothing. So I look away from her.

Sydney drops her stick to the ground. "Fine." She turns sharply on her heel and walks off into the woods, no teacher or a student realizing it or telling her to stop.

Jackson takes his arm away from me and slaps me on the back. "There. That should be the last you hear from her."

I let out a long, slow breath. "Do you think so?"

"It should be. But I guess only time will tell."

Chapter 32

Audrey

I'm already lying awake in my sleeping bag when the alarm on Lyla's phone goes off the next morning. I watch as my sister goes to hit the snooze button.

I give her a gentle shake. "Come on, Ly. We have to get up."

I barely slept last night, but I don't even feel tired. Knowing that Mr. Reeves is Warner's biological father—and that I'm the only one who knows about it—has suddenly made him a million times more interesting. Before, I always found Warner to be sort of boring. A classic good guy who will skate through life under the radar, being nice to everybody because he doesn't want to hurt anyone's feelings. I like to joke with my friends that Warner is a nerd trapped in a hot guy's body.

And in just one single night, my entire opinion of him has changed. Now Warner is mysterious. A sweetheart. A silent, tortured soul, having to carry around the weight of not knowing who his father is. I can't imagine what that's like. He must feel like a giant chunk of his soul is missing. I feel awful for him. And I have no idea why his mom is keeping his father a secret from him. Especially when Mr. Reeves is such a good guy. He would make a great father. It doesn't make any sense.

Beside me, I can hear that Lyla has started up with her soft snores again, but I don't try and wake her. I'm too busy lying here thinking about the meal I had with Warner last night. How I sat down next to him, completely uninvited, and he talked to me as if we've been friends forever. Part of me wanted to tell him the truth about what I learned because I feel that I am much more loyal to him than his mother, whom I don't even know. But the second I looked up at the teachers' table last night and saw Madeline glaring at me, I grew too afraid. It's a huge secret to keep to myself, but maybe it's none of my business. Just because I heard something I wasn't supposed to doesn't mean I need to do anything about it. Maybe if Warner is supposed to know that Mr. Reeves is his dad, it will happen another way.

So then when Warner and I chatted about random stuff instead, I was worried it would get weird and awkward, but it didn't. Not to mention that Ryan Copeland kept eyeing me, too. That was another plus.

I also liked that Maddy couldn't take her eyes off of me. It felt good to make her stressed out and worried. I liked showing her that she doesn't scare me. Even if she does. That's why I had been hoping to get more information out of Mom when Lyla and I went down to the docks to talk to her yesterday. However, I clammed up when I saw Mr. Reeves standing there. But as soon as he left, I hoped we would get Mom to cave and explain exactly why it was that she and Maddy stopped being friends however long ago. I thought maybe Mom would say that Maddy had threatened her, or something along the lines of what Maddy had done to me.

Lyla and I should've known we weren't going to get much out of our mother, though. Mom has never been very open to talking about her past.

I finally stop thinking about Warner and his mom when Lyla's phone goes off a second time. When she tries to hit the snooze button again, I snatch the phone away. "No," I say. "We have to get up. I heard there are cinnamon rolls for breakfast." I want to make sure to get my hands on one of the delightful sounding pastries before they're all gone.

My sister groans and slowly sits herself up, looking disoriented as she stares around our small two-person tent.

"Are you okay?" I ask with an eyebrow raised. Maybe she didn't get that good of sleep last night.

Lyla nods her head and checks the notifications on her phone.

"Okay," I reply with a shrug. I already feel very awake. "Then, since you're up, I'm leaving to hit the showers."

"You didn't have to wait for me to wake up," she argues.

"But what if you overslept?" I say.

"Who... cares?"

I roll my eyes and turn to open my suitcase and rummage through it for today's outfit—straight-leg jeans and a crop top—and climb out of the tent. As much as I don't want the trip to end later today, I am looking forward to not having to sleep on the ground again tonight. My queen-sized bed feels like a luxury compared to that.

I say hi to some of my friends outside the tent, then I hit the showers, fight with some girl over an outlet in front of the mirror like I had to do yesterday, and get ready for the day.

I take longer getting ready than usual because I want to look extra cute today, so I'm a little bit late heading into the mess hall. If there are no more cinnamon rolls, it will be worth it—I look and feel good.

The thing is, Ryan Copeland complimenting my boots and staring at me yesterday when I ate my meal with Warner reignited the spark I felt last year whenever I was around him. But not only that; I am finding that I also want to look cute in front of Warner, too.

I get in line once I enter the mess hall, which is short now that most people have already gotten their food. I snag the second to last cinnamon roll, fill my Hydro Flask at the water station, then I go to sit with my friends.

The moment I take a seat, I can tell Sophia, Danielle, and Olive all know something I don't.

Then when I turn and look around the large, full mess hall, it seems like a lot of people know something I don't. It's much quieter this morning, and a lot of people are talking and hushed whispers.

"Is it weird in here, or is it just me?" I ask the girls. Sophia is on my right, wearing a denim jacket and black leggings, her hair curled, and Olive and Danielle are across from me. Olive has on a green crop top and her hair in a cute scrunchy. Danielle is wearing a two-piece athleticwear set, her Auburn hair in her natural short waves.

"Did you not check your phone?" Sophia asks me in a voice full of attitude. Sometimes I really hate how condescending she is towards me.

"I haven't yet..." I trail off uneasily. "I was busy getting ready. Why?" I pull my phone out of my back pocket and see that I have some Snapchats from them.

"Sydney Hutton, the new girl, is missing," Olive says. I'm not sure if I heard her right.

"Wait. She's missing?"

They all nod in unison.

"Sydney is?" I ask.

"Yes!" Sophia says impatiently. "Apparently her tent-mate, Jeanette Trujillo, had been crashing in her other friends' tent because...you know... she felt uncomfortable sharing it with Sydney. Sydney had the tent to herself and nobody knows what happened. When Mr. Sawyer went around and did the attendance this morning, he found that she was unaccounted for."

"I hope they find her and that she's okay," Danielle says next to Sophia.

"Oh, shut up," Sophia snaps at her. "You don't even like Sydney."

Danielle scoffs and gives Sophia a nasty look.

"Do you think maybe she just wants the attention?" I ask, tearing a piece of my cinnamon roll and slowly eating it. I can't say I blame Jeanette for not wanting to share a tent with Sydney. Not only is Sydney not very clean, but to state the obvious; she's also weird.

"Probably," Sophia snorts.

Danielle isn't done being annoyed with Sophia. "Just because I am not crazy about Sydney doesn't mean I don't care if she's okay," she argues. Instead of replying, Sophia just rolls her eyes.

When Lyla comes and sits beside me, all she has on her tray is a juice box.

"Sydney is missing?" she asks me immediately, not even greeting her old friends. Or looking at them, for the matter.

"I guess so," I reply.

"Hello to you, too," Sophia says to her. Lyla still doesn't look in her direction.

Her eyes are focused on me and me only. "How is that even possible?" she asks.

"No idea," I say to her. "Did you talk to her at all recently?"

"No," she quickly snaps at me. "Why would I? We're not friends."

I bug my eyes out at her. "Just wondering, jeez."

Mr. Reeves stands up on his bench at the teachers' table and talks to us through the megaphone. "Everyone needs to stay put in the mess hall, got it?" he asks us. "Just stay put and we will get the day started shortly."

He turns the megaphone off and steps down, his face a shade of green. All of them at the teachers' table look really worried as they mutter to themselves in a huddle.

I look back at Lyla to see her reaction to Mr. Reeves's announcement. She's sitting there like a stone, not even poking her straw through her Juicebox.

Lyla says she's not friends with Sydney Hutton, but I don't know. Call it my twin-telepathy or something.

But I think my twin might be lying to me.

Chapter 33

Maddy

When it's clear that keeping the kids confined to the mess hall isn't going to help us find the missing girl—Sydney Hutton—any quicker, we let everyone loose and tell them to stay close to their tents. I, on the other hand, call Warner and tell him to meet me at my cabin straight away.

When he walks in through the screen door, he looks tired. His shaggy brown hair is even messier than usual and his eyes are slightly bloodshot. I hope it's from lack of sleep and that he hasn't been crying because of Sydney. He told me he doesn't even like the girl.

"Are you okay?" I ask from over on my bed.

"Yeah. What's going on?" he asks, not moving away from the door. It's as if he's going to turn and run back out at any second. "Any word on Sydney?"

"No," I say. "You don't know where she could be, do you?"

"No. If I did, don't you think I would've told someone?"

I bite my thumbnail nervously. "Okay. I was just checking. It's just that... I was watching you and Jackson with her at the campfire yesterday. I saw how Jackson was talking to her."

For some reason, I'm an anxious, jittery mess. I've always had an overactive imagination, so my mind is coming up with the worst scenarios in my head.

"So?" he asks. "I barely even know her, Mom."

I get the feeling he's not telling me the full truth. "I know it was her that came to our house the other day. You went and hung out with her, remember?"

He is quick to reply. "Yeah, I hung out with her once. I don't know her whole life! I don't know where she is or what happened to her."

"Warner, I will always protect you," I tell him. "No matter what. But in order for me to do that, you have to be one-hundred percent honest with me. So please tell me the truth. Did you have anything to do with why Sydney is missing?"

"No!"

He looks offended. Hurt. Astonished that I would ever accuse him of being involved in something bad with her.

I chew on my nails some more. "Okay! I just had to check. I believe you, I promise."

We both sit there quietly for a bit before he seems calmed down enough to resume speaking to me again.

"Do you think they'll find her?" he asks me. His voice is much softer now than it had been when I asked him about his involvement with her.

"I don't know," I say. Then I stomp my foot in frustration. "Ugh, I really hate these woods!"

Chapter 34

Lyla

With so many junior and senior kids at the camp, I still don't understand why they wouldn't let us stay and help look for Sydney. It just doesn't make any sense to me. Why am I on the bus going back to Toxey when Sydney is still out there somewhere, possibly alone and afraid and desperate for help?

My stomach hasn't stopped turning since I first heard the news about Sydney this morning. It's progressively gotten worse as the hours have ticked on because no one has heard from her or found her yet. I'm mad at myself. I wish I had done something. I wish I had stopped her from disappearing somehow. I wish I had been hanging out with her. Or at least texting her on my phone so that I could have known her whereabouts. If we had been texting, maybe she would have told me that something bad was happening, or maybe I would have figured out something was wrong because of how abruptly she had stopped replying.

I look to Audrey next to me, who is staring out the window on the bus. I don't know what she's thinking, but what I do know is that she's not acting like herself. Usually, my sister is always trying to make sure I'm okay. Always trying to cheer me up and tell me everything's going to be fine. So seeing her sitting here like this, silent and frozen, is worrying me.

"Ree?" I ask, putting a hand on her shoulder. She snaps to me with a start, almost like she had been having an intense daydream about something, and I brought her back to the present unexpectedly. "Are you alright?"

I wonder if there is something else bothering her other than the fact that Sydney went missing. I just don't think she would be this concerned about Sydney missing—my sister didn't even like her.

Audrey nods her head at me vigorously. "Yeah. All good. Just... a weird day, I think."

I settle back in my seat. "Definitely not how I expected the trip to end," I agree.

She gives me a thoughtful expression but doesn't say anything back.

"What?" I ask.

"Um... nothing." She turns back to look out the window.

My stomach dips yet again. This time, it's because I'm worried she knows something. More so, I'm worried she knows something I did. Something I did... last night.

There is a lot about this situation that feels super familiar to me. It's familiar to The Trinity Thing. For some reason, it feels like it's my fault that Sydney is missing right now.

The truth is, Sydney Hutton had texted me last night. I was laying in my tent with Audrey after curfew, scrolling through Instagram like usual. Sydney's text had said:

Sydney: *When everybody is asleep, come meet me at the docks. Give it another hour.*

Her text did not give me any reason why. She didn't offer any explanation as to what it was that she wanted to do once we were both out there. Part of me figured she just wanted to hang out but that she was being dramatic and playing the whole "don't let anyone know we're friends" game she thought I was trying to play. Even if it was a little true.

But I didn't want to go meet her. My sister was laying right next to me, for one. And I didn't necessarily think that Audrey would tattle on me if I decided to sneak out, but she would have definitely wanted to know where I was going, and I'm not good at lying—especially to her.

Two, I didn't want to get caught doing something I am not supposed to be doing. Not for the second time since being on the trip. Everyone is already starting to think I just like the attention, even though that is far from true.

So last night, I didn't text Sydney back. And she hadn't ever texted me to follow up, either. I never got a, "Where are you?" or a simple, "Just let me know you're coming so that I'm not standing out here alone."

Nothing. Was that because it had already been too late by that point? What was the exact moment that Sydney Hutton went missing? How long had she been standing at those docks before something happened? Before she decided to run away. Or before she was kidnapped. Or killed. Or eaten by wolves. Who knew?

At some point in the night, eventually, I did go check on her. Much longer than an hour had passed because I had to wait to be absolutely sure that Audrey was in a deep enough sleep to where she wouldn't possibly wake up. I originally had every intention of not going, but as I lay in bed, staring up at the boring brown tent ceiling, I just kept tossing and turning, trying to sleep off the fact that I was ignoring Sydney. It made me feel bad. Guilty. I felt like I should see her. She was just a lonely new girl trying to make it through high school. What if I was her only friend? Besides, I had told myself I wanted to get to know more about her. The Sydney I had come to know so far hadn't opened herself up to me a whole lot, so

I wondered if maybe this was the night she might finally let me in a little.

So nearly 45 minutes past the time that she had originally said in her text to me, I finally snuck out of the tent and walked to the docks. When I got there, alone, I stood there, pulled out my phone, and tried to shoot her another text.

Lyla: *I am here. Was waiting for Audrey to fall asleep. Where are you?*

I waited around in the open moonlight, my body clearly visible from the trail that went back up to camp, for about ten minutes. Then, deciding she had probably got sick of waiting for me and gone back to her tent to go to sleep, I slowly make my way back up the trail. I could've sworn I heard some voices in the trees as I walked, but I didn't pause or give it much thought. I knew I couldn't be the only kid who wanted to sneak out of their tent and go on a late-night adventure after curfew.

I simply crawled back into my tent, found that Audrey was still fast asleep, and quickly joined her in a slumber of my own. Little had I known; by then, Sydney was probably already gone.

Chapter 35

Amelia

I had turned around to check on my daughters on our bus ride back to Toxey around 400 times—give or take a few. Neither of them talked to each other or anyone around them. And as tired as they both looked, neither of them slept, either. They just sat there, Lyla staring straight ahead and Audrey looking out the window, like a lot of the other kids on the bus. It struck me as odd that even cheery, optimistic Audrey didn't seem to have anything to talk about. It made me sad for my girls. Worried about them.

I didn't know the missing girl at all, and from what I can tell, no one else really seems to know her, either. It was still a scary situation, nonetheless. It could've been either one of my daughters who was missing right now. But out there somewhere, that girl's parents or guardians, whoever they are, are worried sick right now. Another family is broken because of a missing child.

I've seen this before. And I had always hoped that I wouldn't ever have to see it again.

The buses take us back to school, where everyone unloads and starts meeting with their parents. I notice right away how all the adults look extra happy to have their kids home safe, even if they had been desperate to get rid of them in the first place. They're all thinking the same thing I was. "Thank God it wasn't mine who went missing."

As I help my daughters load our luggage into the back of the Range Rover that I kept parked in the lot while we were gone, I look at them. "Remind me to tell your father not to take Joey camping in those woods if they go. Clearly, they're cursed."

Audrey nods her head while Lyla numbly walks around to the backseat and climbs in. Audrey gets in the passenger seat up front with me and, not stopping to say goodbye to anyone, we pull out of the parking lot and start driving home. I'm glad the girls are just as eager to leave Blackfell High as I am. I'm glad they didn't want to stop and talk to their friends and teachers, trying to hear updates about Sydney Hutton's disappearance and partaking in spreading rumors about her and what could have happened to her. It was pointless. They are either going to find Sydney, or they aren't.

But while deputies and forest rangers and volunteers comb through those woods, what else are they going to uncover?

I shudder at the thought and try to concentrate on my driving. The dark thoughts I keep getting threaten to take me under, but I must remain focused.

"Uh," I start, looking at Lyla through my rearview mirror. "I'm sure everything is going to be fine, girls. Sydney will be all right."

"Hopefully," Audrey says in a soft voice. In the backseat, Lyla sniffs dryly.

I drop my fingers on the steering wheel. "Were you guys—are you guys close to her? Sydney?"

Audrey turns in her seat and looks at Lyla. Lyla shoots her a funny look back.

What is that all about? I wonder.

"I'm not," Audrey says.

"Me neither," Lyla adds in. The way they're acting towards each other—it seems familiar somehow. It's making memories resurface. Ones I desperately do not want to think about. They slam to the front of my brain and try to force me to pay attention to them, and for a split second, I do. Those words. The forest rangers. The news vans. This is not the first time.

"MOM, LOOK OUT!"

I jump back to the present just as the Range Rover hits a curb. Over-correcting myself, I swerve the other direction and drive off the road, all of us heading straight for a large oak tree. I hear Audrey scream and I look in the mirror for a flash of a second and see Lyla's eyes bulging out. Her terror is silent.

I turn my wheel sharply again and nearly miss driving straight into the wide, sturdy trunk. Then I slam on my brakes in the middle of a grassy field outside our neighborhood.

"What is wrong with you?!"

I turn in my seat and look at Lyla, feeling worse than horrible. "Honey, I'm so—" My heart is pounding, as I'm sure theirs are, too.

Lyla's face is red. She looks like she detests me.

"You nearly killed us! Why were you driving like that? How could you just stop paying attention?"

"Ly, we're fine!" Audrey snaps. But I don't expect her to understand why Lyla is panicking so much right now. Audrey hasn't experienced the PTSD that Lyla has.

"I... I don't know what happened," I say. And it's true—I don't.

What was it that I had even been thinking about?

Lyla unbuckles her seatbelt and opens the car door. "I'm walking the rest of the way."

"Lyla, I'm sorry!" I cry to her.

Lyla gets out and puts her hands on her knees and bows her head. "I don't care!" she says through slow, deep breaths.

"Lyla, are you having a panic attack?" I ask. "Remember the breathing tricks!" I just want to do anything I can to make her feel okay. To make up for how much I probably scared her just now. How much I probably pushed back all the progress she's made since her accident.

Lyla straightens herself up, not looking at either of us. "I'm fine!" she shouts, even though she's clearly not. Then, she takes off in a run.

"Lyla!" Audrey calls after her, clearly shellshocked. I put my hand on her shoulder. "It's alright. Just let her go."

Chapter 36

Warner

The entire last day of the upperclassman camping trip went by without anyone finding Sydney.

And since not finding her for some reason means she is definitely still alive, school is still in session today. I'm dreading going because I already have heard some of the horrible rumors involving her disappearance and I am not super eager to hear more. Especially the ones that involve me.

Some of my peers are saying that Sydney ran away because I wouldn't accept her love. That the scene Jackson caused between me and her at the campfire had been her breaking point.

Others are saying she did something worse than running away; they're saying that she drowned herself. Because of me.

"That is some intense love," Jackson says to me at the school steps before the bell rings to head to first period. He has a smirk on his face like he finds this whole thing with Sydney and the rumors amusing, and that, for some reason, makes me mad. I have to physically hold back shouting at him. I don't even know why I'm so bothered. They're just rumors. I know none of them could possibly be true. Of course, they're not true. Right?

"Jackson, don't be insensitive," Lyla says, sitting in the middle of us on the stairs. I ignore both of them and pull my phone out and shoot Sydney yet another text. She hasn't replied to any of them so far, which makes me feel sick to my stomach, but I am still holding out hope that any second now, my phone screen will light up with a text from her. She'll say something like. "I'm fine, you goofball! Want to hang later?"

Me: *Sydney, just let us know that you are alright.*

If I have the power to make her want to leave the trip and run away like everyone is saying, maybe I also have the power to make her come back. I'm sure everyone is thinking so, too. I feel like people are relying on me to produce her return.

"I'm just saying," Jackson says to Lyla before turning back to me. "Isn't it funny how sometimes being the nice guy can only make things worse?"

"What are you talking about?" Lyla says in an irritated voice. I give him a look that matches her tone.

Jackson shrugs nonchalantly, still addressing me. "Well, think about it. You were nice to Sydney. You made it to where she thought, for some reason, in her twisted messy head of hers, that you liked her. Just because you were nice. So that means you were so nice that you caused her to run away. Crazy."

"I wasn't even that nice," I try.

This gets a laugh out of Jackson. "Yeah, you were. If you had just told her off from the start, rumors like these wouldn't even be surfacing right now."

Lyla gets to her feet. There is a storm cloud brewing around her as she looks down upon her boyfriend. Her jaw is tense and her eyes are narrowed at him. "You can be such a jerk, Jackson."

Jackson glares up at her. "What are you talking about? I'm not trying to be a jerk. I'm just telling Warner he could've avoided this! I am helping him learn from his mistakes."

I stand up, too. I throw my bag over my shoulder and walk away from both of them, not saying another word. Jackson is always trying so hard to be funny and alpha. Lately, he often forgets what it's like to be an actual friend.

"See, look!" I hear Lyla shout at Jackson as I pull open one of the school entrance doors and storm inside. I don't turn around to look back at either of them, and they better not try to come after me, either. I need to be alone right now.

At lunchtime, I'm surprised to see Lyla in the cafeteria for once. Last year she was here every day, sitting with Audrey and the rest of their clique. But so far this year, she's hardly made a lunch appearance. I wonder where it is she goes during her break if not here.

I see that she's by herself, so thinking quickly but not deeply, I decide to step up behind her in the lunch line.

"Sorry I bailed on you guys this morning," I tell her as a way of greeting. She looks cute today. I like her slightly ripped jeans and the black short-sleeve T-shirt that has a flaming Obey logo on it. Her shoulder-length hair is half pulled back in two small pink translucent butterfly clips. I'm wearing a plain white tee, beige cargo shorts, and my white Nikes with white socks.

She looks surprised to see me standing beside her. "Warner! Hi!"

"Hi." I give her a smile. She looks like she wants to smile me back but doesn't. "Look, I'm sorry I dipped on your guys earli—"

she interrupts me, stopping me from finishing my apology. "Don't worry, I totally get it," she says. "Jackson was being a complete jerk. I don't get him sometimes."

I shrug and wait behind her in the line while she orders from the lunch lady. A Caesar salad with grilled chicken and one extra packet of dressing.

I order next—a bean and cheese burrito, then we slide our trays down the counter together and wait for our orders.

"This whole thing just has me pretty stressed out," I admit to her. "I know it's all just rumors, what everyone is saying about Sydney and why she disappeared, but it is honestly starting to get to me."

"Don't listen to anybody. It's not your fault." She's looking at me intently. I stare back.

"I don't know" I argue. What if it is my fault?

"It's not."

I don't want to tell her this, but if I don't tell somebody, I might explode.

"Well... the thing is..."

"Yeah?" she asks when I don't continue.

"Syd did sort of...text me. That night."

At this, Lyla freezes. Slowly, she turns her head to look at me. She looks confused. Suddenly I'm wondering if maybe she is trying to blame me now, too.

"That's not the worst part," I go on to say anyway.

The lunch lady hands Lyla her salad with extra dressing, and she's slow to set it on her tray. I'm not sure why she's turned so sloth-like all of a sudden. Something in my gut is telling me maybe I shouldn't say anything else. But I'm too far in.

"What do you mean?" she finally asks. She doesn't move away from me even though she has her food now. At least she wants to finish this conversation. That's a good sign, right?

I lean in closer to her because I don't really feel like letting anyone else hear this. "Sydney asked me to meet her."

The lady practically chucks my foil-wrapped burrito over the counter at me, and I scramble to catch it. When I set it on my tray and walk away from the line with Lyla, her eyes are huge. And even though we're walking, she won't take them off of me.

"I didn't go," I quickly reassure her. "Because... you know. I was trying to get her to take the hint that I didn't like her. I didn't want to keep leading her on. But still. Maybe if I had gone..."

For some reason, I can't finish the sentence.

"You feel like if you had gone to see her, she might not have disappeared?" Lyla asks. Both of us have stopped walking and are kind of just standing in the middle of the cafeteria, letting kids walk around us, the both of us getting lots of stares from our peers. Right now, I wouldn't be surprised if Lyla, Sydney, and I were the most talked-about kids in the entire school.

"Well... yeah," I admit. "Don't you think?"

She sucks in a deep breath. "Well, maybe more than you know, actually."

I raise an eyebrow. "How?"

"I..." Lyla looks around to make sure no one is listening in, just as I had done in the lunch line. Then she steps closer to me. "I got a text from her that night, too. Asking to meet me."

CHAPTER 37

MADDY

Normally I wouldn't have Craig come over to the house, but Warner told me practice was going to be running late today and that he and his friends were going to get food somewhere afterward, so I figured—why not?

"How was the trip?" Craig asks after kissing me on the cheek when I let him inside. Then he hangs his jacket up on a hook of my coat rack and surveys the room. I hastily picked up as much as I could before his arrival, but it wasn't much. There are still the cups on the coffee table and dust all over the end tables.

I groan loudly to answer his question as the two of us walk over to the sofa and take a seat. We turn so that we're facing each other and resting our arms on the back of the cushions. Instantly, he links his fingers through mine. It feels nice, and I smile at him a little.

I had made the mistake before of bringing guys I was dating around Warner while he was growing up, and needless to say, those relationships never went anywhere. As Warner got older, the angrier he became about this. He hated meeting and spending time with all of these potential fatherly figures just to have me break it off with them and tell Warner he is never going to see them again. So eventually my son and I came to an agreement that I won't introduce him to any of my significant others unless I know it is starting to get serious.

"I take it you had an amazing time, then?" Craig asks sarcastically. He has an adorable lopsided smile on his face that's making me want to do less talking, more kissing. But venting about the disaster of a trip sounds kind of nice, too.

"Well, it was pretty much a nightmare straight from the start."

One, because I don't like seeing Mia and Dean together. Two, because I'm not a big fan of being in the woods. Especially the Boldosa Redwoods. Three, because I had to work alongside Mr. Sawyer. And four, because Audrey Bailey found out that Dean Reeves is Warner's biological father and I don't know if I can trust her to keep it a secret.

But Craig doesn't have to know about all of that.

"Yeah, they still haven't been able to locate Sydney Hutton yet," Craig says.

Oh yeah, I knew there was a fifth reason.

"Hm. What is it they say about missing people after a certain amount of time?"

Craig looks grave. "Let's just say it's less and less likely that she is going to be found alive. If found at all."

My stomach dips violently. For the shortest moment, I think maybe it would be for the best if Sydney didn't get discovered. But how wrong of me is it to think that? It's not like I didn't like the girl, I just feel a hideous overwhelming need to always protect Warner and make sure he comes first.

"Do you know anything about what might've happened to her?" Craig asks. His tone is casual, and he is still holding my hand, but there's something inquisitive about the way he's talking, too.

"Not a clue," I decide to tell him.

"Did you talk to her at all?"

I think about it for a moment. "Maybe a little. She was in my group."

"Huh."

I gave him a flirty smile and reach for the remote on the coffee table. Even though it's only been a few days, I am finding that I missed Craig. More than I probably should. Especially considering the fact that I still don't even know what we are.

Craig doesn't want to change the subject yet. "What was she like?"

"She definitely was a weird girl," I tell him. "Not anything like the usual ones Warner brings over."

"Hold up," Craig says, letting go of my hand and leaning forward as I scan through the channels on the TV. I pause on the current channel I'm on—The History Channel.

"You want to watch this?" I don't know what show is on, but I see aliens on the screen. I had no idea Craig was into aliens.

"You're telling me Sydney Hutton has been over here before?" he asks. "Warner hung out with her?" Apparently, he hadn't been referring to the TV channels.

"Um..."

I stare at him as I rack my brain to try to find the words to say. I don't want to implicate my son in this in any way. If I say the wrong thing to one person, suddenly the entire town will be talking.

For a second, I'm relieved when I hear the screen door of my house open, followed by the front door. But then I gasp and leap to my feet, getting as far away from Craig as possible.

Warner enters the house, then he stands there in his uniform, holding his football helmet, looking back and forth between Craig and me.

"What is this?" Warner asks. Craig gets to his feet as well.

I scramble around the couch, closer to my son, and stutter as I speak. "I-I wasn't expecting you back so s-soon! This is... this is Craig."

Great. I did it again. Everything I do these days seems to make Warner madder and madder at me. If I have a couple more of these incidences, I might lose him for good.

Craig walks forward and holds out his hand to him. "Nice to meet you, Warner. Your mom has told me a lot about you."

Naturally, Warner doesn't move to shake it. He stares at it with a tense jaw.

I try to smile. "So, um... why are you home so soon?"

"Coach Reeves told me to leave practice today. My head's not in the game, apparently."

I nod slowly as Craig gives up on the handshake and puts his hand in his pocket instead.

Warner scratches the back of his head and twists his face in anger. "I'm sorry," he starts, glaring at me. "Didn't we have an agreement about you bringing guys over?"

"Warner, we can talk about this later," I try through my teeth.

"It's alright, Maddy," Craig tells me, heading over to his jacket and putting it back on. "I'll take off. Just give me a call later, okay?" Then he addresses Warner. You have a good night."

Warner shakes his head, then turns and heads down the hall to his room. I follow Craig to the door with an apologetic wince on my face.

"I was not expecting that to happen," I tell him.

Craig leans in and kisses me softly on the lips.

Suddenly, I don't feel so sad.

"It's okay," he tells me. "I get it."

I sigh and nod, and then Craig leaves.

When the door is shut and locked, I turn off the porch light and walk back into the living room. I stand there for a long while, my hands on my hips and my heart beating loudly. Thinking quickly, I turn back and march straight into Warner's room, throwing the door open as I enter. He's just standing there in the middle of his room with his back to me and his fists balled.

"What?" he hisses at me, only turning his head to look at me through his peripherals.

"Why are you so mad right now?" I ask. "You are the one who said you weren't going to be home until late."

This makes him turn to me full. "And you're not supposed to have guys over at all!" he shouts. "What are you even doing dating, anyway? None of your relationships ever go anywhere! Don't you think you should just give up already?"

I blurt the words out before I can even think about them. "I'll have you know that I'm actually in a serious relationship with Craig!"

Sure, we've been seeing each other for a while, but we don't even consider each other boyfriend and girlfriend yet.

Still, the lies keep coming from my mouth. "I was planning on introducing you to him next week!"

Thankfully, my son's shoulders lower a tad bit. "Wait... you're—you're serious with that guy?" His tone has quieted a bit, so I lower mine, too.

"Craig," I remind him. "He's actually a really decent guy."

I know it's shocking for him to hear me say these things. Ever since we came up with the agreement for me to not bring anyone home unless it was serious, there hasn't been anyone serious. And the agreement was made years ago.

"Oh," Warner says, not looking at me. "That's..."

I offer him a small smile. "You could try saying you're happy for me?"

He pushes his muscular neck back. "I'm not gonna go that far."

I playfully roll my eyes, glad the fight is over.

As far as his response to me goes, I figured as much.

Chapter 38

Audrey

It was insanely difficult to stop checking my phone even when I was in the middle of class. Now that I'm home, I am pressing on my phone screen every three seconds to illuminate it, waiting to get a news alert about Sydney's disappearance. A text from somebody saying they heard from her. Anything. I even installed the Toxey News app so that I can receive updates on her case right away.

I feel bad for Warner. About how everybody is talking about how Sydney's disappearance is all his fault. For one, I don't think that's true. Two, he's a good guy, and he doesn't deserve any of this. Even if Sydney Hutton ran away because of him, that doesn't make it his fault.

Seeing Coach Reeves send him home today at practice had been sad enough. And I was honestly surprised Mr. Reeves and Mrs. Greene didn't just cancel the football and cheerleading practices, or at least end them early. Nobody felt particularly cheerful today, even if none of us really liked Sydney. It's not every day someone goes missing from Toxey. Especially a new girl. Especially a teenager.

The only person at cheer who hadn't really seemed to mind Sydney being gone was Sophia. She had even had the audacity to say, "Well, Sydney didn't fit in here, anyway. Maybe she figured that out, and that's why she left."

Currently, I am sitting on my bed trying to get some reading done for English. Then Lyla comes walking in.

"Can I use your phone to call myself?" she asks me. "I can't find it anywhere."

I pick up my phone and toss it over to her. Her face—unfortunately—unlocks the screen on my phone so she doesn't need to know my password to get on it.

"Thanks," she says. "I'll be right back. I'm pretty sure I'll hear it buzzing somewhere in my room."

I nod my head at her and try to focus on reading the same paragraph for the hundredth time these past ten minutes.

Lyla disappears, but only for a quick moment. Then suddenly she's back. However, instead of her own phone that I assumed she already found in her hand, she's staring at my phone screen still.

"Uh… Ly?" I ask her. "What are you doing?"

"I opened up your text message thread to find my name so I could call myself. But… this distracted me." She walks towards me, holding my phone up and showing me the screen.

My heart skips a beat as I realize what she's seen. It's a text.

From Sydney.

The night she went missing.

Sydney: Hey, it's me. Sydney. Meet me at the docks after everyone goes to sleep. I have to talk to you about something.

I set my book down on the bed next to me and feel my throat go dry. "Um… I have no idea why she texted me," I say.

My sister looks angry. "Why did she text you? Do you guys talk often? When did you even get her number? I thought you didn't like her."

"She told me she was going to be throwing a party at her house soon," I explain. But then I realize I'm not the one that should have to do the explaining right now. Lyla can't actually be mad at me. It's not like I actually went to see her that night.

"Well... did you go see her?" I ask, ignoring all of her questions. "Is that why you left the tent that night?"

She looks caught red-handed.

No backing yourself out of this one, Lyla.

"Did you?" I ask again. I hate that I'm slightly afraid of her answer. I'm afraid about what might've happened between her and Sydney that night.

It takes a second, but eventually, Lyla's face falls. "Okay, well yes, I went to go meet her," she answers, her hand holding my phone, dropping by her side in defeat. "But I waited too long or something. She wasn't there when I went."

I know I should have told Lyla right when I heard her sneaking out of the tent that Sydney had texted me. But I didn't. I wasn't even entirely sure it was Sydney she was sneaking off to go meet. But if it was, I was going to be mad at her for not being honest with me about the two of them being friends.

"After Sydney texted me," I start explaining. "You didn't say anything to me about getting a text from her, too. But then, when you snuck out, I sort of wondered if you had gotten one."

"So we both kept it a secret from each other," Lyla concludes. She looks sad, and it matches how I feel. Keeping things from each other is not exactly something we typically do.

"Lyla, I'm not friends with her," I say. "But... are you?"

"Honestly?" Lyla gives me a nervous look. "Yes."

Before I can start complaining about it, Lyla keeps talking.

"She is super weird and kind of needy, but she is nice to me. And she's a good listener. She almost reminds me of...Trinity."

Is.

We're still talking in the present tense like Sydney alive. But... is she?

"There's something else," Lyla adds. I am afraid to know what it is. "Sydney also asked Warner to meet her. I don't know if there was anyone else. But definitely us three."

"What, do you think she was just trying to get some sort of dock party started or something?" I wonder. "I don't understand."

Had Sydney texted everyone's number she had gotten since school started?

Lyla sighs and runs her hand through her now short hair. "What was she trying to pull?"

"I wonder what it was she claimed she needed to talk to me about," I add.

"So then... did Warner go?" I ask. "Did he tell you?"

"He didn't go," she replies. "He told me he wants her to get the hint that he doesn't like her. And now he's feeling horrible about not going. Like he could've stopped it or something."

If I had replied to Sydney's text and gone to meet her, for some ridiculous reason, would I have been able to stop her, too? Are all three of us to blame?

"So, you're the only one who went, but you didn't see her."

"Yes. I think I went too late or something. I don't know."

Something feels off inside my stomach. With a missing person case, please are bound to ask questions. They are bound to try and dig into what happened at night. Is my sister telling me the truth? Did she actually meet with Sydney and didn't want to tell me what happened while she was with her?

Chapter 39

Amelia

The majority of the people I went to high school with still live in Toxey with me. My Facebook feed is consistently full of their posts. When I look at it now, I see lots of information, headlines, news updates, and questions being posted about Sydney Hutton.

But with a teen missing out of Toxey, a new student who apparently lives with foster parents, my old classmates and Facebook friends are also bringing up something else. Apparently, this incident is reminding them all too well of our beloved classmate, Carson; he disappeared, too.

Eventually, I close my laptop shut and take deep calming breaths. I don't need to be looking at that stuff. It's only going to make me freak out inside.

In the distance outside my office in my home, I hear the doorbell ring. The clock on my desktop reads close to nine p.m. Joey is in bed. The girls are up in their rooms. Gentry is... gone again.

So, who could that be?

In my slippers and robe, I walk to the door and look through the peephole. To my surprise, it's Craig Fritz.

I unlock and crack the door open. "Craig?"

I see him around town and at functions sometimes, but we aren't close. Still, I can't help but notice the resemblance to him now compared to when he was a kid in high school. I dated his younger brother, Parker. The two of them were both very good-looking.

"Sorry to bug you this late, Mia. I was hoping I could ask you some questions regarding the disappearance of Sydney Hutton?"

My throat tightens. One main difference from him in high school to him now, is that Craig Fritz is a detective. If I'm not mistaken, I think he might be Toxey's only one.

"Now?" I ask.

"I meant to come earlier; the day just got away from me."

"Are you asking all the chaperones and teachers that were on the camping trip?"

"Yes, of course. Nothing to worry about. You're not a suspect or anything like that."

I step aside and let him in, and I motion for him to go into the front room. If we talk in the living room, there's a chance my kids will hear the echo from upstairs and wake up and come see what's going on.

Craig and I sit across from each other in the room, and surprisingly, we end up having a nice chat. We don't only talk about Sydney and the camping trip. We catch up a little bit about how our lives have been since high school. In high school, I always remembered not really caring for Craig. I much preferred Parker. Now, I'm not sure why.

"So how is Nora?" Craig asks, flipping his notebook closed, signaling that we're done talking about the investigation for the night. Still, I'm finding myself glad he wants to keep talking.

"Nora? I rarely even get a postcard from her. Or gifts to the kids on their birthdays."

"That's a shame."

I change the subject. "What about Parker?"

"Still living it up in NYC. Some sort of wolf on Wall Street or something." Craig heaves a big sigh, and it's clear that he's jealous.

"Do you see him much?"

"Oh, maybe a little bit more than you see Nora."

We both chuckle.

"Well, I for one, don't blame Parker for not coming back," I tell him.

Craig thinks about this for a moment, then nods his head. "Yeah, same here. The ones that make it out of here sure are lucky."

He couldn't be more right.

The next night, Sydney still hasn't been found, and I'm surprised to find Craig at my doorstep yet again. This time at least, there's plenty of time before dinner starts.

"I'm so sorry to bug you again," he says, looking genuinely like he means it. "I just need to review your list of activities for your team. Yellow, was it?"

I haven't gotten the chance to change out of my work clothes yet because I was at the office all day, but now I'm glad I didn't. For some reason, I want to look cute in front of Craig.

I nod at Craig and let them inside. "Yes, it was yellow. I was on Dean Reeves's team."

Craig winces. "Yeah, I could've gone to ask him for it instead of bugging you again. But... he and I don't exactly see eye to eye."

"Right. Of course."

We go back to the front room, and I go on the calendar on my phone and run through the activities for that camping weekend with Craig. He takes detailed notes and asks me to email him a copy, which I do.

Finally, he stands. "Thank you for all your cooperation. I'll get out of your hair."

"Oh, actually… do you want to stay for dinner?"

He raises his eyebrows at me. I hope I haven't overstepped my boundaries by asking. It's just that I am enjoying reminiscing on the past with him—something I never do—and it is close to dinnertime, after all.

"With you and your kids and your husband?" Craig asks.

"Gentry is out of town," I say, feeling a little guilty. "But my kids, yes. Don't worry, they'll like you."

But if my kids do like him, they don't do a good job showing it to either of us during dinner. I whip up some grilled chicken and veggies, and even though I explain to the kids that Gentry knows Craig is over and that he's a childhood friend of mine, they still act weird and standoffish all throughout dinner. Maybe none of them are used to being around cops. Craig did have on his full uniform, after all.

"Are we allowed to ask you if you found Sydney yet?" Layla asks him. We just finished eating and putting the plates in the sink, and now Craig is getting to his feet to head home.

"Right now, the investigation is still ongoing," he tells them. "I'm actually heading to join the search party right after this."

I look out the pitch-black window. "You're driving all the way over to the Boldosa Redwoods right now?"

Craig just shrugs. "When duty calls…"

"Do you think she's still out there?" Audrey asks. "Do you think she's still alive?"

Lyla leaps from the table. "Don't answer any of those! Not while I'm in the room!" She races around Craig and me and dashes up the stairs, leaving Audrey sitting there with big puppy dog eyes while Joey continues to look down at the gun in Craig's holster.

CHAPTER 40

WARNER

After school, I head to the soccer complex located at a park near the fire station of Toxey. It might not be the best paying job in the world, but it's better than nothing, and at least I am doing something I actually like. Coaching these young kids is fun and fulfilling for me, and I can almost see myself becoming a coach for some sort of sports team in the future.

I finish setting up the cones just as the last kid arrives and the practice is about to start. The head coach, Michael Carrillo, blows his whistle at everyone and tells them to gather around. "All right! Today we are going to start off with some soccer dribbling drills!" Michael is an interesting character. He is one of those guys who looks mean and threatening with his harsh facial features and the way his eyes are always narrowed because he doesn't like to wear sunglasses. But when he speaks, his voice is light and pleasant and he smiles often at his players. He isn't a very big yeller—nothing like Coach Reeves, anyway. He just wants these guys to have fun. That is his main goal, and it's one that I can get behind.

The kids all listen happily, the team a mixture of boys and girls who are ages ten through twelve. They have on their shin guards and cleats, along with gym shorts and

T-shirts. The city doesn't have the budget to give them actual uniforms, so when they do have soccer games, they get to wear colored mesh vests over their regular T-shirts.

"Your assistant coach here, Coach Carpenter, set up these cones," Coach Carillo explains. "You will break into teams of three and weave the balls in and out of the cones. Sound good?"

"Yes!" they all shout back. The coach breaks them up into teams and has them line up in front of these separate drill stations. I stick with the team that is at the last station since it's somewhat more difficult and needs more one-on-one teaching compared to the other two stations, where Coach Carrillo can bounce back and forth.

"Remember to use the side of your foot, not your toes!" I tell the kids. "And once you got the hang of that, try to keep your eyes more focused ahead of you instead of looking down. It's always good to know which direction you're headed!"

A small tan kid with a black bowl haircut and super bushy eyebrows pauses when he finishes kicking his ball through the cones. He looks at me and tilts his head. "Do you go to Blackfell high?"

"Yeah!" I tell him.

"What grade are you in?"

I know I shouldn't be making small talk with the players right in the middle of practice, but I don't want to be rude to the boy. "I'm a senior. Going to be graduating this year."

His face falls slightly, which confuses me. "Oh. You probably don't know my sisters then. They're only in the eleventh grade."

"You'd be surprised," I say. "I actually know a lot of people at Blackfell. What are their names?" The more I look at him, the more familiar he starts to seem.

"Lyla and Audrey. They're twins!"

That's when it hits me—Joey is Lyla and Audrey's younger foster brother. I give him a pleasant smile. "I definitely know them! Lyla is dating my best friend." As I say it, my stomach dips uncomfortably.

"Really?! Your best friend is Jackson? That guy is the coolest!"

I chuckle. Of course, Jackson would be close with their foster brother. He loved kids too, and if there was another opening for this assistant coaching job, I don't doubt he would want to be working here as well. "Isn't he?" I ask.

I look over Joey's shoulder at the next person working on the drill, knowing I need to get back to coaching them. Joey doesn't take the hint and keeps talking.

"Did a detective come over to your house, too?"

His question almost makes me forget I'm even coaching a team in the first place. "What do you mean?"

A detective was over at their house? Was it about Sydney? And if so, why?

"A detective came over to our house to speak to my mom. His name was Detective Craig Fritz. He even stayed for dinner. It was kind of weird."

Detective Craig? Was that the same Craig that my mom is dating? Meaning my mom is dating a detective?

"Oh, that guy," I say. He hadn't been wearing a uniform when he was over at my house, but Joey doesn't need to know that. "He did come over, actually. He's just doing his job. Nothing you should be worried about." I have no idea if I'm telling the truth or not.

"He had a gun," Joey pointed out.

"Yeah, all cops do. It's their job to keep everyone safe." I look over his shoulder again at the next person starting the drill. I cup my hands at them. "Great job! Keep your head up!" Then I look back down at Joey. "Joey, right?"

He nods.

"Alright Joey, we should talk more later. But get back in the line. We're going to be running through the drill three times each."

Joey gives me a smile and turns and re-joins the rest of the team. I try my hardest to let the assistant coaching job distract me from all the questions flowing through my mind. It isn't without difficulty. The detective, my mom and Lyla's mom, Jackson, Joey, Sydney's disappearance... There's a lot of people that keep tying Lyla and me together, and I don't know if it's all coincidence or if there is something more to it.

When practice ends, I decide to dig a little deeper. I grab my phone from my drawstring bag on a metal bleacher seat and compose a text to Lyla.

Me: *Do you think you can meet me at Delilah's in a little bit? I was hoping to talk to you about something.*

I help the coach pack up the supplies and listen to his advice and ideas for the next practice, then I am let go for the evening. I grab my bag and get my car keys and phone out and see that Lyla has texted me back.

Lyla: Sure. *I can be there soon. Taking my bike.*

I also have a text from Jackson.

Jackson: *When are you done with your practice? Want to meet up?*

Me: *I can't. I gotta do some stuff.*

Instantly, I feel guilty after I send it. I should tell him I'm meeting up with his girlfriend. It's a harmless meeting because I just want to know what her thoughts are on the situation with our parents. If there's something bigger going on that we don't even realize. It's not a date or anything, but something inside of me tells me that if Jackson knew I was texting her and meeting up with her, he would not be happy about it.

Chapter 41

Audrey

Lyla and I are watching a teen drama show on The CW Network in the living room when Lyla snaps her head up at me, her phone balanced on her kneecaps that are tucked into her body on the couch.

"What?" I ask her. We're both in our comfy clothes already, me in leggings and a baggy T-shirt and her in sweat shorts and a cami. We just finished eating dinner with mom before she left to go pick up Joey from soccer practice down the street.

"Warner just texted me," Lyla says to me. Her eyebrows are furrowed in confusion as she stares at her phone screen again. "He asked me to meet him at Delilah's. He said he needs to talk."

"Wait, Warner did?" I ask, feeling just as confused as she looks. Warner is her boyfriend's best friend. What is he doing trying to meet up with her? What could he possibly have to talk to her about?

"It must be about Sydney, right?" Lyla asks, slowly getting to her feet.

"Wait, you are going to go?"

Lyla shrugs. "I guess so."

I stand up. "Well, if it's about Sydney, then I should come, too. She texted me before she disappeared too, after all."

I can tell by the look on my sister's face that she doesn't think I should come because I wasn't exactly invited, but I don't care. I want to know what's going on. I refuse to be left out of the loop. And I still think it's weird that Warner is asking Lyla to hang out without Jackson around. So this will help make sure nothing weird is going on between the two of them if I am there to supervise. Besides, something sweet would hit the spot right about now.

"I told him I was going to ride my bike over there," she says.

"It's dark," I point out. "And Delilah's isn't in the safest part of town. I'll just drive us. Come on."

We don't even change before we get in my car and head to meet up with Warner at the old ice cream parlor. Everyone still comes here for the nostalgia factor and because it has the best ice cream in town. I like to come here because my mom told me when she was my age that this was where she worked. It's a small joint with chrome barstools, old red booths, and faded, dirty checkered flooring.

When we get inside, Warner is already sitting in a booth, a chocolate fudge sundae sitting in front of him, hardly touched. He's wearing a Nike T-shirt and looks a little sweaty, like he just finished a workout.

But the fact that he looks like this doesn't deter from how handsome he is. I don't like how I suddenly notice it. It's as if the fact that I know who his father is has suddenly made him more interesting to me, which is weird.

Warner doesn't exactly smile at the sight of us. He just nods his head as we approach. Lyla slides into the booth first and I sit down on the same side as her, the both of us facing him.

"Hey, Audrey," he says, acknowledging the fact that I came uninvited. Thankfully, he doesn't look too disappointed about it.

"You guys want menus?" a man asks from behind the counter, wearing a pin-striped apron and a paper hat.

"Yes," I say the same time Lyla says, "No, thank you."

The guy grabs two menus and brings them over to us, anyway. Then he stands there hovering like he wants us to decide on what we want to order right then and there so that he doesn't have to make another trip over here. "Uh, I will just take a strawberry milkshake," I tell him.

"I'll do a hot chocolate," Lyla says.

The man picks our menus back up and walks away.

"Thanks for meeting me," Warner starts off. "It's a little random, I know, but I just felt like we might be able to put our heads together about something."

"What are you thinking?" Lyla asks. It still feels weird for me to be around Warner because of the secret I know about him. It feels wrong to sit here and know something so private and personal about him that he doesn't even know about himself. I wish I had never overheard Maddy and Mr. Reeves speaking to each other back in her cabin during the upperclassman trip.

"I don't know," Warner says, itching his chin briefly. "I met your foster brother today. He's on my soccer team. I am the assistant coach."

"No way!" I say with a smile. It's funny how small the world can be sometimes. Next to me, Lyla doesn't look surprised or amused. She is all business, sort of like how Warner is looking at us right now.

"Yeah. He told me something about a detective coming to your house. Detective Craig Fritz? Is that true?"

Lyla and I look at each other for a moment before turning back to him. "Yeah," Lyla answers. "Has he been to your house, too?"

"Uh, well, yeah... But not as a cop, I don't think."

"What do you mean?" I ask. The loud mechanical noise of the blender mixing together my milkshake is heard behind the counter, so we have to speak up now to hear each other.

"When I met him, I didn't even know he was a cop. A detective. Whatever. He was wearing normal clothes. Apparently, he's my mom's... boyfriend."

Lyla and I look at each other again, both of our eyes wide in surprise.

Across from us, Warner chuckles. "It's funny how you guys do that," he comments. "You guys even have the same facial expressions."

Then Lyla and I don't even react to this. We hear it too many times.

"Do you think he's going over to all the parents' houses?" I ask, placing my hands on the tabletop and clasping them together.

"I'll try to find that out. I'm not sure how much he knows about Sydney's disappearance. Or what our parents might have to do with it," Warner says. "Don't you guys think it's strange how we all keep somehow being connected to each other?"

"There are a lot of small coincidences, aren't there?" Lyla asks. "Did you know that our parents used to be friends? Like, good friends?"

"Friends?" Warner asks. "They hate each other."

"Apparently they had some sort of falling out," I say, wanting to give him some information, too. I can't let Lyla do all the talking. "She wouldn't give us much information on it when we asked her, though."

The worker walks over and sets down our orders. The three of us talk some more about our parents and about Sydney while we have our sweets, then Warner says he needs to get back home before his mom loses it on him again for being gone so late.

During the drive home, Lyla is quiet. "That was weird, right?" I ask to fill the silence. "It seemed like a pretty uneventful meet-up."

Lyla shrugs. "I guess so. But I think he's right to be concerned. It feels like something weird is going on. I just don't know what."

When we turn onto our street and get closer to our house, I notice an unfamiliar sedan parked out front. Lyla notices it too and leans forward in her seat and squints at it.

"Whose car is that?" I ask. Detective Craig's normal civilian vehicle? Is he over at our house again?

"No idea," Lyla replies. As soon as I park and turn off the vehicle, she flies out of the front seat and dashes inside. I hurry to follow in behind her.

"There you guys are!" Mom says to us in the kitchen with a smile on her face. It looks pained, like she doesn't really want it there. "Look who has come to visit!"

Sitting at the counter behind her, a steaming hot mug of either tea or coffee in front of her and two suitcases and a duffel bag sitting on the floor next to her, is someone I haven't seen in years.

I'm about to say her name in a shocked voice, but my twin beats me to it.

"Aunt Nora?"

Chapter 42

Lyla

"I can't believe you have never had roller coaster pancakes," Aunt Nora tells me, Audrey, and Joey at breakfast the next morning. She has the Beatles blasting on a portable Bluetooth speaker as she dances around the kitchen happily, whipping us all up some sort of breakfast she refers to as roller coaster pancakes. "My mom—our mom—used to make these for us all the time! It's a cherished family recipe."

I still have no idea why Aunt Nora has decided to come to visit. I don't think my mom quite knows either. If she does, she refuses to tell us about it.

"Uh… is it going to be done soon?" Audrey asks, glancing at the clock. "We have to head to school."

Nora smiles pleasantly at Audrey. She looks weirdly like my mom, only her face is more rounded and her hair is more of a hazelnut brown. She and my mother both have the same narrow chin and slight circles under their eyes that never seem to fully go away, no matter how much eye cream or concealer they use.

"Audrey, your hair would look so cute if you cut it like Lyla's," Aunt Nora tells her.

Audrey's face twists into something unamused and insulted. She sits at the table and says nothing as Nora turns back around and puts her concoction in the oven.

"What's going on down here?" Mom asks as she enters the kitchen from the staircase. She is all done up and ready to head to work. She has on a leopard print long sleeve shirt, black skinny jeans with tiny holes at the knees, and black leather Chelsea boots.

Nora is still in her pajamas: striped pants with an XXL yellow shirt. Her hair is a tangled unbrushed mess and her face has makeup on it from yesterday. She reminds me a little bit of Sydney.

"Are you cooking something?" Mom stares at Nora in horror. "You don't cook."

Nora looks personally offended. "I can cook some things," she says. "Like mom's roller coaster pancakes. I can't believe you've never made those for them before!"

Amelia smiles a little bit. "I completely forgot about those," she says. "It amazes me how little I remember from my childhood. Well... that can just be something special that only aunt Nora makes." She walks over to the Keurig, which brews a pot every morning automatically. She pours herself a cup and leans against the counter while Nora dances along to I Want to Hold Your Hand.

It amazes me to watch them. Two completely different people, somehow born from the same set of parents.

As the week goes on and turns into the weekend, I only notice more differences between my aunt and my mother. How quirky Aunt Nora is. Strange. Weird. Goofy. The best word I can use to describe her would probably be eclectic. She has a variety of likes and interests, as well as a large variety of dislikes and opinions. While she is a little out there, almost like a hippie, my mom is not. Mom is idealistic, practical, efficient, and straightforward. With my mom, things are black and white. With Aunt Nora, apparently, there are allowed to be a lot of gray areas.

Dad came home a few days ago from another trip, and he had given Aunt Nora a hug with that same strained expression that Mom had had on her face when Audrey and I first saw her. Then, when Dad's workweek was over, he said he had a busy weekend planned. Right now, for example, it's around noon on a Saturday, and he is out golfing with some work buddies. Part of me is getting the feeling that neither my father nor my mother really wants Aunt Nora here, but they don't know how to tell her so.

I'm in my room scrolling through Instagram on my phone when I hear laughter downstairs. Not only in my mom's voice, but a man's voice as well. I leave my bedroom and head to the staircase, seeing Aunt Nora at the bottom of it, peering around the corner, spying into the front room. I go down the stairs and Aunt Nora turns around and looks at me with one eyebrow raised.

"Who is your mom talking to?" she asks me, her voice a whisper as she points around the corner.

I copy her and stealthily peer around to see who Mom is in the front room with. My stomach dips when I notice that it is a Craig Fritz again.

Then Joey walks out of the kitchen and sees Aunt Nora and me standing here. I'm pretty sure Audrey would be with us too if it weren't for the fact that she is currently at cheer practice.

"Who is that?" Joey asks us, having heard the voices as well.

"Shh!" Nora and I say together.

"That's Detective Craig Fritz," I whisper to them both. Then I fill in Aunt Nora. "This girl went missing from our school camping trip. I don't know if you know. He's been routinely asking all the parents and teachers that volunteered to chaperone questions to try and figure out what happened to her."

"Did you say Craig Fritz?" Nora asks, forgetting to whisper.

I widen my eyes as we all freeze and notice how the talking in the front room has stopped. Then suddenly there's a loud burst of giggles; clearly, Mom and Detective Fritz hadn't heard us.

"Yeah," Joey says, continuing our conversation with Aunt Nora. "He's been coming over here a lot."

"Not that much," I argue. Although, is it necessary for Craig to come over for the fifth time? And does it always have to be when my dad just so happens to not be home?

I look up at my aunt Nora and see that she is gnawing on her bottom lip, her eyes downcast and her toes wiggling in her slippers.

"Aunt Nora?" I whisper.

When she looks up at me, her eyebrows are narrowed. "I have to go... do something." She starts walking up the staircase, but three steps up, she stops and turns back around to us. "Does your mom always act this way?" she asks. "Or has she been sort of strange lately?"

"She's been weird," I agree. Next to me, Joey nods his head. She was weird on the camping trip, she was weird after the camping trip, and she got really weird when Aunt Nora showed up.

"Huh." Aunt Nora looks deep in thought for a moment longer, then she turns and resumes heading back up the staircase.

Chapter 43

Amelia

"I just don't get why she doesn't leave," Gentry says to me. We're in the bedroom folding laundry and putting it away in our closet. "You guys weren't even ever close." He's referring to Nora and the fact that it's been quite some time now and she is still staying in our guest bedroom with no plans of leaving and with no hint as to why she is even here in the first place. Every time I try to bring it up to her, she gives me the same answer. "Cheese, Sis, I really have to have a reason to come see my family?"

I sigh as I hang up one of my favorite shirts from the boutique next to my office. "What do you want me to do, Gentry?" I ask in an irritable voice. It's not his fault, but it's frustrating to keep having this conversation with him.

"I don't know, at least figure out what it is she wants?"

"Maybe she doesn't actually want anything? Maybe she just actually wants to spend time with us," I try. I know he doesn't believe me, and I can't blame him—-I barely even believe myself. I just feel weird trying to ask her too many questions. I don't want to push her to a place she doesn't want to be. And I feel guilty about all of our missed communication over the years. Nora is good at making me feel guilty. She always has been. Even though our lack of communication has been a two-way street—for the most part.

"I just don't believe that." Gentry shoves some balled-up socks into his sock drawer. We have one of those smartly designed closets that have drawers and cupboards, and shelving to place our shoes. There's even an ottoman and a rug in the middle and a full-length mirror on one of the walls. "I mean, look at her. I don't think she has a lot of money. And she clearly knows that we do."

"You seriously think my sister came here to ask me for money?" I'm even angrier now. "She's my sister, Gentry. She wouldn't do that. And if she did need money, she would've asked by now. And she would insist on paying me back, too."

Suddenly, Joey appears in the doorway, making the both of us jump.

"I can hear you guys fighting from the hallway!" he complains. His eyes are heavy with sadness and his shoulders are slumped. It's clear he is disappointed in us. "You guys fight all the time. You never see each other, and then when you do, you're fighting."

It kills me to hear him talk like that. I don't mean to raise my voice when I am getting in a heated conversation with Gentry, but sometimes it's inevitable. Unavoidable. Gentry knows how to press my buttons.

Gentry kneels down in front of Joey and puts his hands on his shoulders. "I'm sorry, buddy. We weren't fighting. We were just talking... loudly."

"Yeah right." Joey won't look at either of us.

"Sweetie, I'm sorry," I chime in. "We were having a slight disagreement. But we're not mad at each other. We are just trying to resolve the issue. It's alright."

"Why don't you go get the Xbox started up and I'll come down and play that new racing game you've been telling me about," Gentry tells him. "Does that sound good? I just have to finish up putting the rest of our laundry away."

Joey side-glances at me before answering. "Okay." His voice still sounds sad, but it's enough for now. He turns and walks out of our room.

I put a hand on my hip and glare at Gentry as he stands back up. "He's miserable. And he misses you," I say. "You and I both know that giving him a happy family is all we are supposed to be focused on right now."

"I know."

"How can you do that when you're never home?" I ask. "You need to do something with him. Take him on a trip or something. I got to go on a trip with the girls, maybe you and Joey should go on a trip just the two of you." I'm sure Joey could use the bonding time with my husband.

Gentry lets out a long breath and finishes putting the last of his clothes away. "I think that might be a good idea."

When the next weekend comes, Joey and Gentry head to the mountains to go on a father-son camping trip. Nora is still here at the house, and she's made herself quite at home. She and I have talked here and there, but not nearly as much as she has talked to the girls and Joey. If one thing is clear, it's that Nora is much more interested in seeing her nieces and nephew than she is in seeing me. Not that I'm surprised.

My stomach dips excitedly when I hear a knock on the door as I'm reading a book in my front room. This time, I already know who it is. Craig had texted me before he headed over to let me know he was coming. We've been texting on and off for a few days now, just friendly stuff. More reminiscing about high school and joking around with each other. It's been nice, and I'm looking forward to talking to him again.

With a smile on my face, I head to answer the door. Before I reach it, Nora comes out of nowhere and stops me. "Who is that?" my sister asks.

"It's just Detective Fritz," I say, the smile wiping off my face.

"Why is he here again?" she asks, not looking happy. "And why were you just smiling like that?"

"Were you in my front room?" I ask, changing the subject. "I've told you it's off-limits." I try to move around her and answer the door, but she puts a hand on it to prevent me.

"What are you doing with him?" she demands. "Your kids are suspicious of all the time you spend together. Especially when Gentry's not home."

"Don't be ridiculous. Craig knows I'm married to Gentry and Gentry knows every time I have Craig over. We're just friends."

"Did you have something to do with that girl's disappearance or something?" she questions.

A knock sounds on the door again. "Sydney?" I ask, feeling myself get defensive. "No, of course not. I'm just cooperating with the investigation in any way that I can."

She crosses her arms. "Because of your guilty conscience?"

Nora's words hang in the air, floating between us like a dark ominous cloud. She has an expression on her face that makes her look nearly unrecognizable.

I say nothing back, and finally, Nora steps away from the door. Usually, she's hiding out in her room when Craig comes over, but this time, she stays.

I answer the door with a smile, though I'm not as excited to see Craig as I had been moments ago.

"Hey, you," Craig says in greeting. I open the door wider so that he can step inside. When his eyes land on Nora, I don't miss the surprise on his face. "Nora Flynn, is that you?"

"Hey there, Craig." She doesn't look nearly as pleasant and happy as Craig does to see her.

"It's been forever! Somehow, you look exactly the same!" He steps inside the house and reaches out to give Nora a hug. She hugs him back and when they pull apart, she stares at him some more.

"So... what brings you to town?" Craig asks, trying to make easy conversation.

Nora crosses her arms. "You became a cop?"

"Sure did," Craig tells her. "It's always been my dream, didn't you know that?"

Nora was only a freshman when Craig was already a junior. They didn't talk that much in high school, and Craig was more my friend than he was hers.

Nora pulls her phone out of the back pocket of her flare leg pants. "I have to take this," she tells us. Then she turns and goes up the stairs, taking them two at a time.

I smile at Craig. "Come to the kitchen. I have some beverages and cheese and crackers."

I watch as he stares after Nora for a moment, then he nods his head and follows me. We take a seat at the kitchen counter, a marble platter displaying an assortment of cheeses and meats and crackers before us, as well as two spritzers. I got the drink recipe from Pinterest last week and have been hooked on them ever since.

"Is everything okay?" I ask, sensing something off about Craig today. He's not being nearly as smiley and goofy as he has been the past few times we've talked.

"Oh, yeah. It was just weird to see Nora like that. You didn't tell me she was visiting."

I shrug. "Didn't think it was important. Why? Did something happen between you two?" I say it in a joking voice, but I am curious.

He chuckles. "Course not. It just brought me back to high school, you know?" I know he's not referring to just high school. He's referring to a specific incident in high school.

When I try to swallow, my throat is dry. I take a sip of my spritzer before I speak again. "You mean... Carson?" I ask with much, much hesitation. He is not someone I ever, ever talk about.

"Yeah," Craig says with a small nod. "I've just always felt horrible about the way it all went down. How they never found them. How they just simply gave up. Much too soon, if you ask me. That's why even though Sarge wants this case closed and Sydney Hutton presumed dead, I just can't bring myself to do it."

I gently grab Craig's forearm, doing it in a comforting matter. Craig and Carson Price had been friends back in high school. "That makes complete sense," I tell him. "I totally understand where you are coming from. I really hope you are able to find out what happened to Sydney. That poor girl." I just want to get the topic off of Carson and back to anything else as quickly as possible. For multiple people's sake.

"Yeah, well... there's been a couple developments that I haven't quite looked into yet," he says, eying me curiously.

"What kind of developments?" I ask.

"Well, I'm assuming you don't know about this, or else you would've already told me."

I put down the slice of Brie I had just picked up to place on a cracker. "Told you what?"

"It seems there are three people in particular that Sydney was interested in getting to know better. Two of those are your daughters. The other one is Warner Carpenter."

"That has to be some sort of mistake. I'm not sure where you're getting your information. My daughters told me that they were never friends with her."

"Did they?" Craig asks. "Because I'm not so sure they're being honest with you about that."

I struggle to find the right way to reply. "Well... I—I assure you, I had no idea if they were friends with her after all."

I had specifically asked my daughters in the car on the drive home from the camping trip if they were close with Sydney. I knew I didn't like the way they had looked at each other after. I should have known then that something was up. The question is now: why did they lie to me?

Chapter 44

Audrey

I don't know why, but Aunt Nora definitely likes Lyla more than me. For one, she gives Lyla way more compliments than me. Two, she nitpicks the things I say and do. Three, she pays much more attention to Lyla, too. Aunt Nora seems to want to spend more time with her than me. The two of them are always giggling and talking to each other. And Aunt Nora always sits next to Lyla at the dinner table. They paint each other's nails and pick out movies to watch together. Maybe I am just too busy with cheer to have as much freedom to hang out with her, but something tells me that that is not it.

"You remind me so much of your mom," Aunt Nora says to me often. At first, I thought it was a compliment. I love my mom and I strive to be like her. I love her ambition and her grace. Her fashion-forwardness and how polite she is to everyone. Why wouldn't I want to be like her? But the more Aunt Nora says this to me, the more I am starting to think it's supposed to be an insult. Especially because it doesn't seem like Aunt Nora and my mom get along very well.

Driving to school today, I try to tell Lyla about how I feel about it. "I mean come on," I tell her. "How do you not see it?"

"I think you're being silly," Lyla says. She's in a lighter mood than I've seen in a while. I am beginning to think spending all of this time with Aunt Nora has made her happier. I can't help but feel a little bitter and resentful about it. I had worked all summer to cheer her up. Aunt Nora comes for a couple of weeks and suddenly Lya is chipper and cheery again? What is that about?

"I'm not," I say to my twin. "You can't tell me you haven't seen it. She's always complimenting you. She hates everything about me."

Lyla chuckles and I know it's because she agrees with me. I laugh weakly and swat at her as I pull into the parking lot of school. "It's not funny!" I whine. I don't know why I want Aunt Nora's approval, especially since she's such a kook, but for some reason, I do. She's the only aunt I have.

I park the car, and we get out and go our separate ways. I'm supposed to meet up with the girls this morning and Lyla is going to be hanging out with Jackson, like usual.

There's still been no new developments or news about Sydney's disappearance. Since a couple of weeks have gone by now, the school has pretty much forgotten about her. She hadn't even been attending Blackfell high for that long. Not long enough to make a very lasting impression, at least. Every day, the school has started returning more and more back to normal.

I go to my locker and unload some of the textbooks I had brought home for homework. I touch up my lip gloss in my small mirror and turn off the tiny battery-powered disco ball I have hanging inside before I shut it and get on my phone to see where my friends are at.

When I click my phone screen on, the first thing I see is a text from an unknown number.

Unknown: *I know your secret.*

My face heats up and I use both hands to hold my phone steady as I reread the message over and over again.

It has to be spam, right? I'm probably going to get another text shortly. It's that your skincare routine is lacking! Click the link to check out our offer!

My secret? The only secret I really have is about Warner Carpenter's father. Mr. Reeves. The only person who knows that I know about it is Madeline Carpenter. She specifically told me not to say anything, and so far I have listened to her. It's Maddy's secret more than mine, anyway. So it doesn't make any sense for it to have been her who sent me the message.

"Hey!"

I jump and look up at Sophia. Over the weekend, she's added some highlights to her hair.

"Changing it up?" I ask. Then I look down at my phone and reply to the text, just to confirm that it is spam.

Me: *Who is this?*

I put my phone in my back pocket.

"I decided that blondes do have more fun," Sophia says, a casual smile on her face. But I know this game. She is jealous of all the attention my sister got when she chopped all of her hair off, and Sophia wants to get the focus back on her, the queen of the school.

"Well, you look like a rockstar," I tell her with a friendly smile.

"I know, right?"

A twinge of irritation raises inside of me. Why can't she ever just say thank you?

"Come on, let's go gossip to the girls about the scandal that happened over the weekend." She starts walking around me towards the cafeteria.

My heart skips a beat. "Scandal?"

"Yeah?" she says with her eyebrows raised. "About Allison Trevino and Orion Potts? How they apparently got in a huge fight at Wrigley Hall's party? It was all over Snapchat, remember?"

"Oh, right." I don't bother to tell her that I didn't check Snapchat at all over the weekend. For some reason, I have been checking social media less than less lately.

My phone buzzes in my back pocket as we go to meet the other girls. I pull it back out and read it as we walk.

Unknown: *Clear your conscience, Audrey. Or else.*

I freeze in my step.

Okay, this clearly isn't spam.

Sophia turns and gives me a weird look. "You good?"

Who the heck is this person? Why are they telling me to clear my conscience? I didn't do anything wrong.

Does this person think I have something to do with Sydney's disappearance? Do they think I'm withholding information from the police? Is it potentially somebody else that knows about Dean Reeves?

"Audrey. Hello?"

I snap out of my thoughts and realize that Sophia is talking still. I put my phone away again. I'm just going to ignore it. "Totally," I say to my friend. "I'm good."

Chapter 45

Warner

I stand with Jackson and Lyla a little bit outside the school before the bell rings, but I really don't like being around the two of them right now. Especially when I had met up with Lyla and didn't tell Jackson about it. If he knows, he isn't mentioning it to me, either. Part of me wonders if Lyla knows I want to keep it a secret and if she wants to keep it one, too.

I feel like such a jerk for having a crush on Lyla. Why can't I like the other twin? The one who is single? They're obviously both equally attractive. I just don't get it. Something keeps drawing me to Lyla, and I don't know what it is. I just need to keep away from her. Maybe the crush will fade. It's just a temporary feeling. If I put all my focus into my assistant coaching job and football, I'll forget about her in no time, I'm sure.

I leave them pretty quickly and go inside the school. When I open my locker, a folded piece of paper falls to the tiled floor. I drop my backpack to the ground and bend over and pick it up. When I unfold it, my breakfast threatens to fly out of my mouth as I stare at it in horror. It's a picture of me. And I'm talking to Sydney. And we are in the woods. In the middle of the night.

I refold the photo and shove it in my back pocket, panicking. Who sent me this? Who took the photo? Why did they put it in my locker like this? What is happening to me right now?

Forgetting about what I was even doing in my locker in the first place, I slam it shut, throw my backpack back on, and head to first hour early.

At practice after school, my friends can tell I'm being weird. I'm not focusing, just like I hadn't been when Sydney first disappeared. Coach Reeves sees it too, and he isn't happy.

"What kind of captain are you?" Coach snaps at me at one point. "You're acting so completely JV right now." We are practicing a couple new plays that the coach had come up with. I was supposed to come up with some too, but it slipped my mind with everything going on. This is another reason why Coach is mad at me today.

When we get a water break a little bit into practice, Jackson elbows me in the side. He splashes some water from the nozzle of his bottle right onto his face to cool himself down. His cheeks get beat red in the sun like this. "What's up with you?" he asks. "You've been pretty crappy at football ever since we got back from the camping trip."

"No, I haven't," I say defensively. I'm great at football. What the heck is the matter with me? Get your head in the game, Warner!

But I can't. My head keeps going back to the stupid photo I found in my locker earlier. The one that's now sitting in the small zipper that's hidden inside of the largest zipper of my backpack. I don't want to chance anyone else getting their hands on it.

So, I hung out with Sydney sometimes. It doesn't mean anything. Is somebody trying to blackmail me with this photo? What are they trying to play at?

There's something else I am considering, too. What if it was Sydney who did this? What if she had somehow set up a timer on her camera or something and got the photo? Is she fine and not really missing after all? Is she just doing all of this for attention? Did she just make up this chaos to mess with me all because I told her I don't like her? Can it be that Sydney is alive and well?

Part of me knows that it's impossible. If Sydney is alive and well, then sending me this photo in the first place is pointless, right? Something happened to Sydney, and someone wants me to know about it.

Chapter 46

Maddy

I go to Toxey's only Starbucks to meet up with my old friend who is in town. She insisted on Starbucks because it apparently has been ages since she has been to one.

I want to look cute and like I have my life together for her, so I put on a red pleated floor-length skirt and a cute summery blouse. My hair is up in a high ponytail out of my face, and my makeup is natural and bronzy. I look like I spend my days lounging out by a fancy pool at a hotel somewhere. Even if that's definitely not the case.

When my friend walks in, she looks just like I remember. Round face. Narrow chin. Long hazelnut brown hair.

"Nora Flynn," I say with a grin, getting out of my seat to give my old friend a hug.

"Hey, Mads." Nora hugs me back with an equally wide smile on her face. Then she takes her sunglasses off and shows me her bright blue eyes.

It's rare that Nora and I get to see each other, but over the years, we've stayed in touch. Even if I've said otherwise to some people.

"I can't believe you're actually here!" I say with an excited squeal.

"I want a Matcha latte," Nora says, squeezing my hand and tugging me along to the back of the Starbucks line. We order our coffees; I get an iced vanilla latte. Then we go back to the table we had set our purses down at. We sit across from each other and sip our drinks, easily diving into a conversation about catching each other up on our lives. I do a majority of the talking because she insists that during our time apart, she has been doing a whole lot of nothing. She decided to come to town because she realized she barely knows her nieces and nephew and wants to be a part of their lives. Even if it means enduring her horrid older sister.

"But you know something weird I noticed about one of the twins?" Nora asks me at one point. I lean in across the table closer, eager to know what she's about to tell me. I love to hear gossip about Amelia's children. Especially if it's bad gossip.

Nora looks serious. "Lyla and your son have been hanging out with each other. Did you know that?"

I sit back in my chair. This is not good news to me at all. It's bad gossip, but not the kind I was hoping to hear. I wanted to hear that one of them was failing out of school. That one of them got into hard drugs or something. Not this.

"Lyla and Warner are hanging out?" I ask. "You mean because she's dating his best friend, Jackson?"

"Lyla has a boyfriend?" Nora asks. She looks totally clueless about it.

"Wait. You're telling me Lyla never mentioned to you that she has a boyfriend? And she's been hanging out with my son?"

Nora shrugs and sips the last bit of her latte, the ice and the straw making a loud noise in her plastic cup. "Apparently so. I don't know... when I saw them together, it seemed like they had a crush on each other. Maybe Lyla and Jackson broke up?"

“Absolutely not,” I say, even though I’m not sure. Would Warner have told me information like this? Wouldn’t Warner ask my advice if he wanted to ask Lyla out? I know he tried to talk to me about her back on the camping trip, but I had shut the idea down. I thought he would’ve taken my advice and stayed away from her after that. I guess not.

I have several reasons for not wanting my son around any of the Flynn-Bailey family. But now, my main reason is because of Dean. Because Audrey Bailey found out that Dean is my son’s father. And I am supposed to trust my enemy’s own daughter to keep it a secret from Warner?

I wish I could talk to Nora about this. But I have kept this secret for a long time. If I start blabbing to people now, the news will get out in no time and Warner will surely hear the information from someone else besides me. I don’t want that to happen.

The thing is, Audrey and Lyla are twins, right? And don’t twins tell each other everything? So even though Audrey told me she won’t tell my secret, did that apply to her own twin, too? Or did she immediately run and tell Lyla that Dean Reeves is Warner’s father? And if they both know the truth, who’s to say one of them isn’t going to confess the truth to him? How can I consider them reliable? They are Bailey’s, for crying out loud!

Chapter 47

Amelia

As I sit at my desk in my office the next morning, scrolling through Pinterest for my newest clients, Mr. and Mrs. Barton, I'm thinking about my girls. About what Craig told me about them. Why on earth had Sydney Hutton been "interested" in them? And why were Audrey and Lyla so secretive about it? Not once did I hear either of them talking about her ever, except for when Audrey had come home from cheer tryouts and made fun of her that one time at the beginning of the year.

It's also embarrassing to be told information about my own daughters that I hadn't already known by someone else. I hated the pitying expression Craig had given me after I told him I hadn't known Sydney had been in contact with my girls.

The whole disappearance of Sydney is strange, too. Where did this girl even come from? Wasn't there anyone who missed her? Why weren't her foster parents on the news, sobbing and holding press conferences to beg the public to help them figure out where she went? Had something bad really happened to her, or had she just simply run away?

If Sydney doesn't have anyone that cares about her, then I am going to try to stick to believing my theory that she ran away and is fine. Maybe Sydney was interested in being friends with my daughters, but I highly doubt those feelings were reciprocated.

I stop scrolling through Pinterest when I realize I've been sitting here not paying the slightest bit of attention. I am supposed to be finding good inspiration images for the look I think Mr. and Mrs. Barton are trying to go for. They have an older house—like most of my clients do, and they want something sleek, minimal, and contemporary, with just the smallest hint of eclecticism. John and Meghan Barton actually remind me a lot of myself and Gentry. They're a part of one of the wealthier families in Toxey. Except unlike Gentry and myself, who are hard-working beings that took a while to get here, the Bartons came from an already wealthy family just outside of town. But I can tell the Bartons care a lot about their outward appearances to other people. And they have a daughter Joey's age and a daughter a year under Lyla and Audrey, too. The fact that we have so much in common already and it's just the start of the project makes me so much more eager to work with them.

I rush home later to cook dinner for the kids—and my sister, I suppose—before the football game tonight. I promised Joey we would go together so that he could watch the game and I could watch his sister cheer. I was hoping Lyla would be coming with us, too, but when I get home, I find that she isn't here.

I text her.

Me: *Where r u? Coming 2 the game 2nite?*

I wait a little bit to see if she is going to text me back right away, but when she doesn't I frown and set my phone on the counter and get started on dinner—a simple house salad with a lemon vinaigrette and some baked chicken breasts.

While cooking, Joey sits at the table and tells me about his day at school. As he gets back into a routine and adjusts to being a middle schooler, I can tell he is getting more relaxed and used to it.

Audrey comes down the stairs as I'm taking the chicken out of the pan and putting it on a serving platter given to me by my mother. When Nora saw me using it the other day, she gave it a look of complete disgust. She doesn't exactly talk to our parents. Now I keep the platter hidden in a high cupboard, just in case she tries to "accidentally drop it". Audrey is dressed in her maroon and black cheerleading uniform, her pom-poms in hand.

"It smells so good in here!" she says pleasantly, walking to the table and sitting next to Joey, who is watching YouTube videos on his iPhone.

"Thanks, you're just in time!" I tell her, checking my phone to see if Lyla has replied yet. "Do you know where your sister is? And did you see Nora upstairs?"

Audrey shakes her head, leaning over Joey's shoulder to watch whatever it is he has on.

"Nora, dinner!" I call. Then I text Lyla again.

Me: Hello?

Nora comes down the stairs from the guest room, wearing sweats and a large hoodie. She looks like she either just woke up or hasn't slept in days. I can't tell.

"Thanks, Sis," she says as she sits at the table. I set it and join them.

“Well, I guess we can just eat without her,” I say about Lyla, glancing at my phone screen again just in case. I hate not knowing where she is. Why isn’t she texting me back? I feel like I am about to start implementing a rule that if they don’t respond to my messages within ten minutes that they’re grounded. Even though I have never really been that kind of a mother.

“Where is Lyla?” Nora asks, looking disappointed and addressing Audrey. My other daughter shrugs and plates herself some food, shoveling it in her mouth quickly.

I’ve noticed that my sister has seemed to take more of a liking to Lyla than Audrey, but I don’t have any idea why. I turn to her.

“We’re going to the football game at Blackfell High to watch Audrey cheer,” I tell her, trying to sound friendly. “You should come. Show your support for your niece.” I don’t actually want to spend time with her, I just want to see if she’s willing.

Nora plates her dinner next. She scoffs. “Yeah, like I’m ever going to step foot back on that campus,” she says in a pointedly sarcastic voice.

“Why not?” Joey asks. He still has a video playing on his phone and hasn’t gotten himself any food.

“Joey, phone away,” I say.

“You’re on yours!” he complains.

I freeze, seeing the phone open to Lyla’s text thread in my hand. “I’m trying to get ahold of your sister,” I say.

He rolls his eyes, clicks his phone off, and turns back to Nora.

“That place will suck the soul right out of you,” she tells him.

“Nora, come on,” I scold. “He’s already scared enough about being in middle school.”

Nora doesn’t look the least bit apologetic. “You’re better off homeschooling him,” she tells me.

My stomach knots. I look at my plate and start cutting my chicken into smaller pieces than usual.

The garage door opens and we all turn to see Lyla walking in, her cheeks pink like she had been out in the hot setting sun.

"Where were you?" I demand, sounding sassier than I want to. Gentry says I need to be gentler on Lyla. But it would have taken her just a few seconds to text me back.

"Sorry," she replies, not answering my question.

I try again. "Where were you?"

"Oh my god!" she snaps. "Leave me alone!"

My jaw drops. I know the others are looking at each other with the same expression. "Leave you alone?" I repeat.

"Ugh!" She walks out of the kitchen and stomps up the stairs with her backpack.

"What's her problem?" Audrey asks with attitude.

I give her a look. She doesn't need to add to the drama.

We get to the football stadium early to get good center spots on the bleachers, right in the middle so I can see in all directions. Audrey is on the sidelines, stretching her legs on the bench. When she sees me in the stands, she waves excitedly. I wave back, feeling loved and happy that she doesn't think she's too cool for me or that I am too lame of a mom to say hi to. I'm also incredibly proud of her. She's been cheering since junior high, and she gets better every year. I wish Lyla had stuck with it.

The stands fill up quickly, and by the time kickoff happens, it doesn't seem like there's a single open seat around. Even the away teams' side is full—and not of the away teams' supporters.

"This is cool and all," Joey says, "but if I see anyone I know, I'm ditching you."

I laugh. I would be more concerned if he had said the opposite.

It's about ten minutes into the game when I catch a glimpse of familiar brown hair a few rows down and a little bit to my right.

Maddy Carpenter is here. However, I nearly choke on the sip from my bottle of Coke Zero when I see who she is sitting next to.

Craig Fritz.

I can feel my heart beating in my ears as I watch them. Our team scores a touchdown, and everyone gets up and jumps and cheers, and Craig and Maddy turn to each other and kiss on the lips, both of them smiling happily as if they've been together forever.

"Mom, they scored!" Joey calls to me, on his feet and clapping.

I swallow uneasily and give a weak cheer.

I'm completely flabbergasted. How many times have I seen Craig lately? And how many of those times did he mention anything to me about the fact that he is dating my ex-best friend?

I feel sick to my stomach.

It's fine, Mia. Who cares? This is nothing you need to stress yourself about.

I close my eyes and take some slow, deep breaths. I have a war in my head that two parts of me are fighting in. The reasonable part of my brain is telling the part that wants to march right up to them and demand to know what's going on to relax and not do anything rash.

I am not the best at relaxing, though. Not when I feel like a fool. When I feel lied to. Tricked. When I feel like everyone seems to know something I don't. I'm Amelia Bailey—I know everything.

I'm not jealous of the fact that Craig and Maddy are together—definitely not. That isn't what has me so angry right now. I feel used. I feel like something is up, and I think I need to figure out what.

CHAPTER 48

LYLA

I don't think my parents need to always know where I go and what I am doing. I think they should trust me enough to know that I am being careful, and I am not making any bad decisions. My dad never tells me where he's going, or even that he's leaving at all. Sometimes I wake up in the morning and he's just... gone. So if anything, it's hypocritical of my parents to think they can bug me about where I am and what I am doing.

Besides, I don't really feel like telling anyone about this specific place I like to visit.

Frequently.

If Mom and Dad knew I was constantly going to Trinity's grave to talk to her and think about her, they would probably put me in a mental institution or something. They would give me those sad eyes that I hate getting. They would be more worried about me being there than they probably are when they don't know where I am. I think keeping it a secret that I come here and visit my dead friend's grave is better for everyone.

"Parents are so annoying, Trin," I say to the headstone as I flop myself down in front of it. The flowers her parents placed a couple of days ago look a little sad, so I pull the scissors out of my backpack and trim the stems and add more water from my Hydro Flask to the vase they sit in.

I talk to her for a little while about everything I have been thinking and feeling lately. Everything I would have told her and only her if she were still actually here. I'll be honest, I have no idea if she can hear me, but I prefer to think that she can. It makes me feel the teeniest, tiniest bit better.

My phone lights up in the grass next to me and I pick it up and see that I have a text message from an unknown number.

Unknown: *I can't believe you killed her.*

I drop my phone reactively.

"What the heck?" I gasp out loud. I get to my feet at lightning speed and look around myself. Is someone playing a prank on me? Spying on me and wanting to hurt my feelings? It wouldn't be the first time someone has tried to blame Trinity's death on me. Little did they know they were right in doing so. Trinity's death is my fault—they're simply pointing out a fact to me that I already know.

I see a brown Station Wagon, the front windows down, slowly driving on one of the small cemetery roads. Usually, only cops, hearses, and people attending graveside funerals are permitted to drive on them.

But the person in the car is a cop. It's Detective Craig Fritz, and he's staring right at me.

I walk across the perfectly manicured grass over to his open passenger window, holding my phone up in front of me.

"Did you just send me a text?" I ask him, knowing I sound crazy and that the idea is highly improbable. But he's the only one I can see around me. He seems to be the only one who knows I am here right now.

Craig's wild eyebrows narrow at me. "Did I what?"

I drop my hand to my side and scratch my head, confused, as I look around myself again. "Never mind," I mumble.

"What are you doing here?" he asks me.

Wait a second. Is he following me?

I know he's a cop, but I really don't feel like being nice to him. What if he is the one who sent that message?

"I don't think I have to tell you that," I say, not sure if I'm right.

He slowly nods his head up and down, his eyes peering into mine with a hard expression, like he's trying to get a read on me. I don't like it.

"That's true, you don't have to tell me," he says. "But listen. I wanted to ask you a couple of questions about your friend, Sydney Hutton."

I have a bad feeling about this entire situation. And Mom always tells me I need to trust my gut. My woman's instinct. I put my phone in my back pocket and cross my arms. "I think my mom should have already told you everything you need to know."

I'm coming off stubborn and mean, but I'm terrified inside. Why does he want to talk to me about Sydney? How did he know I would be here? Has he been waiting for a moment to get me alone? A moment when I am weak and vulnerable?

"Your mother seemed to not know that you and Sydney were friends," he says.

"Were?"

"Are you still?" he asks. "Do you know where she is?"

I shake my head repeatedly. "This is ridiculous," I tell him. "One, I wasn't friends with her. Two, I find it really fascinating that you think you can come here, behind my mom's back, no doubt, to try to corner me into answering questions for you about Sydney. Just like I think it's fascinating that you have been spending so much time with my married mother when you have a girlfriend of your own to be hanging out with. Does Madeline Carpenter know how often you're over at our house?"

I watch as Detective Fritz's jaw tightens. I also can see inside of his car some fast food wrappers and a tall soda cup in his cupholder. It looks to me like he's been in his car for a while. Doing a stakeout, maybe?

But why me? I don't know where Sydney is. I don't know what happened to her. I don't know why she was so determined for my friendship.

"How did you know I was dating Maddy?" he snaps. "My personal business is none of your concern, Miss Bailey."

I'm glad to get an angry reaction out of him. It's what I was going for. "Just like you have your ways to get information on people—apparently—I have my ways, too."

"When did you last see Sydney Hutton?" he asks, trying to get the subject back to her. "Did you see her the night she went missing?"

"Yeah, we were on the camping trip together," I tell him, laying the attitude on thick. "Everyone saw her."

"What about after curfew?"

Shoot! He was getting me to answer questions!

"You never answered my question, Detective," I say, smirking. "Does Maddy know you come to our house?"

He doesn't answer me. He just continues to give me that same menacing "I hate kids" stare. Then finally, he puts his car in drive. "You should go home. It's not safe for you to be wandering around the town alone. Especially when a girl from your town has gone missing."

I glare at him as he drives away.

Chapter 49

Warner

Evergreen I feel like Lyla is the only one who I can talk to right now. With the Sydney situation and the fact that our parents hate each other for some mysterious reason, there are multiple reasons I keep gravitating towards her company and wanting to talk to her.

I text her when I get done with football practice. Jackson is right next to me in the locker room, packing up his duffle bag and joking around with the guys, and I know I should tell him I am talking to her. But I don't.

Me: *Can you meet me right now? Parking lot in front of the Evergreen hiking trail?*

I pack my own duffle bag, and when I look at my phone again, I see that she's replied already.

Lyla: *On my way*

"Who are you texting?" Jackson asks, leaning over my shoulder.

"My mom," I lie, quickly putting my phone back in my pocket. I ignore the weird look he gives me and tell him I need to get going.

When I pull into the parking lot outside of Evergreen hiking trail, it starts to rain. My windows slowly start to fog when I turn the heater on in my car and wait for Lyla to show up.

When she does, I feel like a huge jerk. She rode her bike, which I should have known, and it's pouring rain out now.

I reach over and open my passenger door for her, where she's approaching on her bike.

"Dude!" I cry to her, having to talk louder because of the downpour. "I'm so sorry! Hurry, get in!"

She laughs and waves it off, then she gets off of her bike, lets it drop to the floor, and dashes into my passenger seat. She is completely drenched.

"A little rain never hurt anyone," she tells me as she closes the door.

"I don't know why I thought you'd show up in your car. I should have come to you," I tell her, still feeling like a horrible person even though she's being so cool about it.

"It's not your fault," she says. "I'm the wimp that won't get in my car."

I turn the heat on higher even though I am already nearly sweating. She looks so cute sitting in my car with her makeup smeared and her hair dripping. I have this overwhelming need to take care of her.

"You are...something else," I tell her with a grin. She smiles back at me and wipes water dripping down her forehead from her hairline.

"I'm sorry I'm getting water everywhere," she says.

"No, don't apologize," I say. "I deserve it."

She rolls her eyes but is still smiling. "Warner, stop. It's fine."

I reach behind my seat, feeling around the back to see if I have a blanket or towel or something she can use. I feel something soft, so I grab it and pull it out. It's my black

Blackfell hoodie, the letters BHS written across it in maroon block lettering. "Here." I hand it to her.

She looks unsure if she should take it, but only for a moment. "Thanks." She throws it on over her dripping T-shirt. "So, why did you want to meet up?"

I clear my throat and sit back in my seat. Oh yeah. I had nearly forgotten there was a real reason I wanted to see her other than because I have a massive thing for her. My stomach dips as I think back to the threatening note I got in my locker.

"Um, something sort of… happened to me the other day," I start off, speaking slowly because I am unsure exactly how to tell her. I want to talk to her about the note, but I can't tell her everything.

I look at her carefully. She has an eyebrow raised in concern. "What happened?" she asks. "Are you okay?"

"Yeah, yeah. I'm fine," I say. "But… I think someone is messing with me."

"Like, Jackson?" she asks.

"Jackson?"

She looks confused. "I don't know. What are you talking about?"

Would Jackson have been the one who left the note? Is this all just some big prank to him or something?

"Uh. I'm being blackmailed."

"Are you serious?"

I nod. When I swallow, my throat feels dry. "I think Sydney might have something to do with it. I don't know, though."

"Wait," she sits back and stares out the windshield as rain continues to slam down onto it. "I got a weird message today. I think someone may be messing with me, too."

"What was the message about?"

She looks hesitant. I shouldn't have even asked her. I don't want her asking the same question to me.

"It… doesn't even matter," she says. Thankfully, she doesn't ask me in return. "But why do you think Sydney has something to do with yours? Do you think Sydney is alive or something?"

I shrug. "I don't know what I think. This is all so…" I don't know how to finish.

She nods her head, still looking out the windshield.

"Do you think it's the same person?" I ask.

She takes her time answering me. "I… I don't know." Her teeth chatter. She slaps her hand over her mouth and looks at me to see if I saw it.

"You're still cold?" I ask in amazement. Maybe I should go stand in the rain right now, then. I could use a cooldown.

She giggles nervously. "I think I am just more anxious than anything. A big part of me wishes I never met Sydney. That she never moved here. Is that bad?"

"No," I say. But then I change my mind. "Or, maybe. But I feel the same way, so you're not alone, at least."

She gives me an appreciative smile. For a long while, we sit there and stare at each other. I would kill to know what she's thinking.

I sigh, my thoughts of her being my girlfriend turning into thoughts of Jackson. "Can I drive you home?"

"Oh, you don't have to do that," she says. Then lightning streaks across the sky outside my driver's window. We both look at it, then look at each other. We start laughing.

"I think I do," I say. Before she can try to protest again, I get out of the car into the rain.

"What are you doing?" she calls after me. I slam the door and race around to grab her bike. It fits easily in the back of my jeep.

My hair feels pretty wet when I climb back in, but it's not anything compared to how soaked she got.

"You could have just left it," she tells me, referring to her bike.

"Then how would you get anywhere?"

She nods. "Oh. Right."

I can tell she's scared as I drive her to her house. She is gripping the door and the seat with her hands and I catch her closing her eyes and taking in deep breaths here and there. It's the first time I am seeing firsthand how much being in a car scares her. And it probably doesn't help that it's raining so badly that I can hardly see.

We make it to her house in one piece. And the rain has finally slowed to a sprinkle, but lightning still streaks across the sky every so often.

She undoes her seatbelt and looks at me. "Do you want to come in?"

I raise my eyebrows in surprise. "In your house?"

"Yeah. Something weird is going on, right? I think we should do some more brainstorming. After I change into something warm and dry so I can think more clearly, though." She is so casual about it that I'm jealous. She seems like she couldn't care less about what answer I give her. And here I am, stammering.

"I...I—yeah. Uh, sure." I park the car and we get out. My nose is immediately filled with the scent of wet pavement, and I breathe in deeply.

Relax, dude, I tell myself.

We go inside her house and right away, we head up the staircase and go to a small sitting area. There are comfortable armchairs, a bookcase, a floor lamp, and a couple of live green plants. "Sit," she instructs, pointing to one of the chairs. "I'll be right back."

I do as I'm told while she changes into dry clothes. I feel stupid for hoping she is still wearing my hoodie when she comes back out. I feel even stupider when I am disappointed that she isn't. She's wearing a giant long sleeve T-shirt as a dress and poofy, warm-looking socks that go to her mid-calf.

She sits next to me. "So. I'll tell you this," she says. "The message I got… what they said… there's only one person who knew about it."

I sigh. "Sydney."

She purses her lips and nods. "I think you might be right. I think she could be messing with us."

Chapter 50

Lyla

Warner and I are still talking to each other—but we've digressed from the topic of Sydney—when Audrey appears at the top of the stairs. She freezes in her step when she notices us.

"Um, Warner," she says. "Hello." She is giving us a suspicious look while she moves towards us.

"Hey, Audrey," Warner says, smiling in a friendly way. He and I had gotten off track and started talking about everything and anything somehow. I hadn't even realized we had been sitting here for that long. Warner is just easy to talk to. Easy to be normal around. Kind of like how I felt about Sydney. Like how I felt about Trinity.

"Where were you?" I ask my sister. She's not dressed like she had a long cheerleading practice and the clock on the wall with the bookcase says it's nearly nine p.m.

She shrugs. She's wearing black jeans and a white shirt with a sunflower in the middle of it. She looks completely dry, too. "What are you guys doing?"

Apparently she would rather keep where she was just now to herself.

I sigh. "Well..." I look at Warner to try to communicate to him with my eyes that I am about to fill Audrey in on what happened with us. I don't know if he's wanting Audrey to know or not, but the way I see it, we are all in this together. "Warner and I are being messed with. And we think it's by Sydney."

Her eyes bulge out. She walks into the sitting room and drops down to sit cross-legged on the floor. "No way," she says. "What do you mean by messed with?"

I give her a pointed stare. "Why, did something happen to you, too?"

She bites her bottom lip. "Uh... yeah. Sorta. I don't really know."

How does she not know?

"Well, I got a... weird text," I say.

"And I got a note in my locker," Warner says. His hair is dry now and slightly sticking up all over the place from when he ran his hand through it while thinking earlier.

I can tell by the look on Audrey's face that something happened to her too. "Yeah, that's what I was going to say," she says. "What were your messages about?"

Warner and I exchange looks. We still haven't told each other what our messages were about. "Just stupid stuff," I say.

"Blackmail," Warner adds.

Audrey frowns. "Mine wasn't blackmail. It was more... threatening."

"Do you think it was a message that Sydney could have sent you?" I ask.

"Definitely not," she responds. "I don't know who it was, but the message I received was not something she knew."

"How threatening was it?" I ask, feeling concern rise up in me for my twin.

"Honestly. It could have even just been spam," Audrey tries, playing with the threads on the oriental round rug.

"I don't know," Warner says. "It seems unlikely you'd get a threatening spam text then same time Ly and I are getting specific, weird messages being left to us, too."

I agree. "Whoever it is, I think it's the same person messing with all of us."

Audrey sits up straighter and looks at us. "Well, Wait. Sydney isn't the only person we all have in common," she says.

Warner and I look at each other again. When we do, Audrey notices it and speaks again.

"So, are you two, like, a thing, or something?"

"No," Warner and I say at the same time. Then I glare at my sister. "What is the matter with you? He's my boyfriend's best friend! We would never..."

"I'm just trying to figure out what's going on," Warner adds in my defense.

Audrey gives us a teasing smile. "Chill, I was just kidding around." Then she stands up. "Our moms don't like each other. And we don't really know why. That's the other thing we have in common."

"Oh!" I remember. "And Craig! He's been hanging with the both of them!" I get mad all over again just thinking about how he acted towards me at the cemetery. I don't bother to tell them about the weird encounter, though. I don't want them finding out where it is I like to disappear to.

"So..." Warner starts, thinking something over in his head. "Are Craig, Sydney, and our moms all tied together somehow, you think?"

I hadn't even considered that being a possibility, but it seems super unlikely.

Audrey wrinkles her nose. "Our mom didn't know Sydney."

Warner shrugs and gets to his feet, too. So I do the same. It's like all of us are about to end a business meeting.

Audrey comes up with the plan easily. "So here's what we need to do then. We need to do some research on our moms. Figure out why they stopped being friends. Figure out how that detective is tied in. And maybe we should try to learn more about who this Sydney chick is, too."

"I guess we all have some homework, then," Warner says.

I have to dig up dirt on my own mother. I've always seen her as a simple, straightforward woman. But how well do daughters ever get to know their mothers?

Chapter 51

Maddy

The hair salon I work at isn't glamorous. It's located in a shopping plaza right next to a grocery store. It's the main grocery store in Toxey, so at least I do get a lot of customers. It has a storefront made entirely of glass with posters and sales brochures hanging in the window, then when you walk inside there's a small waiting area with a few black and chrome plastic chairs, a coffee table full of magazines and hairstyle books, and a small fountain along the wall that trickles very quietly.

The reception desk is to the right when you walk in, a shelving display of different shampoos, conditioners, and hair products you can buy when you go to pay for your haircut. There are about six stations inside the main area of the building with the shampoo stations and hair drying stations in the back. Then where nobody can see is a minuscule break room, a storage closet, a bathroom, a waxing room, a laundry room, and an office.

My coworker, Rochelle Bautista, and I are gossiping about a customer that neither of us can stand. She's been coming into this hair salon since the beginning of time, apparently. But she is rude to anyone that isn't her normal hairstylist, Betsy Crawford, who is nearing retirement.

"I just don't want to have to be the one that takes over for Betsy," Rochelle is complaining to me. She has long braided hair, a dark complexion, and a somewhat eclectic sort of fashion sense. She likes to pretend like she's a witch sometimes. As interesting as she is, she's also probably my favorite coworker here. "She's going to hate me. More than she already does!"

I roll my eyes and sit in her stylist's chair. We both have a little bit of a break in between clients. "Honestly, even if we got her hair exactly how Betsy does it, I guarantee you she would still complain and tell us it was wrong so that she could get some sort of discount from us." I wouldn't put it past Betsy's customer. People do that all the time around here. Anything to get free stuff.

Rochelle's brown eyes bulge out as she nods at me in agreement. "And just think about having to—"

The entrance to the store opens, jingling a small bell hanging above it, making Rochelle and I both turn around to see who it is. I have a one o'clock appointment with a new customer, apparently. The receptionist, Mariah Haas, a young girl who graduated from high school last year, told me she requested me specifically.

The bad mood I was already in because of Betsy trying to make Rochelle and me pick which one of us wants her customer when she retires worsens at the sight of the person. It's Amelia Bailey-Flynn.

She goes right up to the receptionist and begins talking to her, a pleasant smile on her face. She's wearing designer head to toe and carrying an expensive leather purse around her wrist. Her blonde bob is already shiny and healthy and doesn't look like it needs a single thing done to it. Why is she here? And she better not be my next appointment.

Next to me, Rochelle gets excited. “Wait a second, isn’t she that interior designer? Amelia Bailey?”

I look at her. “Trust me, you do not want her as a customer. She’s worse than Betsy’s regular.”

Rochelle winces. I can trust her to take my word.

I sit back in Rochelle’s chair and wait for Mariah to walk over to us. I don’t even give Amelia the satisfaction of looking in her direction. I refuse to make eye contact with her and pretend like I didn’t notice her.

Mariah looks directly at me when she speaks. “Your one o’clock is here, Maddy,” she tells me. “Her name is Amelia. She’s booked for a simple trim and style for about an hour.” She looks absolutely clueless standing there smiling at me and bouncing a little on the toes of her feet. “Want me to send her back?”

“This is the one that requested me specifically?” I ask her with an arched eyebrow.

Mariah gives me a simple head nod.

Irritated, I get to my feet. “Let me handle this,” I say. Then I march right up to Amelia, who’s pretending to be very interested in the selection of hair supplies behind the receptionist desk. I highly doubt she buys any of these products. I see them as super expensive already, but she probably sees them as dirt cheap. She wouldn’t waste her time with anything we have here.

“Can I help you with something?” I ask her with a hand on my hip. “Because I know you’re not here to get a haircut with me, Mia.” I had seen enough of her during the camping trip. Before then, I hadn’t talked to her for years. And now here she is again? What gives?

When she looks at me, I half expect her to put a fake smile on. But she doesn’t. “I booked you for an hour,” she says. “I’ll pay, too. I figured it would be the only way to get you to actually talk to me."

"You want to pay me to talk to you?" Is she nuts?

"Well, I had a feeling if I sent you a simple text or a message over Facebook that you wouldn't reply to me."

Well, she's right about that much. "What is this about?" I ask her. "I don't really have time."

Amelia smirks at me. Then she looks at the appointment book open on the receptionist desk. "Well, according to this, you have an hour."

I look to Mariah and Rochelle, who are still hanging at Rochelle's styling station, whispering to each other, and looking over at us.

"I'm going to have this appointment outside," I tell them, conveying my best with my expression to show them how annoyed I am about all of this. They give me concerned looks and Mariah nods her head while Rochelle holds up a thumb.

I don't bother grabbing any of my things because I'm not going to go far. This conversation better not take the full hour. I rush past Amelia out the door. Then I head through the parking lot.

Amelia follows me, her heels clicking loudly as she struggles to keep up. I walk across the lot over to a green patch that sits before the sidewalk in front of the main road. There's an old picnic table that hardly anyone ever uses underneath a large old sycamore tree.

I don't really feel like sitting, but I do anyway. I don't need Amelia thinking that I'm nervous about this conversation. Because I'm not.

Really.

Amelia hesitates before sitting.

"What, this seat too poor for you?" I ask.

This gets her to sit down. "No, it's just a little dusty," she snaps back. "I have on light-colored pants." As usual for my job, I have on all black. We look like polar opposites. And that couldn't be more true.

"Whatever," I say. "Why are you here?"

She sits there with her back straight and her hands in her lap, her purse gently placed on the grass by her feet. I used to know everything about this woman in front of me. I knew stuff nobody else did about her. It's weird to look at her as a stranger now.

"I'm going to be very straightforward with you," Amelia starts off. "I know that you are dating Craig Fritz."

I blink at her for a moment and don't say anything. Was it supposed to be some sort of secret? Did she think I was going to reach out to her to let her know when we started dating for some strange reason?

"Okay?" I ask.

"What are you doing?" she asks back. She looks angry for a reason I can't quite place.

"What do you mean, what am I doing?" I snap back. "It's just like you said. I'm dating him. I didn't know that I wasn't allowed."

"Cut it with the lies, *Madeline*," she says to me. "What is it you guys are trying to do? You're planning something. Working together. I want to know why. And I want to know what it is exactly Craig and you think I did."

"Am I missing something? What makes you think we're planning something?"

"Because Craig has been coming over to my house so much, that's why!" she hisses. "And he failed to mention to me that he's dating you, which I found a little funny. Until I realized it's because you two are keeping it a secret on purpose."

"Okay, you have officially turned into a crazy person," I say. "Good to know." I shake my head and go to get to my feet. I don't know what Miss Paranoid's deal is and I don't know why she's saying that Craig has been at her house, but I'm not buying into it.

"Why did that missing girl have such an interest in our kids?" Amelia asks, stopping me in my tracks.

I turn my head slowly to her. "What did you just say?"

"Sydney Hutton. Craig told me she only seemed interested and befriending Lyla, Audrey, and Warner. I want to know if you know why." She looks uncomfortable, and she still does that same thing she always did when we were little, when she was uncomfortable or nervous about something. She sniffs like she had been crying, even though she hasn't been.

I had lifted my butt from the bench, but I sit back down now, my hand still on the tops of the table. "Is that... is that what Craig told you?" I ask her.

She looks me dead in the eyes. "Yes."

There's definitely something strange going on in this town. The more I sit here and think about it, the more I become hyperaware. I straighten up in my seat the way Amelia is in hers and clear my throat. "Well, Mia." I say to her. " One thing I thought you would be very aware of, out of all people in this town, is that nothing in Toxey is ever what it seems."

I'm excited after I get home from work that day as I wait for Craig to come over. Even though I told Warner that I am dating him, I still don't really love the idea of Craig being around when Warner is home, so when Warner had told me he would be out with friends tonight, I seized the opportunity and invited Craig over.

He looks handsome and scruffy as ever when he shows up on my porch. He brought over beers and bratwursts, along with some propane and hotdog buns.

"What is all of this?" I ask with a smile after greeting him with a hello kiss.

He beams down at me in excitement. "Thought I could grill you up some grub," he says. "I saw that old barbecue wasting away on your back porch."

"I would be amazed if that thing even worked at all," I tell him. "Be warned." The people who sold me this house left it here. I don't even know the first thing about barbecues.

Craig laughs and heads to the back porch. I follow him.

"So how was your day?" I ask him in a pleasant voice. "I missed you."

He had called me earlier to chat like he normally does around my lunchtime, but I hadn't answered because I was... otherwise engaged.

"Yeah, I'm bummed we didn't get to have our afternoon chat," he tells me as he holds the back door open and the two of us walk onto the porch. My back porch is a cluttered, dusty mess. There are two chairs that hardly ever get sat in, an overflowing storage closet, some planters that don't have anything alive in them, and then the rotting barbecue. Craig quickly sets all of his stuff down and gets to work on the grill.

"Yeah, me too," I tell him, wiping off one of the chairs with my hand before sitting down in it.

Craig pops a cap off of one of the beers with a keychain on his keys and hands the beer to me. I take a sip, loving how refreshing it tastes in the warm evening air. The sun hasn't set all the way, so the chill air won't breeze in until a little bit later.

"Well, my day was slow," Craig says as he switches out the propane. "I haven't been getting much done over there lately."

"Oh yeah? Because you can't find anything out about that Sydney Hutton case?"

He pauses briefly, then resumes work. "Something like that," he says vaguely.

"What do you think happened to her?" I ask.

"Well, it doesn't much matter what I think. There's a big difference between thinking and knowing. And I don't want to say anything until I know."

I want to do it, but I don't. I want to ask him about Amelia Bailey and why he's been going over to her house and spending time with her. When Amelia told me about it earlier today, I'll admit—I had had absolutely no idea about him seeing her. And Craig apparently kept it a secret from Amelia that he was dating me. He also decided to keep it a secret from me that he was going over to her house and asking her questions in regards to Sydney Hutton's disappearance. If he's keeping it a secret from me, there must be some sort of reason. I would just really like to find out what that reason is sooner than later.

"You okay?" he asks me.

I look at Craig and see that he's turned around and is staring at me with a funny expression. I hadn't even noticed that I had gone into a trance.

I give him a smile. "Definitely," I say. "I just hope you guys are able to figure out what happened to her soon. Just so I don't have to worry about Warner anymore."

"What reason do you have for being worried about Warner?" Craig asks. I could be crazy, but I could swear there was a slight edge to his voice.

I furrow my brows. “Because he’s the same age as her. And something happened to her. If it was something bad, who’s to say it won’t happen to him?”

He stares at me for a long while before finally turning back to figuring out the barbecue. I tense up in my seat. Other than the fact that he’s been talking to Amelia, I can’t help the feeling that there’s something else Craig isn’t telling me. And I’m a little nervous about finding out what that is.

Chapter 52

Warner

When I get home that night, I go straight to my room so I can do some digging on my laptop. Digging on my own mother, who I discover asleep on the sofa the second I walk in. There was a long while where I would have woken her up and told her to go to sleep in her own bed. I'm not sure at what point it was where I gave up trying to be the responsible and caring one in the family. She can sleep out there every night for all I care.

I set my stuff on the ground, kick off my Vans, then crawl into bed, where my laptop is already sitting on it charging. I unplug it and open it up, putting my back against my headboard and extending my feet out in front of me. I go to Google and type in Amelia Bailey first. I'm a little too afraid to start with my mom right off the bat.

I don't get much information about her. Just about her interior design company, how she's married to Gentry and has a foster son along with her twins, and how she was born and raised here. I also see that she went to a college out of state, where she actually went for a degree in interior design. So apparently Amelia Bailey has always known what it was she wanted to be when she grew up. I highly doubt my mother always dreamed of being a hairdresser.

When I go to the images tab, I see countless photos of Amelia's interior design company portfolio. All the remodel she's done around Toxey, and a few out of town as well. She's good at what she does, I'll give her that. And she's good about keeping her presence off the internet for anything other than that.

I try my mom next and find virtually nothing. I find the massive house my grandfather used to live in, which somebody else bought forever ago. I can't help but look through the photos of it off of the realtor's website. It's just crazy to me that my mom was related to somebody who had so much money. I don't know a single thing about my grandparents. Mom has always refused to talk about them and, just like my unknown father, they don't exist in her life.

I sit there and think for a minute, feeling frustrated that I'm not finding any good information. Then I do some math and determine that Mom and Amelia graduated from Blackfell in 1999. I try to google Blackfell High graduating class 1999, but don't get much information. I hover my mouse over the Google tabs, about to click on Images but then I pause at the news tab. Wondering what this will lead to, I click on it.

The top result is from a local news website with a heading that says,

Teen Missing.
Search Over for Carson Price, Who Has Been Presumed Dead.

My heart beats a little quicker as I click on the link to read the article. Already I am learning something that Mom never told me. When she was in high school, a teenager went missing. I think it's strange that she would keep that from me, seeing as I am going through the same thing right now.

The more I read the article, the stranger it gets:

On Saturday, April 24, 1998, teenagers at Blackfell High School, who were attending their prom, were mortified to learn about the disappearance of their junior classmate, Carson Price. Price was last seen at the prom. However, he left early, according to witnesses, after getting into a fight with his girlfriend, Nora Flynn. The last person who claims to have seen him was Nora Flynn, a sophomore at the time of the dance who had attended as his date. She claimed she saw Carson Price's lifeless body in the Boldosa Redwoods about an hour outside of town after he had called her and asked her to meet him. However, after doing a thorough search of the area over the span of several days, no such body was discovered.

I Google 'Nora Flynn' because her name sounds super familiar to me. This time I use the images search, and when I find a photo of the woman that had been inside Lyla and Audrey's house, I put two and two together. Nora Flynn is Audrey and Lyla's aunt. Their aunt had a boyfriend who went missing. "

"That's so weird," I whisper to myself as I click on the photo. It takes me to some amateur cold-case blogger's website. This post in particular tells me more about Nora Flynn and how she was considered the girl who cried wolf after Carson Price disappeared. How her fight with him on prom night had been physical, and he had broken her nose. Apparently, a lot of people questioned whether or not she really saw his body, or if she had something to do with his disappearance, or if she simply just liked getting the attention.

I close my laptop, thinking. I don't know what Nora Flynn could possibly have to do with any of this, but it's worth telling Audrey and Lyla about. I have a feeling they don't even know that any of this happened.

When I get to school the next morning, I find it strange that Jackson and Lyla aren't hanging out together on the front steps before the bell like they usually are. Especially because Jackson was supposed to get a ride with me to school this morning but bailed. He didn't even text me to let me know, and I was running so behind that I didn't have time to message him and ask where he was.

I go inside the school and head to my locker to get my books for first period. The halls are full of everyone gossiping with each other and slamming lockers. I close my locker and take my phone out of my pocket to send a text to Lyla and Audrey in a group chat so that I can ask them when they can meet up. The info I found on their aunt is something I would rather talk to them about in person.

I am standing there leaning with my shoulder against my locker as I begin to compose the message to them.

"Warner!"

I look up to see Jackson striding towards me with his chest puffed out and his face red. I step away from the locker, but before I can ask him what's going on, he slams his fist into the side of my face, and I nearly fall over.

It hurts. A lot. I am temporarily blinded by the force of it, unable to do anything but keel over and hold my head in my hand while squeezing my eyes shut. When I finally manage to open them, Jackson is right in my face and all of our classmates are racing over to see what's going on.

"I'm done with you!" Jackson shouts at me, jabbing a finger inches from my face. "You stay away from Lyla. And stay away from me!"

I am instantly angry because I have no idea what I did and why he punched me, so I stand myself up straight and get ready to fight him back. As soon as I raise my right hand, a teacher forces his way through the crowd of kids, yelling and recording us, and pulls Jackson away. "That's enough!" he says. "Everyone disperse before I start handing out detentions!"

The kids do what he says. I stand there still fuming and wanting to hurt Jackson.

"Jackson, you're going to the principal's office. Now." The teacher looks at me. "I saw the whole thing. Someone take a Warner to the nurse!"

Audrey steps forward. "I'll do it," she says. She looks a little shaken up and pale but otherwise fine. She stands between Jackson, the teacher, and me and swallows audibly.

"Fine." The teacher pulls Jackson along and the two of them turn. Jackson tries to look over his shoulder at me but the teacher forces him to face forward.

Audrey grabs my elbow and starts pulling me along. "Hurry before everyone tries to talk to you," she says.

My face is throbbing, and the room around me is spinning slightly as we walk. "What the heck was that?" I ask her. "Why did he punch me? And why is he telling me to stay away from Lyla?"

Where is Lyla, anyway? Why don't I see her anywhere? Why hadn't she been with Jackson when he approached me at my locker? I'm so confused and worried and it's only making my head hurt more.

"Get out of our way," Audrey says to everyone else as we push our way through the throng of students. Then she talks to me in a little voice that only I can hear as we turn the corner. “Well, what did you expect?” she asks me.

“What are you talking about?” I knew I should’ve just told Jackson that I have been meeting up with Lyla. If I could just explain to him that it was only to figure out what’s going on with our parents, he would understand, right?

“Warner,” she says in an exasperated voice. “You texted him that you were in love with Lyla! How else did you think he was going to handle that? He’s not some mature, practical, calm adult. He’s a testosterone-filled jock.”

I stop walking and yank my elbow away from her. "What?!" I ask her loudly. “Are you insane? I didn’t say that!”

“Well apparently you did!”

“When?” I ask as I get my phone back out and go to mine and Jackson’s text thread. I’m about ready to keep complaining about how ridiculous this all is, but then my voice dies in my throat. There it is, the last text I sent to my best friend:

Me: *I know this might make you mad. But I have to be honest with you since you’re my best friend. I’m in love with Lyla. I have been for a long time now. And I don’t want to keep hiding it from you. I just can’t help the feeling that she would be a much better fit with me than you anyway. Do with this information what you will, I just thought you should know.*

It was sent around one in the morning last night.

How is that possible?

The first bell rings, and everyone around us starts heading towards their classes. I look up at Audrey in horror. “You have to understand,” I say. “I didn’t write this.”

Chapter 53

Amelia

I opt for meeting Craig at a coffee shop by my office this morning instead of over at my house around my children and my husband. It's a family-owned shop that plays a lot of acoustic versions of popular pop songs. A lot of people like to come here and work or study on their laptops at one of the many tables inside. I personally think all the noises—the music, the sound of people talking, the whirring of the coffee machines, and the grinding of coffee beans – would be a little too much for me to be able to focus. But I'm glad that it's loud in here now. That way, nobody will be eavesdropping.

I'm already seated with my coffee when Craig walks into the shop. He smiles at me and nods his head, then he walks over to order his drink before joining me at the table by the window. Outside, the sky is dark and gloomy and some of the leaves on the trees are slowly starting to change color and settle into the fall.

Craig sits down with a heavy sigh. Then he offers me a smile. One I return even if I don't want to.

"Thanks for meeting me here," I tell him. "I know it's not as close as the station is to my house." I sip my Americano and he sips what I assume is plain drip coffee in a to-go cup.

"Don't worry about it," he says. "I guess it's good for me to get out and about every now and then."

I tilt my head at him. “You don’t get out much?” I ask.

He shrugs casually. “Not lately. Been too busy with work to do anything other than eat and sleep and work.”

And date Madeline Carpenter, apparently.

“I see. Any new developments on the Sydney Hutton case?”

He shakes his head slowly. “Still digging.” Then he notices the look on my face. “Digging for the answers. Not digging up trying to find her body.”

I put a hand over my heart and pretend to be relieved. “I was going to say!”

He sips his drink some more. “So, was there a reason you wanted me to meet you this morning?”

“Well, the last time we talked I know you said you wanted to meet up again soon, and I knew I didn’t have much on my calendar today and was thinking about you…” I trail off.

He gives me a smile that I didn’t see as flirty until now. All this time I thought Craig was just somebody I got along with and could talk to.

But now I’m seeing everything a little clearer. I think I need to watch myself around him from now on.

“That’s sweet of you,” he says. “And your husband really doesn’t mind us hanging out so much?”

I fiddle with my to-go cup. “Well, I’m just cooperating in your investigation, that’s all,” I say as I avoid his eye contact and try to sound slightly flirty myself. “I know you mentioned Sydney being involved with my daughters. Did you have any more questions about that?”

“Why? Have you talked to them at all?”

I nod. “They’re still insisting that they were never friends with her,” I say. “But you said that Warner Carpenter was also seen as a person she was interested in knowing. Have you… talked to him or Maddy about it?”

Craig stops drinking his coffee mid-sip at my question. He sits there paused like a frozen buffering TV screen, then he slowly sets his cup back on the table. "Of course I have," he says. "Almost as much as I've been seeing you. Kind of weird, isn't it?"

Why isn't Craig Fritz admitting to me that he and Maddy are a couple?

"Weird?" I ask.

He stares deep into my eyes. His face looks more serious right now than I think I have ever seen it. "Feels a little bit like being back in high school."

I am unwinding on the sofa watching HGTV when Gentry gets home with the kids after spending the evening taking them out to dinner and dessert. Nora is upstairs in the guestroom doing who knows what like usual. I'm beginning to worry that she's turned into a permanent resident here, but I'm too stressed out with everything else going on in my life to try to do something about it right now.

I sit up straighter. I throw the maroon-colored throw blanket from the couch over my legs . I smile at them as they all enter the kitchen behind me. "How was it?" I ask about their night out. "Did you guys have a good time?"

"I need to get some homework done before bed," Lyla says, waving at me before turning to head up the stairs.

"Yeah, we had fun," Gentry answers for them.

"We played Heads Up while waiting for our food and Dad and I won pretty much every round," Joey informs me.

"Only because you're a little cheater!" Audrey snaps. But she sticks her tongue out and smiles at Joey, so I know she's only messing around with him.

Joey smiles back. "It's impossible to cheat at that game!"

"Whatever." She walks over to me on the couch and gives me a hug. "I am dead tired from practice today. I'm going to bed early."

"Are you sure?" I ask. "A new episode of House Hunters is on."

"I'm going to watch it in bed," she replies. I let her go. At least she had the decency to give me a hug, unlike Lyla.

I chat with Joey and Gentry a little more until Joey heads up to his room to go watch YouTube and I follow Gentry to our master bathroom. We start brushing our teeth and getting ready for bed.

"So..." Gentry starts. "I have to talk to you about something."

I have my toothbrush in my mouth but I try to say something like, "Go ahead."

He sighs and leans in close to the mirror to take out his contacts. "Well, our daughters asked me about why you and Madeline Carpenter stopped being friends tonight."

I lean over the sink and spit out my toothpaste, nearly choking on it.

He continues. "I'll be honest, Mia. I didn't like lying to them."

I rinse the sink out and grab the edge of the counter tightly. "What did you tell them?"

Why do they keep trying to figure this out? Who cares that Maddy and I stopped being friends? It's not anything the girls need to know about.

Gentry closes the lid on his contact case and looks at me through the reflection in the mirror. "I just said I don't know," he says. "They didn't believe me and bugged me about it for nearly all of dessert, but I stuck with it."

I timidly touch his hand. "Thank you."

He looks at me reproachfully. I don't blame him. But it's really not something I'd rather get into with my daughters. Ever.

Gentry isn't done with me. "And Joey also mentioned to me that he's mad that Craig keeps coming around. Just so you know."

He walks out of the bedroom, leaving me there to lean against the sink and cross my arms. I stare at the ground, feeling the anxiety build up inside of me. I try my hardest not to let myself feel overwhelmed. But in times like this, there is absolutely nothing I can do about it.

Chapter 54

Lyla

I don't get it. It just doesn't make any sense.

At all.

Why on earth would Warner tell his best friend that he's in love with me? Warner never cared to mention that fact to me—the one that he's actually in love with, apparently.

But did he really mean it? Is Warner Carpenter actually in love with me? Because that also doesn't make any sense. Warner has always been nothing but nice to me. But then again, he's nice to everyone. Audrey, too. I didn't think I was anything special. I didn't think he was flirting with me or trying to date me. I was vaguely aware that he wasn't telling Jackson that we had been hanging out, but I figured it would just complicate things if he did, so I understood why. It's why I didn't say anything to Jackson, either. I didn't feel like he needed to know that Warner and I were meeting up over personal family matters. It wasn't anything intimate, and it wasn't because we like each other.

Or so I thought, at least.

I head straight to Audrey's car after school and wait for her to give me a ride home before she goes back for her cheer practice. The second she gets within my eyesight, she wiggles her eyebrows at me like she has something juicy to tell me. I have a feeling I know who it's about.

I tug on the door handle before she has unlocked it. "Let me in," I say.

She fishes her keys out of the front pocket of her backpack while still giving me that look. "You'll never guess what Warner said to me," she starts. She unlocks the car and I climb in, dreading whatever she's about to tell me. She gets in the front seat and tosses her backpack in the back. She turns her car on and closes the door. "Close your door!" she demands. Apparently, she doesn't want anyone to overhear us.

I do as I'm told and buckle in. I try not to look at her but it's impossible when she's leaning in closer to me every second.

"Oh my God, what?" I finally ask.

"So you know how Jackson punched Warner this morning in the hallway?"

"Wait, he did?" I fake a shocked expression. I am well aware this happened. I had been hanging out in the cafeteria before school started with Jackson when he confronted me about it. I tried to tell him it was probably a mistake and then he just needed to talk to Warner about it. He told me instead that he was going to beat the crap out of him, and when I tried to stop him, he pushed me away. Like really, actually pushed me. And people saw it, too.

She rolls her eyes at me. "Anyway. I walked Warner to the nurse. He's got a nice shiny black eye. But he told me something crazy, Ly. I mean crazy."

"Either tell me or just freaking drive already," I say.

She giggles. "I don't even know why I'm laughing. It's really not funny. It's just that this whole thing is so outrageous. Warner told me that he didn't text Jackson that."

"He didn't text Jackson that he was in love with me?" I ask. "Audrey, Jackson showed me the text. It was from Warner's phone number and everything."

Audrey doesn't look so sure. "I know. Warner told me that already. But he looked completely shocked when he pulled up the text thread between him and Jackson. He said he never sent it and that he was asleep. Asleep. How crazy is that? Like he either texted you in his sleep or somebody somehow got a hold of his phone."

"Do you really believe that?" I ask. I don't want to sound conceited or full of myself at all, but now I'm wondering if Warner is just pretending like it never happened because he wants everything to go back to normal. He's not one to particularly enjoy confrontation. Especially with his best friend.

"I think I do," Audrey tells me. "I mean, the look on his face... and someone has been messing with us, you know."

"Like Sydney?"

Audrey huffs. "As much as it doesn't really make sense, it kind of does, too. It probably was Sydney."

"She must have got a hold of his phone somehow."

"How creepy is that?" she shutters. "She probably saw you and him hanging out and wanted to get some revenge or something."

"Do you think we should go to the police about this? If Sydney is messing with us, that means she is alive. I feel like the police are going to want to know that Sydney is alive. They probably all think she's dead. Just like the rest of our classmates do."

"Well... you do whatever you want to do," she tells me. "But with what Sydney has on me, I can't go to the police." She turns to face forward and puts the car in reverse. Apparently, she wants to be done talking about it, but I'm not quite there yet.

"You can't tell the police about what she's threatening you about?" I ask. "Audrey, what is it?"

"Oh my God! Don't you love this song?!" She turns up the volume on her stereo to the max and the two of us drive back home without speaking again.

I decide to hang out with Aunt Nora later. I'm too stressed out and conflicted about everything that happened at school today to want to check my phone or do anything else. So hanging out with Aunt Nora seems like the best distraction.

The two of us sit in the living room and put a movie on Netflix. It's some mystery about the wealthy father who passes away and everyone thinks his children killed him so that they can get the money left to them in the will.

I am wearing a fluffy robe and some giant socks because whenever Dad is home, he likes to keep the temperature at a crisp 69° regardless of what the season outside is. Aunt Nora is on the opposite couch wearing sweats and a hoodie with the maroon throw blanket over her. Her long brown hair is wet from getting out of the shower only a little bit ago, and her face is slightly pink from the exfoliation she just finished doing after that. How did mom get the blonde genes and Maddy got the brown genes? Especially since both of my grandparents were blonde?

"Why are you staring at me?" Aunt Nora asks. "I swear my face isn't going to be this pink forever. It just needs time to calm down."

I giggle. "No, I know that," I say. "I'm just trying to find the similarities between you and Mom."

She rolls her eyes. "I got all the good genes," she teases.

"Oh, stop, you're both beautiful."

"If you say so," she jokes. "Now pay attention!"

That's one thing I've learned about my aunt Nora since her visiting here. If we watch movies together, no one is supposed to talk. Everyone is supposed to pay deep, deep attention and not even check their phones. She likes to have the lights off and blankets on, and popcorn is preferred but not a necessity.

"Sorry, sorry," I say.

We watch the movie for a little bit longer, but on the couch to my right, I notice how my aunt Nora is getting a little fidgety.

I don't say anything because I know that she wants me to pay attention to the movie. But I'm wondering what she's thinking about.

"Do you like high school?" she randomly asks me towards the end of the film.

"Do I like it? Why?"

She looks at me. "Nothing. It's just that... I didn't have the best time. I was just wondering if you were in the same boat. Everyone says high school is the time of their lives. The favorite part of growing up. It just wasn't the case for me."

I tuck my feet under me, suddenly feeling colder."I don't know, I guess," I admit. "I used to like it. But ever since last year..."

She nods, understanding. "With your accident and your friend passing away, right?"

I look away from her.

"Well, it might not be exactly the same, but I kind of know what you're going through."

"You do?" Mom has never mentioned anything to me about Aunt Nora getting into a car accident when she was in high school. Mom hasn't really told me anything about her and Aunt Nora being in high school.

Aunt Nora tucks some hair behind her ear. "Yeah. I... I sort of discovered my ex-boyfriend's dead body in the woods when I was sixteen."

My jaw drops open unexpectedly. "Oh my God!"

Aunt Nora cringes and sits up straighter. She brings her feet under her just like I did. "Yeah, it was pretty horrible. He wasn't the best boyfriend to begin with, and he asked me to meet him. So I did. But when I found him... it was too late. And I don't even know what happened to him."

"You mean, you don't know how he died?"

It's clear that she's uncomfortable talking about it because she won't even look at me. "Yeah. When I finally went to go get help, the police came into the woods for him and never found him. Sometimes I think I imagined it. But then other times I am absolutely certain."

"They... they didn't find your ex-boyfriend's body?"

She shrugs simply. "Technology wasn't as good back then."

My brain feels like it's going to explode. "Why didn't Mom ever tell us this story?" How come I never knew?

"Oh come on," she says, smiling a little to lighten the mood. "It's not exactly the easiest thing to tell a child. And your mom knows I don't like to talk about it. This family has a way of sort of just pretending things never even happened at all."

Chapter 55

Audrey

When I get back to the locker room at school after dropping Lyla back at home, all of my friends are dying to know more details about what happened this morning with Warner and Jackson.

"Your sister is such an attention chaser," Sophia says.

"I just can't believe they actually got into a fight over her," Danielle says. "They're like the two cutest guys in the school."

"Warner is kind of, like, a terrible person, isn't he?" Olive says.

I roll my eyes and grab my cheer shoes out of the locker and sit on the bench to put them on. "It's all just a big misunderstanding," I tell them. I almost want to say that somebody is sending us all texts to mess with us, but for some reason, I don't. I guess I have to be careful who I trust, and right now, I am not sure I trust any of them. They're all supposed to be my best friends, but who knows what they're hiding from me? From everyone?

And if I even so much as mention that I think Sydney is alive, they won't let me live it down. They will tease me about missing my secret friend and they will probably say something horrible about how they hope she is dead. They can be kind of heartless like that sometimes. Sophia and Olive at least. Danielle has a little bit more heart.

"I'm so mad I didn't see it!" Sophia continues, putting lip gloss on in the mirror by the sinks even though we're about to get really sweaty, so I don't really see the point of it. "I hit like every single red light on the way here this morning."

"I saw it," Danielle says with wide eyes. She walks over to the sink to join Sophia, holding her hand out so that Sophia will give her the lip gloss afterward. "I've never seen Jackson look so angry. And poor Warner didn't even get the chance to fight back!"

"Wait, really?" Olive asks. She finishes tying her own shoes and hops up to go join them over at the sinks for the gossip. "Because I didn't see it, but people in my third hour were saying that they were both punching each other and that they were both bleeding and all that."

"No way!" Danielle argues. "Didn't happen. Jackson just punched Warner right in the face when he was on his phone. He didn't even see it coming."

Beside me, my own phone lights up. I pick it up and walk deeper into the row of lockers, not wanting them to ask me who I'm texting. I hate that they feel like they need to know every single bit of my business.

But I won't be able to tell them who texted me even if they ask. It's from an unknown number again.

Swallowing audibly, my hands instantly begin to sweat. I use my face to unlock the phone and read the text.

Unknown: *You were warned.*

Feeling frustrated, I type a reply.

Me: *Sydney? Seriously, knock it off.*

I hit send, not feeling very good about it. Sydney is probably not even going to reply to me. And she might get mad if she figures out that I know it's her. Who knows what she will do then? I don't even know what she's talking about anyway. Clear my conscience? I was warned? Warned about what? What am I supposed to clear my conscience about, exactly? The fact that Mr. Reeves is Warner Carpenter's father, and Mr. Reeves, Miss Carpenter, and I are the only three people in the whole world to know about it? Oh, and the mystery texter, whoever that is.

It wouldn't be Mr. Reeves texting me this, would it? What if he somehow found out I had overheard the conversation between him and Maddy that night? Mr. Reeves wants Warner to know that he's his father. That much was clear from the conversation. Is it possible he is trying to get me to spill the secret so that he doesn't have to?

But if so, then why is he threatening me? That's my own teacher!

"Girls!" Coach Greene yells at us. "In the gym, now!"

I toss my phone and my car keys into my gym bag, shove the bag in my locker, and slam it closed.

"Are you okay?" Sophia asks in a voice that makes me feel like she does not, in fact, care if I'm okay.

"I'm good." I walk ahead of them and get into the gym for practice.

Chapter 56

Maddy

Craig is early picking me up for dinner the next night, so I ask him if he will be fine waiting in the living room while I hop in the shower. I have barely gotten home from work and checked the mail by the time he is already knocking on my front door. He tells me he didn't mind waiting and that he will just watch TV in the living room.

So, I hop in the shower and try to be quick about it. I don't want to keep Craig waiting and I don't want to give him a reason to tell me that we should just reschedule our date. I have my reasoning for wanting to resume dating Craig. Even if he wasn't telling me about Mia.

When I hear talking, I turn the shower off and freeze, trying to hear who it is. At first, I think it's maybe just the TV in the living room. But then I can hear two clear voices, one clearly Craig, and one clearly my son.

I step out of the shower and throw a baby pink towel around myself and walk out of my bathroom and towards my bedroom door. I quietly put my ear against it to see if I can hear what they are discussing. I want to know if Craig tells Warner anything he won't tell me or vice versa.

All I hear is mumbling at first. Then I hear a clear, "I already told you!"

That was definitely my son shouting and getting angry. I quickly throw my bedroom door open. Out in the hallway, I see that Craig has backed Warner into a corner near his bedroom door. He is grabbing my son harshly by the shoulder and sticking his nose very close to my son's face in anger.

My son has a black eye. This is the first I've seen it.

"What are you doing?!" I shout defensively at Craig. "Get your hands off of him!"

Craig steps away quickly, whirling around me with an infuriated look. His hair is messier than usual and his clothes are wrinkled. He has dark circles under his eyes like he hasn't gotten much sleep. Behind him, Warner is frozen, his face narrowed, and his fists balled as he stares between Craig and me.

Craig is the first to speak. "I think it's about high time you tell me what you know!" he shouts at me. I stop for a second, shocked. I have no idea what happened between greeting him after I got the mail and getting out of my shower now.

I keep the towel tightly closed around me. "Know about what?!" I snap.

"He keeps demanding I tell him what I know about Sydney's disappearance," Warner answers for him. "But I don't know anything! I didn't even know the chick!"

I race past Craig, slamming my shoulder into his as I go. I put an arm behind Warner and gently usher him away from the hallway into the living room.

"This is absolutely ridiculous," I mutter as I walk with him.

"Mom, I already told him everything. I don't know what happened to Sydney."

Craig follows behind us. "And I just happen to think you're lying!"

I let go of Warner and spin back around to Craig. "Craig!" I shout. "You need to leave."

"Maddy, it's not a big deal. I was just asking him a simple question."

"You cornered my son in my house and raised your voice at both of us. It is a big deal."

"You're just being sensitive."

I point at the door. "Craig, please. Get. Out."

Craig stands there glowering at Warner and me for a moment longer, then he lets out a growl and storms out of the house, the screen door slamming behind him.

Chapter 57

Audrey

Practice goes on for hours because Coach Greene keeps insisting that we are messing up the routine and that we should be at a much further point in memorizing the choreography than we currently are. It's pitch black out by the time I leave the school and walk to the parking lot to my car, my friends walking alongside me.

"I hate being here when it's dark," Olive complains. "It creeps me out."

"Except for when there's like, a football game, or like, prom?" Danielle reminds her.

Olive rolls her eyes. "Well yeah, obviously. Those don't count. It's like we're here when we're not supposed to be. It's eerie."

After the creepy text message I got before practice, I can't help but agree with her.

"Hey, do you guys wanna come over? Or hit Delilah's with me?" Sophia asks. "Dad gave me a hundred dollars today for no reason. It can be my treat." She smiles at us excitedly. Her dad is always giving her money to do stuff and she pretends like she thinks it's the greatest thing in the world. But I know Sophia better than that. She would rather just have a dad that wants to spend time with her. Who gives her hugs every once in a while and compliments her. Her dad doesn't know how to do any of that.

"Yes!" the others cry. We stop at my car, the first one out of ours in the parking lot, and I dig through my gym bag for my car keys.

"What about you, Audrey?" Sophia asks from behind me.

I prop my knee up on the side of my car and rest my gym bag on top of my leg so that I can dig through it further. I can't find my keys anywhere. Didn't I remember to put them in here?

"Yeah... one sec, I'm trying to find my car keys."

A sudden breeze blows by and my hair flies back. Chills go down my spine and across my arms. I'm still a little sweaty from practice, so I'm surprised that I also feel cold, too.

"Do you think you left them in your locker?" Danielle tries. I give up searching and sigh, throwing my gym bag back over my shoulder and turning to them. "Probably," I say.

Olive looks freaked. "Do you want us to go with you to check?"

And listen to Sophia complain about how forgetful and annoying I am? No thank you.

"You guys go ahead and meet me at Delilah's, okay? I'll just run in and grab them, and I'll meet you there."

Danielle and Olive hesitate, but Sophia is quick to smile brightly at me and say, "Okay!"

I smile at them weakly and head back towards the school.

Please still be unlocked, I think to myself. I try the door, grateful to find that it is. I'll just be quick about it. I'll get to the gym locker room before any janitors or teachers try to stop me, then I will get my keys out of my locker and get to Delilah's. I could use something sweet after such a tough practice. Hopefully Coach isn't still in her office. If she sees me, no doubt she'll try to stop me and talk to me about my form or something stupid.

I pass by Coach's office to find the door closed and the lights inside off. I pull on the door of the locker room and find it still open. Inside, my shoes echo on the cement flooring. I walk past the closed bathroom stalls and the showers that have the curtains pulled tightly shut on all of them. A light flickers above one of the sinks and I jump a little. I'm getting goosebumps again.

I go down the row of yellow lockers and stop at mine.

"That's weird," I say aloud. My locker is slightly ajar. I look around at all the others. None of them appear to be left open. But I shut this when I left, didn't I?

Taking a deep breath, I pull open my locker further. My cheerleading shoes are still there. So are my pom-poms. Some extra workout clothes. Everything seems to be in order, except my keys are not anywhere inside of it.

"Ugh." I groan and close the locker. I turn around and throw my gym bag on the bench. I unzip it and dig through it more thoroughly. My keys have to be in here somewhere because I didn't get here without them.

The noise of one of the showers turning on stops me in my tracks. Then I hear the sound of one of the plastic shower curtains slowly opening, the metal rings sliding across the metal pole they're hanging from.

"Hello?" I call. Then I wonder why the heck I'm even doing that. That is only the stupid thing the cheerleader does in horror movies.

And I'm not about to be a stupid cheerleader from a horror movie.

Leaving my stuff behind me—except for my phone—that is staying in the pocket of my biker shorts—I walk down my row of lockers over to the showers. I'm sure it's just a janitor getting a head start with cleaning, but I want to be absolutely certain. For some reason, I keep thinking that it could also be Sydney.

And I keep thinking about that weird text.

When I turn the corner, nobody is there. But the shower is on, steam filling the air and slowly moving towards me, fogging up the mirrors at the sinks.

I turn around in a slow circle. I don't see anybody in here at all.

Feeling scared and uneasy, I decide to leave the locker room. I will feel much safer when I see another adult around.

I knock on Coach Greene's office, just in case there's a chance she's inside. But nobody answers.

Just keep walking, Audrey, I tell myself. Maybe my friends are still outside and I can just catch a ride with them to Delilah's while I try to figure out where my keys could be, or if I have a spare set at home.

I look over my shoulder before resuming my walk back towards the school exit. Then, when I round the corner, I see a figure down the hall ahead of me. They're tall and wearing all black. They're also holding a long, sharp silver knife in their right hand, and they also have a mask on their face that looks like it's supposed to represent a creepy, smiling man. It's made of plastic and is overly shiny. All the facial features are overly animated, including the cheeks, eyebrows, chin...

And that smile.

I don't say hello this time. I don't pretend that I think it's somebody just playing a joke on me.

The stranger and I are equal distance to the hallway in the middle of us that leads to the school exit. If I want to run that way, I'll be running towards him. So instead, I turn around and sprint in the other direction. I have no idea what other door I'll be able to get out of, but I'll try anything.

"Get away from me!" I scream as I sprint down the hall. I can hear the echoing of their shoes running after me, but they don't say anything back.

"Help me!" I scream. "Someone!"

It doesn't seem like anybody is here. Just me and them.

I turn another corner and dive into the cafeteria. I look over my shoulder and see the man gaining on me. I quickly grab some lunch chairs and throw them in his path before I continue running. Anything to slow them down, even if for a moment. Then I run back behind the kitchen counter and go through the doors in the kitchen, just in the hopes that there is a teacher or someone back here prepping for tomorrow's lunch.

"Help!" I scream again.

But as I go through the kitchen, nobody's here to help me.

Right before Lyla got hit by that drunk driver, did she have the chance to actually think in her head, "I'm going to die?"

Because if she did, I know exactly how that feels now.

Chapter 58

Warner

My life is basically a mess right now. All I can think about is the fact that it's all Sydney's fault. Every part of it. The fact that my mom is dating the stupid detective. The fact that the detective cornered me in the hallway and shouted at me the way he did. The fact that Jackson got mad at me over the text that I did not send to him about my love for Lyla. The fact that Coach doesn't think I'm good enough to be captain of the football team. Everything. It all comes down to Sydney. She's been screwing with my life ever since she started at Blackfell High, and even from wherever she's hiding, she is still continuing to screw with it.

I go to my secret little spot I have here in Toxey. It's a place that I like to go to when I want to be alone, where nobody bugs me and nobody can find me. I just want to be somewhere where Sydney can't spy on me and where nobody can tell me I need to come home or deal with my responsibilities.

"This is so stupid!" I shout at no one. It just feels good to put out some of my anger and frustration a little bit. I turn to my left and punch a tree trunk. It was an extremely stupid idea because instantly my knuckles split and my wrist throbs. "Ouch!"

I shake my hand out, ignoring the bleeding, and climb on the hood of my red jeep and sit down. I put my knees up and rest my elbows on them, wishing I could somehow get a sign. A sign about what I'm supposed to do next. About how I'm supposed to make this all go away. About how I can make everything go back to normal. My senior year was supposed to be easy. Simple. All I was supposed to have to worry about was getting into college. Telling my mom that I don't want to stay here. Now, that concern seems minuscule compared to everything else.

I grab my phone and go back to the text message I supposedly sent Jackson. I'm in love with Lyla. I have been for a long time now.

I'm completely confused about the whole thing and a little bit terrified, even. The possibility that I somehow did it in my sleep, subconsciously, seems more of a likely possibility than the fact that somebody else snuck into my room while I was sleeping and somehow managed to get my password and get on my phone so that they could send the message. But both possibilities are equally alarming.

I just can't help feeling that she would be a much better fit with me than you, anyway.

Everything that was sent to Jackson is true. I am foolish to try to deny it now that it's out there. Whoever did this knows exactly how I feel about Lyla. And since I haven't really told anyone, it's another reason why I think I might've been the one that did it. I self-sabotaged myself unknowingly. Either that or...

My phone buzzes with a new text, snapping me out of my thoughts. It's from Audrey. I tap on it.

Audrey: *I need to tell you something important. Now. Can you meet me somewhere alone?*

I sit there and stare at the message for a second. When I don't reply right away, she texts me again.

Audrey: *It's seriously an emergency Warner. Please.*

What if this isn't even Audrey? What if somebody stole her phone to send me a text from it? What if it's Sydney? And what if when I go to meet Audrey at whatever location alone, Sydney is there instead?

Me: *Sure. Where?*

I hop off the roof of my car and climb into the driver's seat, starting my car up while I wait for her to tell me where to go. I don't know what she's freaking out about, but I guess I wouldn't mind talking to her. She had been so chill about the whole Jackson-Lyla situation this morning. She seemed to believe me when I told her I didn't send that text message to Jackson. Even if maybe I did.

Besides, I still need to tell her and Lyla about what I learned about their aunt Nora.

A few minutes go by, and she still hasn't replied. I text her again.

Me: ???

I sigh when she still doesn't immediately reply, then I switch apps. I go to the Toxey news app, something I've been doing a lot more than I ever have. I don't want to miss any information about Sydney's disappearance.

The first headline I read shocks me to my core.

Body Pulled from Lake Oshwano Believed to be Missing Blackfell High Student, Sydney Hutton.

I click on the article and read it over a thousand times. The body was found a few hours ago. Apparently, they are still waiting to identify the remains. But it's obvious who it is. I'm pretty sure not many bodies wind up in Lake Oshwano.

Sydney Hutton is dead.

So then, who the heck has been messing with us?

CHAPTER 59

LYLA

After my and Aunt Nora's movie ends, she gives me a sweet smile and tells me she's going to bed. Joey comes downstairs when he hears the sound of me watching Jurassic Park. It's one of his favorite movies and it's the first choice that popped up on my Netflix suggestions after the mystery movie ended.

"Jurassic Park?" Joey asks when he appears at the bottom of the stairs. "Which one?" He walks into the living room and gets comfortable on the spot that Aunt Nora had been. He doesn't care which one it is, he's going to watch it regardless.

"I think I'll put on the very first one," I tell him.

"The best one!"

The time on the clock above the TV tells me that it's after nine p.m. I look at Joey. "Aren't you supposed to be in bed?"

He shrugs. "Mom's not here," he tells me. "She is the only one that sends me to bed. Dad doesn't care. He's playing video games in his office."

I look behind me into the kitchen. "Mom isn't here?" I ask. "Where did she go?"

He shrugs again. "She just told me out. I wonder if she is talking to that Detective Craig guy again."

I lean forward in my seat. "Yeah, so do I." It's not like Mom to not tell us where she's going. It's also not like her to be out after seven p.m.

"And isn't Audrey usually home from practice by now?" Joey continues.

"Sometimes she goes to Delilah's after," I remind him. "Maybe she knows Mom isn't home, too." Usually, the curfew is nine. Apparently, I am the only one who is out of the loop on what everyone is doing.

"Looks like it's just us then," Joey comments. He doesn't seem annoyed about it. It's actually kind of sweet.

I smile at him. "Fine by me," I say.

On the cushion next to me, my phone lights up with a text message. I pick it up, my stomach sinking when I see that it's from an unknown number. And it's a picture of something.

I don't want to unlock my phone, but I do it anyway. When I go to the message, I'm confused as to what I'm looking at for a second. The picture is dark and unfocused.

I zoom into it and squint my eyes. Slowly, I come to the realization that I'm looking at a photo of Sydney and Warner. They're talking to each other. Somewhere where it's nighttime. They're outside, surrounded by a bunch of trees. The photo looks like somebody was standing pretty far away and had to zoom in close to get the picture of them together.

"Hang on a second," I say out loud as I try to focus in on their outfits.

Joey gets up from his seat and walks over to my sofa, wanting to look over my shoulder. I let him. I'm too shocked to say or do anything.

At first, I think the photo was taken tonight and sent to me just now. That it's proof that Sydney is alive and that she and Warner are hanging out together.

However, this is the outfit Sydney was wearing the night she disappeared.

"What am I supposed to be looking at?" Joey asks beside me. "Is that Warner? I like him!"

My throat is dry, and my stomach is aching. I don't know who sent me this photo, but it has revealed one thing to me that I hadn't known before.

Warner had told me he didn't go talk to Sydney when she texted him to meet her that night. There's a timestamp on when this photo was taken. And it's definitely after curfew. After Sydney had texted him. Warner had met with Sydney.

The next time my phone buzzes, it's a news alert from the Toxey news app. Joey isn't looking at it because he's gone back to watching Jurassic Park, although he still sitting next to me on the couch.

"Oh my God, turn on the news!" I shout.

Joey jumps. "What's wrong? Why?"

I push him a little. "Turn on the news!" I demand again. "Or give me the remote!"

Joey scrambles, clearly startled and worried, and reaches out onto the coffee table to get the remote and give it back to me.

"Oh my God oh my God oh my God oh my God." I cannot stop saying it.

"Lyla! What is the big deal?" Joey cries.

My hands are shaking as I take the remote and turn Jurassic Park to a news station on our regular cable TV.

Dad comes from out of the hallway where the office is, wearing glasses, his hair slightly messy. "What's going on out here?" he asks.

I don't say anything to anyone. All I do is listen to the news anchor.

"Detective Craig Fritz has been working tirelessly on this case, recruiting detectives from neighboring towns even to help with the search for Sydney Hutton, a teenager at Blackfell High School who went missing at the Blackfell High's biannual upperclassmen camping trip."

I put a hand over my mouth as my eyes widen in horror. I don't even notice the tears as they fall down my face.

"Just a few hours ago, after endless days of looking, the search for Sydney Hutton might finally be able to come to an end. A team of police officers were doing a good thorough investigation and search through Lake Oshwana. This time around, they were able to pull a body from the water. It has not been confirmed if the body belongs to Sydney Hutton, but I'll be reporting live when we receive the DNA test results. It seems very likely that the body might be that of the missing girl. And this nightmare that Toxey has been facing might soon be over."

"Turn that off," Dad demands, walking over to where Joey and I are sitting on the couch. "You don't need to be seeing that."

I can feel Joey staring at me in concern. I know I shouldn't have let him watch it. But I don't care. All I know is in the span of thirty seconds I discovered that not only did Warner lie to me about seeing Sydney the night she disappeared, but shortly after seeing him, Sydney somehow died in that lake.

Chapter 60

Audrey

There had been a back door in the cafeteria that I discovered while running from the crazy masked man behind me. I had pushed it open and sprinted out of it, running not like my life depended on it, but because my life depended on it. I don't even know how long I ran for. I never even looked behind me to see when it was that he stops chasing after me. All I know is that when I finally collapse into a green bank somewhere in Toxey, I do not see anyone in a mask coming towards me from any direction. Finally, I had gotten rid of them.

I sit there and dry heave for a long while on my hands and knees, worried that I'm going to throw up into the grass. Then when I'm able to calm myself down, I roll over and sit on my butt, trying to collect my thoughts.

Somebody had messaged me telling me to clear my conscience. I did not listen.

Somebody messaged me and told me I had been warned. Again, I didn't listen.

Somebody is messing with Warner and Lyla, too. And we are all wondering if it's Sydney.

But the person who just chased me through the hallways of Blackfell High School had a build of a man. Not some skinny teenage girl.

What lengths was Warner's father willing to go to get me to tell Warner the truth?

Feeling desperate and never wanting to experience something so horrifying ever again, I take my phone out of the pocket of my biker shorts and compose a text to Warner.

Me: *I need to tell you something important. Now. Can you meet me somewhere alone?*

I have to tell him. I don't know what Maddy is going to do to me once I do, but I don't really have the luxury of worrying about it. Not if I want to stay alive.

It takes him too long to reply. I text him again.

Me: *It's seriously an emergency Warner. Please.*

I fall back onto the grass and look up at the stars. My own English teacher tried to kill me.

Because it had to be Mr. Reeves who did this, right?

Warner: *Sure. Where?*

I don't know how long I lay there before I finally manage to get myself back on my feet. I don't even recognize this area of Toxey I have run to, but it's definitely not a place I go often. It's a little rundown on this part of town. The houses are small and dingy. The grass isn't kept up with. There's trash littered about. Everything just looks more old and gray over here.

I put my address in my maps on my phone and start following the walking directions. Constantly, I check over my shoulder to make sure I'm not being followed again. I make sure to stay on the sidewalk next to the streets with cars driving past, that way if the crazy guy does come back, they can't kidnap me or murder me in front of all these witnesses. Right? Then once I know where I am, I can tell Warner to meet me.

About five minutes into the walk, I pause outside of an unfamiliar house. My mom's car is parked on the street in front of it. I know it's hers because she has a bumper sticker on the back of it advertising her interior design company.

"Mom?"

The house sits in the middle of a plot of overgrown grass. There's no fencing anywhere and the house itself is in the shape of a small, simple square. Steps up to a front porch lead to a screen-covered front door. The yard in the back is vacant and matches the front, at least from what I can tell standing out here.

Through the windows of the dingy house, I can see lights on inside. The last time I tried to spy on people through their window, I learned something I shouldn't have. Do I really want to try and do that again?

Before I can stop myself, I slowly creep around the front of the house towards the backside of it. I pause just before rounding the corner to their back porch because I hear voices talking. One of them is my mom's.

"Even if he is cute, it's all just so weird, don't you think?"

"Are you jealous?" the other voice asks.

"Shut up!" my mom cries. "You know I'm not." The two women giggle.

"Okay, well, you have to promise me we can get Thai food next time," the other woman says. "I know Mr. Lang has the best Chinese food, but I'm telling you. You will be a new woman when you try Thai Express. Don't let the name scare you."

My mom chuckles again.

I didn't know my mom had any friends besides my dad. I peek around the corner to see who she's hanging out with, but then I nearly fall back on my butt as I try to hide again.

Mom is sitting on the back porch of Maddy Carpenter's house. And it's Maddy that she's hanging out with.

"I'll try to keep an open mind," my mom tells her. I sit there and listen to what else they talk about. My mind scrambles to understand what is even happening right now. The two of them aren't supposed to be friends. They hate each other. They made that very clear the entire time they were forced to chaperone together during the upperclassman trip!

I'm about ready to turn and walk away before Maddy can catch me spying on her yet again, but the sound of Maddy gasping makes my ears perk up.

"What is it?" my mom asks her. I peek around the corner again to see that Maddy is looking at something on her phone.

"Oh my God, you have to see this." She clicks on something and turns her phone sideways and scoots her chair closer to my mom. The both of them look at the phone screen, watching a video.

I hear the whole video. Every single word.

Sydney Hutton was found dead in Lake Oshwana earlier today.

The vomit inside me is dangerously close to coming out again. I have to get out of here.

"I think I should get home to my kids," I hear my mom say to Maddy. Her voice is full of sadness and worry.

I hear the sounds of them getting out of their chairs. Before they can come over here and catch me, and before I can throw up on Maddy Carpenter's lawn, I take off running again.

Chapter 61

Maddy

I am a shaking, stumbling, frantic mess after Mia goes home. I've tried calling Warner fourteen times now, and he still isn't answering me.

"What is happening?" I ask nobody. I run my hands through my hair, not caring how much I am messing it up and how greasy I'm making it. This news about Sydney Hutton has me completely freaked out and I would like to know where my son is.

It's not that I think he has anything to do with Sydney Hutton's death. I just don't want it to ever be his body they're pulling from Lake Oshwana.

I don't want there to be any other dead bodies found there ever again.

I just can't believe this is even happening.

I call Warner again, and while I'm waiting for him to answer or not, I hear someone stepping up the creaky stairs on my front porch. I race over to the door and throw it open, hoping it's Warner and that he left his phone somewhere.

Instead, as Warner's call goes to voicemail, I see Craig standing there in his police uniform on the other side of the screen door.

"I need to talk to you," Craig says in a threatening voice. I haven't spoken to him since I kicked him out of my house after he yelled at Warner and me the last time he was here. He's tried to call me and text me, and even message me on Facebook, but I haven't replied. I just want him to leave me alone. And Warner, too.

"What are you doing here?" I ask.

"Why do you seem so out of breath?" he asks back. "Where is your son?"

This makes me angry. "I don't know where he is, do you?"

"No ma'am. Is it okay if I come in?" He puts his hand on the screen door handle like he's done so many times. But right now, it feels menacing and violent. And I don't want him near me.

"Actually, I'd rather you didn't."

"Maddy, are you really still mad at me for the other day?" he asks. "I'm sorry I got so angry. I was just under a lot of pressure to figure out what happened to that girl. And Sydney Hutton was discovered dead today at Lake Oshwana, in case you didn't already hear the news."

I cross my arms, suddenly feeling cold. "I heard."

We stand there, the screen door between us, for a while. Then Craig finally lets out a low chuckle and looks at the ground. "Strange coincidence, isn't it?"

"What are you talking about?" I hiss.

"Look, Maddy. You couldn't keep it a secret forever. I know that you and Amelia are in cahoots."

My stomach dips violently. Amelia and I had agreed to keep our friendship a secret from everyone. How had Craig discovered the truth?

"Sydney Hutton's death was most likely just an accidental drowning. Isn't that what the news said?" I ask.

"Sure, it's what the new said. But that doesn't mean that I'm still not interested in that son of yours. And Mia's kids, too."

"What do you mean you're interested in them? Are you seriously trying to tell me you think that they did this?"

"I'm not trying to tell you anything. Not until I know."

"You're nuts," I snap.

He laughs some more. Then he steps closer to the screen door so that I'm able to see his face more clearly. "Am I, Maddy?" he asks me in a dark voice. "Well, be that as it may. I want you to be very clear about something. You and Amelia Flynn, or Bailey, or whatever the heck her last name is, are persons of interest in Carson Price's disappearance. Always have been. And I don't plan on stopping until I get to the bottom of this."

Normally I would've had something snappy or witty to clap back at him with. But as he turns and walks away, stepping slowly down the steps and heading towards his police cruiser, nothing comes to me. Every single word I say to Craig Fritz, he is destined to use against me later on. So I better keep my mouth shut.

Chapter 62

Lyla

There's no possible way Audrey or I are going to be able to get a wink of sleep tonight. When she gets home from practice—which she walked from—she and I curl up together in my bedroom on my bed. Neither of us has bothered to shower and get ready to go to sleep. Audrey is filthy. She is covered in dirt and sweat and is still wearing her muddy shoes, even. But I don't care. She's clearly terrified, and so am I.

"I need to tell you something," Audrey says to me when we finally turn off the news on my TV. We don't need to hear any more about how Sydney Hutton's body was found in Lake Oshwana and we don't need to hear the DNA test results proving it was her. We already know the truth.

I also don't want to hear anything else about how it was supposedly an accidental drowning, because right now, I don't know if I believe it. I don't know what I am supposed to believe.

"What is it?" I ask my sister. We have our arms linked together and our temples touching each other.

"It's the secret that I was afraid to tell you about. The one I was worried about even going to the cops with. At the upperclassman trip, I was looking for Mom's cabin and I overheard Mr. Reeves and Madeline Carpenter talking inside of her cabin. I accidentally discovered that... Mr. Reeves is Warner's biological father."

My stomach sinks. I don't know how much more news I can take. "Are you serious?" I ask. "Does Warner know this?"

"No. Mr. Reeves wants him to know, but Maddy does not. They've kept it a secret from him his whole entire life."

I move my head away from her so that I can shake it and put a hand over my mouth. Audrey told me she already threw up today. I might be pretty close to it, too. "That's horrible."

She nods her head sadly. "Somebody else knows. Either somebody else knows besides us, or it's Mr. Reeves messing with me."

She launches into a detailed retelling of her experience inside the school after her cheerleading practice today. I start to cry as I learn about the horrific experience she had. I feel terrible because she doesn't feel like she can go to the police, and I very much understand why.

"I texted Warner and asked him to meet me so that I could tell him," Audrey says, tears streaming down her face, too. "But then I discovered Mom hanging out at Maddy's house because the two of them are apparently friends, and I got so distracted because they were watching the news and I heard about Sydney's death and—"

"Wait!" I shout. "What do you mean, Mom and Madeline Carpenter are friends?"

"Apparently. Because the way they were hanging out and talking and laughing made it very clear. But anyway. I asked for Warner to meet me and he said that he would, but I was so overwhelmed with everything going on that I just didn't even reply to him. I have to tell him, right? I don't know what else to do. When his mom caught me overhearing her and Mr. Reeves, she told me that very very bad things would happen if I told anyone. But then the texts that I was getting were telling me that I need to do the opposite. It's all so confusing."

"Okay, well thank God you didn't go talk to Warner," is the first thing I say.

She gives me a confused look. "Are you serious? It might've been Mr. Reeves that was chasing me through the hallway, Ly. If I don't tell Warner, how soon is he going to try that again? How can I even show up at school after this?"

I pick up my phone and go to the message from the unknown number. I click on the photo of Warner and Sydney again and swallow audibly before turning my phone so that Audrey can look at it. "Warner lied to us, Ree. He did see Sydney before she... died. This is from that night at the upperclassman trip. Look at the time the picture was taken."

Audrey stares at it for a long while. Then, out of nowhere, she groans so loudly that I jump in my seat. She rolls over and puts her head in my pillow and screams at the top of her lungs into it.

I run a hand through my hair, feeling stressed out and overwhelmed like she is. When she lifts her head, she turns and looks at me with a red face. "That doesn't make any sense! What is going on? Why are all these horrible things happening? It feels like nothing is adding up or making any sense at all!"

I go to lean the back of my head against the bedroom wall that my bed is backed up against, but I slam it a little too hard. At least the pain is a nice distraction from how I'm feeling right now.

"I wish I had just gotten to Sydney that night. I wish I had seen Warner and her together. I wish I had talked to her and hung out with her like she wanted. I just..."

Audrey reaches out and takes my hand. "None of this is your fault," she tells me. "At all."

When I change my sheets after Audrey got her mud-covered shoes all over them and finally crawl into bed for the night, I try to remember what Audrey told me. That it's not my fault. That regardless of whether or not I had gotten to Sydney sooner the night she died, all of this still would've happened.

I try to leave my phone charging on my nightstand and not look at it again. I close my eyes for a good ten minutes at least, trying to get myself to fall asleep. But it seems impossible. Eventually, I give up and pick up my phone. I have endless messages from people from school talking about Sydney's body being discovered.

But then I also have another text. From an unknown number.

Before I read it, I remind myself that it's not from Sydney. That it never was from Sydney. Whoever is messing with me is somebody else.

Unknown: *Now you've killed two of your friends.*

TO BE CONTINUED

"Up Next" by Brett Monk

Yes, I said there would be a cliffhanger, but don't despair! All the characters you've come to love (and hate) and waiting patiently for you to join them in "**Sealed With A Lie**", Book #2 in the "**Moms Who Lie**" series.

In "**Sealed With A Lie**" ...

Warner Carpenter's life is going downhill fast. That girl that went missing on his high school camping trip turned up dead and there's still a cruel stalker trying to destroy his life and the lives of his friends, Lyla and Audrey Bailey.

Now the police, led by his mom's ex-boyfriend, are trying to blame him for the girl's murder. And the creepy oppressor is now harassing his mom and the Bailey twins' mom as well.

The teens and the moms are fighting hard to stop these attacks and to find the actual killer. But The tormentor knows so much, they must be somebody close. Everyone has secrets and nobody is sure whom to trust.

Can these two families survive?

*"**Sealed With A Lie**" is the second gripping novel in the 5-book "**Moms Who Lie**" domestic psychological thriller series by Brett Monk and McKenna Langford.*

*If you like **twisty psychological thrillers** with **relatable teen and adult characters** and a **drop-the-mic cliffhanger** at the end of each book, then you'll love the "**Moms Who Lie**" series!*

Here's what some readers and professional editorial reviewers are saying about "***Sealed With A Lie***"...

*"Brett Monk and McKenna Langford do not disappoint with the thrilling continuation of their **Moms Who Lie** series, **Sealed with a Lie. Sealed with a Lie delivers mystery and action in equal measure, in this expertly crafted whodunnit.** Readers will be easily drawn into the many angles of this complex plot, with the narrative hopping from one point of view to another, which adds layer upon layer to the mystery. This installment will keep readers hooked from the start with its fast-paced storytelling and high-stakes drama that drives the plot forward to a satisfying finish."*

- Self-Publishing Review

"A fascinating look into the lives of the members of small-town families embroiled in a mix of lies, deceit and selfishness. Each character is described realistically so that you form a bond as the story and crises unfold. The plot and the characters pull you in and spin you on every turn, all the way into the shocking ending that will haunt you and make you want to reread it all over again!"

- The International Review of Books

"I enjoyed the slow burn as clues were revealed and information gained in this suspenseful thriller. I found this one more action packed than the first and it reminds me a lot of the fun teen horror movies I enjoy. As the twists and turns progressed I quickly began to realize that any suspects I had would soon be matched by a new one. I would recommend this book for fans of Scream and Christopher Pike's Chain Letter. The gripping cliffhanger at the end will leave you craving to know all the answers and all the gaps in between. This is a planned five book series and I am looking forward for the new installments and finally getting to know who did it."

- Bridget Ball, "Booked With Bridget"

Claim your copy of "**Sealed With A Lie**" now!

Author's Notes by Brett Monk

We hope you enjoyed the first story in the **MOMS WHO LIE** saga, and that you will join us for the next novel, ***"Sealed With A Lie"*** and all the rest of the books in the series.

If you really liked it and would like to support the series, please consider leaving a glowing review with lots of stars at the **AMAZON REVIEW PAGE.**

So we know that something odd happened back when Maddy and Amelia were teenagers that set the current drama in motion. If you want to learn what REALLY happened back when Maddy and Mia were in high school on the night Carson disappeared, you can download the free bonus novella, ***"The Lying Begins"*** at the link below.

https://www.brettmonk.com

When you join the community, you will not only get free books and other content by me and some of my friends, but you will get the inside scoop on discounted products and upcoming releases. Plus, I share some personal thoughts and "behind the scenes" photos and notes about my life, media adventures, and favorite grilling recipes. :-)

Community members also get to vote in polls and make suggestions for upcoming books and projects. You might even want to consider being a "beta reader" or an "advance review reader", both of whom get to read the books before they're available to the public!

Best Regards and Happy Reading!

Brett & McKenna

About the Authors

Brett Monk

Brett is an author, movie director, and voice artist. He holds degrees in Communications and Psychology and spent over 25 years producing training films for businesses and government agencies in the Washington, DC area before turning his attention to feature films, books, and audiobooks. He was also a church-planting pastor for 10 years.

Originally from the Shenandoah Valley area, he now lives in Northern Virginia with his family and a rambunctious Bernedoodle named Merlin.

McKenna Langford

McKenna lives in Arizona with her husband and two goofy Boxador brothers.

Before she dove into the world of ghostwriting and co-writing, she got her bachelor's degree in interior design and published her first five novels. She worked in a boutique interior design firm in the valley for two years, moved to

Seattle with her husband to explore for another two years, then moved back to Arizona and made writing her full-time career in 2021.

Made in the USA
Middletown, DE
11 February 2023